Failed Moments

A. Robert Allen

ISBN: 1505814677
ISBN 13: 9781505814675
Library of Congress Control Number: 2014922945
CreateSpace Independent Publishing Platform
North Charleston, South Carolina

To my family, past and present, who provided the inspiration.

PART I

Patrick

CHAPTER 1

The Boigen

"No picture. No name. No background," he whispered to himself as he realized none of this missing information mattered. In his experience, first impressions made all the difference. Details offered nothing more than preparation for yet another first date. This time, however, roles would be reversed. She would need to find him. Patrick Walsh chuckled as he settled back into the snug couch inside the lobby of the elegant Boigen Hotel on the West Side of Manhattan.

The Boigen had to be new, Patrick thought, as he flipped through a small corporate brochure. The hotel, which was south of his old Hell's Kitchen neighborhood and in the vicinity of a few favorite hangouts, boasted "Classic Swedish Charm in the Heart of the West Side." *What an excellent tagline,* he thought.

A beautiful chandelier in the center of the lobby, situated directly above a multi-colored table, demanded Patrick's attention. The light passing through the table's colored shelves reflected off the marble floor and mesmerized him. A large bouquet of white tulips occupied the small, purplish tabletop. *Perhaps amethyst,* Patrick thought. Below that were three shelves: The first level, ruby, the second, emerald, and the third, sapphire. Noticing the colored flecks of light on the floor again, he looked up. *Where have I seen this fabulous chandelier? In a magazine? A catering hall? Or somewhere else?*

Patrick's mind turned back to his social life as he contemplated the newness of a first date and the anticipation of a second, both acting as a lovely build-up to the third date—the highlight of most of Patrick's relationships, when the increasing ease that came from being somewhat acquainted was roughly equal to the remaining sense of the unknown. Third dates provided Patrick with a brief and welcome opportunity to smile. Fourth dates, however, brought on the inevitable question: "Where is this going?" or the new phrasing he'd heard twice this past year, "What is your end game?" Whatever the form of the question, it always marked the beginning of the end for Patrick, although he preferred to think of it as the need for yet another new beginning. *She's late. Where is she?*

Patrick continued to survey his surroundings and tried to relax. The one modern aspect of the hotel, a full-length glass wall, featured three oversized doors with pearl handles, which provided access to Tenth Avenue. The Limerick Liar, one of Patrick's favorite Irish bars, became visible in the distance as a large delivery truck pulled away from the front of The Boigen. *How could I have missed this hotel?*

Two distinct groups of people assembled in the lobby. The larger group clustered around the ornate table with the white tulips. *Tourists*, Patrick guessed as he detected a sense of anticipation when a big luxury charter bus pulled up to the Tenth Avenue entrance. The second group in the lobby lacked the excitement of the first and displayed more control, as they sat in a collection of chairs about ten feet away from the doorway that led to 20th Street. Patrick didn't know what this group was waiting for and realized he had no theories. That was unusual. This game of analyzing the behavior and motivations of strangers relaxed him when he got anxious, which was often. Patrick's blood pressure eased as he continued to watch.

The tourists left the lobby and headed toward the charter bus on Tenth Avenue and the more sedate group departed onto 20th Street. Patrick found it peculiar—actually rude—that each of the tourists peeled a single petal off a tulip as they passed the bouquet and left for the bus. He was tempted to say something to them, but realized as much as it bothered him, he would not want to be seen in any kind of a confrontation when his date arrived. *First impressions dictate the outcome*, Patrick reminded himself. A young hotel employee quickly replaced the ravaged bouquet as if it were a standard duty. Patrick smiled. Good service standards, well executed. It was a tightly run ship.

The Boigen lobby was almost empty and all of the energy that had filled the room a few minutes earlier exited with the two groups. His date was late. As Patrick glanced again at his watch, he felt a tap on his shoulder and then a brief, searing pain just below his right ear. The extreme discomfort forced him to hunch over while pressing his hands against either side of his head. After a few moments, he straightened up and tried to regain his composure. He was unsuccessful. So much for first impressions—Patrick turned to meet his date.

"Good evening, Patrick, it's been a while," she said.

He didn't know how to respond.

"Patrick. This must be upsetting to you, but we need to talk."

His heart was pounding and beads of sweat started to gather on his brow. Patrick loosened his tie and took several long, deep breaths. Finally, he stammered, "I don't understand. The last time…the last time I saw you…" His words failed him.

She smiled gently. "I understand your confusion, but before I answer your questions, I have one for you." She paused. "Do you remember the last time we were together?"

"Yes."

"I thought you would. So when was it?"

Patrick cleared his throat and muttered, "April 11, 2008," as he examined his surprise visitor who hadn't changed at all in the past five years. *How could this be?* Patrick asked himself. *April 11, 2008, was the day she died.*

CHAPTER 2

The Reflektions Cafe

PATRICK NEEDED A way to process his thoughts as they headed toward the hotel café. Logic didn't help and imagination made matters worse; he was about to enjoy a cup of coffee with his dead Aunt Grace. *Am I dead too, or is this some type of terrible dream?* As Patrick realized there were no good answers to this question, his arms started to shake and his lips began to quiver. He knew he needed to relax by thinking about something else, and his mind turned to the café. First, he considered the name–Reflektions. *Probably not a misspelling. The Boigen is a Swedish Hotel, and Reflektions must be the Swedish version of Reflections. Not a bad name for a café,* he thought.

The small footprint of the Reflektions Café enabled Patrick to survey the entire operation in an instant. He started with the limited menu, which consisted of coffee, tea, and assorted cookies. *Not up to the standard of a Manhattan hotel.* Patrick quickly developed a short list for additions-- muffins, cakes, and a selection of sandwiches. *Yes, that would be a good start.* Next on Patrick's "to do" list, the review of the clientele. Couples sat at the few occupied tables. Some were older, some younger, and a variety of ethnicities were represented. The only area of commonality involved the lack of audible conversation. *Why aren't they talking?* The more Patrick continued to focus on the café, the less his arms and lips shook and quivered. He searched for something else, anything else, to analyze.

Grace and Patrick had been close through Patrick's thirties, when he made a series of investments that would change his life. Some people made fortunes on the rise of the dot-coms, and others, like Patrick, profited when they fell. Once he no longer needed to work, Patrick quit his job as a professor of finance and began a solitary daily routine from which he never wavered. The morning began with a workout, and continued with hours of reading about business trends. In the afternoon, he sat at his computer and traded his portfolio. Every day was the same. Every day he was alone and that's how he liked it. No more impressionable students who viewed him as a role model and hung on his every word. No more freshmen orientations, graduations, and endless birthdays, weddings, baptisms, and the like with high maintenance colleagues. Patrick had his computer and the market, and they provided him with what he needed, asking nothing in return.

In the evenings, Patrick went out because even he required some variety. The agenda either involved a date or hours of wandering the streets of the city until a random bar or restaurant in some way distinguished itself from the scenery. He could be quite social with strangers and some of his best evenings came about as a result of one of these urban walkabouts. The variety of the city suited Patrick because he never wanted to be a "regular" anywhere.

Finally, they settled in their chairs.

"So, how've you been enjoying your apartment? Sorry, I'm not being specific enough. You've probably lived in at least two or three places since I passed away. Tell me about your latest place."

"Tell you about my latest place?" It hardly seemed relevant.

"Patrick, you're an anxious mess. If I can't calm you down, I won't be able explain what you need to understand. So tell me about the place, and start with a deep breath..." Grace wasn't usually sharp, but sometimes with Patrick it was necessary.

Patrick recognized he needed to calm down and he did enjoy talking about his apartments. Despite his wealth, Patrick always rented and insisted on one-year leases. He didn't believe in being locked in and sought out upscale apartments in luxury buildings with either a balcony or a terrace. As much as Patrick needed the outdoor space, even in the cold New York winter, he didn't need much of it--only Patrick and his laptop computer needed to be accommodated.

"Okay." He took a breath then stopped, unsure why he was hesitating. "I... I moved to the other side."

She laughed. "Let me guess, for you the 'other side' is the East Side. Were you growing tired of the West Side, Patrick? Or was there another reason? Perhaps it was something about a terrace?"

"Well, yes." He looked at her for a long moment. *How did she know?* "I'm on the 35th floor facing midtown and my apartment has two terraces. The first has a beautiful, unobstructed view of the Manhattan skyline, but the second is the special one."

"What makes it so unique?"

Patrick smiled as he started to describe his favorite terrace, the best he ever had. "Well, first of all, it looks like a castle. Of course, the top is open to the elements, but then the sides have four walls with cut out windows reminiscent of those you would see in a medieval castle. The windows are large, so my view is still unobstructed, but the walls block strong winds and prevent me from getting sunburned. The castle is my favorite part of the apartment."

"So while you can look across the city from the vantage point of your chair in the castle, it would be very hard for anyone else to look in. Is that right?"

"Well, yes, but I burn so easily. The walls give me protection from the sun."

She hid a smile. "Yes, protection from the sun. I'm sure that must be the reason. Irish skin is so sensitive."

Patrick had always been a headstrong child who grew to be a stubborn man. In recent years, he had intentionally distanced himself from the rest of the family. His Aunt Grace was the only family member with whom he'd stayed in touch. Maintaining contact with Patrick was not easy, however, so Grace often broke little things around her house or caused minor glitches on her computer, which could be easily repaired, and then asked Patrick to come to her assistance. They would talk while he worked; she calmed him down and tried to help him manage his highly introverted, but occasionally explosive, personality. While she recognized that her nephew was a brilliant man, she knew better than anyone he was also a personal train wreck. His inability to commit was not limited to his dates, and Grace had realized that his constant moves from apartment to apartment enabled him to remain the new neighbor while never becoming a trusted old friend.

Aunt Grace sat with her back erect, her posture almost as classy as her diction. "Let's first order some coffee and then we can talk."

An elderly, well-dressed man interrupted. "No need," he offered as he placed two paper cups with lids on the table. "A Chamomile tea for the lady and a black coffee for the gentleman." Patrick had noticed this same employee earlier at the front desk and admired his neatly sculpted white beard, perfectly tailored three-piece suit, and monogrammed "P.S." on his shirtsleeve. The gentleman continued with an air of authority, "I think it might be best if the two of you finished your chat in your room. Here is your key card." The man turned to Patrick, paused for a moment, and then said, "And Patrick, I wish you the best of luck." As the man walked away, the big ring of keys dangling from his belt jingled, and Patrick became even more confused. *Who was that man? How did he know my name? Why do we need a room? Why did he wish me luck?* Aunt Grace seemed to understand the urgent need for answers and responded, "Patrick, you'll get all of your answers upstairs. Let's take our drinks and go up to the room."

Chapter 3

West Side Story

THE HAND SHAKING evolved into involuntary flexing as Patrick began extending and clenching his fingers. Aunt Grace wasn't sure if this was pure nerves or indecision as to whether he should form a fist. She tried again to calm her nephew, and while being strong and assertive always worked, she thought kindness would be the better approach.

"Perhaps you'll be more comfortable up here in our room. Look at these lovely accommodations. Did you notice the room number, 1010?"

Kindness didn't work.

"Why are you asking me about numbers and who cares about the accommodations? If you're dead, am I dead as well? I'm only 46. How about that number? How could I be dead? Yes, how could I be dead? I go to the gym almost every day and I eat the right things. I can't understand. Tell me already, am I dead? Tell me. Answer my question!" Patrick demanded.

She tried again with kindness.

"Patrick, my dear. Slow down. Please. I don't want to give you answers you cannot yet comprehend. Let's take a look out the window…"

Kindness failed, again.

"Take a look out of the window? Answer my damn question! How could you possibly say I would be unable to comprehend such a basic thing as to whether I'm dead or alive?"

So much for kindness.

"Tone, young man. Tone. Pissing me off was never a good idea when I was alive, and I assure you, it will be an even worse strategy now that I'm dead. You will sit quietly, shut your mouth, and mind your manners. Do you understand?"

Patrick always respected true strength. After being put in his place by his aunt, he did calm down, but he felt like he was about eight years old.

"The answer to your question is not a simple yes or no. You are rushing me, and I am trying to carefully choose my words in order for you to understand things properly. I will jump ahead just for you, my impatient nephew, but don't push me." Aunt Grace paused for a second to regroup and try to find the best way to present such a highly disturbing message. After another sip of her tea provided a few extra moments to think, she decided a straightforward approach would be best. "Your body is forty blocks north of here on Tenth Avenue in St. Luke's Roosevelt Hospital and you are on life support." *Much too direct, much too cold, much too businesslike,* she thought to herself as she watched Patrick's reaction. Rushing her message made matters worse and Aunt Grace needed to regain control of the conversation. A single tear began to stream down the side of Patrick's face as he asked, "But how can this be true? I'm sitting with you in this hotel room. I still don't understand."

"Patrick, please go over to the computer and turn the power on. I set up a feed from your hospital room for you to view. You've always needed to see something to believe it--sometimes you lack faith, my dear. Go take a look."

Patrick Walsh walked slowly over to the desk, settled into the chair and prepared himself for what he assumed would be distressing. He turned the computer on and the screen was divided into quadrants. Patrick tried to focus, but tears welled up in his eyes.

"Patrick--the upper right quadrant. The upper right."

Patrick stared at the screen and another tear began to travel toward his lip. This tear, however, had company. Patrick wiped his eyes with his shirtsleeve as Aunt Grace walked over to her favorite nephew, hugged him, and said, "Take your time. It's been far too long since you've shed any tears. Far too long. Too much isolation. Not enough laughing and crying with the people who care about you. The laughing and crying, my dear boy, is what represents true living. Get it out, Patrick. Get it all out."

Patrick tried to regain his composure and looked again at the quadrants on the screen. The other three patients had friends and family around their beds. He was alone. "Why is no one there for me?"

"Because you've not been there for them for a long while. I'm not sure you're even aware of what became of a few of your family members over the last few years. Enough of this, let's go admire the view!"

They both walked to the window, which faced north. Aunt Grace reached up to try to hug Patrick, who at 6' 2", 250 pounds, probably didn't go to the gym quite as much as he claimed.

"Do you see the building on the far left? Yes, The Victory, your old building, I believe. What a marvelous terrace you had! In my opinion, this was your best one. You always intended to invite the family over for a big party, am I right? Never happened, did it, Patrick?"

"You're right. Never happened."

"Who do you think is to blame for that?"

"Me."

"Good boy. Take responsibility. You made the poor choice to lead a solitary life. I'm pleased to see you understand."

"What happened, did I suffer a stroke or a heart attack? My blood pressure spikes when I get upset."

"Neither. You were hit by a stray bullet below your right ear. Do you remember that quick, but strong pain when I tapped on your shoulder?"

"Yes."

"Well, that was the bullet. I spared you the prolonged agony. Please understand, however, that this bullet was not the random act of violence it was assumed to be. I've been waiting for you for a long time at The Boigen and it was your time to come meet me."

"You say it was my time, but I'm only 46. How could that be?"

"Your life was not going in the right direction and you had already travelled too far down the wrong path. You can still fix things, however, and get back on track."

Patrick's hands stopped their frenetic movements. He slumped in his chair as he started to come to grips with the gravity of his situation. "How could I possibly fix it? I don't even know what was so wrong!"

"My dear Patrick, I know it's hard, but I do need you to perk up. I will tell you how you can fix things, but you must be resourceful. Can you do that for me, my dear boy?"

Patrick answered by sitting up straight and taking a breath. Time to under-stand. Time to assess. But before any of that, it was time to listen.

Aunt Grace took note of his improved posture. "That's better. I'm going to try to help. Maybe I can be as clever as my nephew the successful trader--why don't we call this your own private West Side Story? After all, you lived here, you were attacked here, you are lying in a hospital here, and the actions you take while a resident of this lovely West Side hotel will determine whether you wake up and return to your life or take some other course."

Patrick barked, "What other course? Speak plainly, this is my life you are talking about!"

"As you wish. Do you remember the happy group boarding the charter bus a little while ago?"

"Yes."

"Well, they were all going back. But you must be patient in order to under-stand the forces at play here. Going back might be the right thing, but the other course may be even better."

"Again, with the other course! You can't even describe the other course properly to me. I'm a successful investor. I don't need some other course. I want to return to my old life!"

Grace took a deep breath and dug deep into her bag of tricks. "Patrick, Patrick, Patrick…" She let the third Patrick hang in the air. He was often chas-tised in this fashion as a child. Patrick got the message and sat forward, tilting his head downward, feeling eight again. He was on his best behavior.

"You don't yet understand what is best, but I am here to guide you. First, we will start with the basic rules of your little West Side Story. Come and sit next to me," she gestured to the easy chair beside her, "and relax. I need you to patiently listen and you must, I repeat—must—stay calm. Can you sit and listen?"

"Yes, Aunt Grace." He felt like he was learning a lesson in first grade, and he was intent on learning this lesson well.

"Let's start with the basics. Remember how you always said you wanted to take a course about the religions of the world? I wish you'd done that…this would be so much easier to explain. Here is the simple truth—no single religion has it totally right or totally wrong. The things which are actually true are in the areas of overlap. The soul is perhaps the biggest of those areas. So this is the first thing for you to understand—when a person's body dies, the soul survives. In many cases, the soul is attracted to a new body, and the next life is dependent, to some extent, upon some lesson not learned in the present life."

Patrick smirked as he asked, "So you are saying I'm talking to your soul, not you?"

"What you're doing is better described as interrupting. May I continue?"

"Apologies. Please do. I'll try not to interrupt your 'soul' again."

"Very cute, my dear. There is some agreement on the soul, but most religions made the concepts of Heaven and Hell too simplistic. Heaven is the ultimate resting place for the most highly developed souls and something to which we should aspire, but it is rare for a soul to achieve that level of purity after just one life. The concept of Hell, on the other hand, would be much better thought of as nothing more than Karma, pure and simple—the old "what goes around comes around" dictum; those people who are abusers and evil in nature in one life, pay the price in the next. So all of those people who boarded the charter bus are going back, but not to their old lives—those bodies are dead. They will be reincarnated."

"But I want to go back to my old life, I still have so much to do. I don't want to start all over. I've achieved so much…"

"Patrick, I know how upset you are but things will all be clear in due time, I promise. Your Aunt Grace will explain everything. Relax. Please trust me. Please, Patrick. Please."

Patrick was as calm as he could manage. Aunt Grace took a deep breath and then finished her explanation, "Souls continue being reincarnated until they are so pure, they would not benefit from another life. Did you notice how each person peeled a single petal off a tulip on their way out of the hotel? Those tulips are symbols of purity and peeling off a petal is our little good luck ritual when we go off to start a new life, which we hope will be more pure than the last. Do you understand so far? Do you get the basic concept? This is important. Any questions?"

Patrick responded, "Lots of them, but I just want you to finish before I ask them. I promise…no more interruptions from me."

"Okay. Let's talk about the hotel for a minute. I'm not sure you realize the meaning of the name. Boigen is actually two Swedish words, 'Bo' and 'igen.' The meaning in English is 'Live Again.' The hotel should be thought of as a place where souls can reflect. When souls arrive, they go for a cup of coffee in the Reflektions Café. Sometimes they are met there by souls like me, who've been with them in many lives and will provide advice related to lessons learned. Most of those souls who got on the bus never checked in—they just had coffee, reflected, and then left for another life. You and I, however, did check in, because our time here will be longer."

Patrick's spirits were improving. Everything was starting to make more sense to him and his beloved Aunt Grace was going to be his guide. He took the risk of interrupting to say something light, "Ah, so I get to move back to the West Side for a while! Excellent. I missed the old neighborhood."

"Yes, indeed!" Aunt Grace exclaimed. "You've regained your sense of humor! This is an excellent development, but let me finish up. Not to worry, we're almost done. You were close to achieving the highest level of purity three lives ago. Yes, that's right, you messed up two times in a row, and you seemed destined to fail again as Patrick Walsh. I almost achieved my level of purity with this last life, but I too had difficulties. Think of our time in this hotel as our opportunity to fix our mistakes as best we can. Depending on how well we do, we may be here for either a short or long period of time, but we certainly require a room. Reflecting over coffee won't be enough for you and I, my dear. I think I've given you a lot to consider. Perhaps we should stop."

"Okay, but only if you're done." She nodded. "I definitely need time to process all of this, but how will I go about fixing my mistakes? How will I know what things I need to work on?"

"You won't be given a report card which will pinpoint exactly where to focus your efforts. Remember, you reflected after each life, and while those thoughts are not currently available to you, they will be soon. We were both so close, we will know where we went wrong. Please understand…we're being given an opportunity to fix things. Think of it like a do-over of certain critical moments in our past lives where we made the wrong choice or took an inappropriate action. You have two prior lives to revisit, and if you fail at any point, a quick fix will not be possible. If you are successful, however, you will regain consciousness and live out your days in this current existence predestined to advance to that ultimate level we just discussed. This is your West Side Story, my dear, a fabulous adventure. Are you ready?"

"Well, I am over the shock. And I want to do better. The fact that I made mistakes in prior lives is not surprising, and I do like the idea of a second chance. Can you tell me what my prior lives were?"

"Yes. The first life you will revisit will be in the French colony of St. Domingue just before the slave uprising in the late 1700's that resulted in the creation of the modern day country of Haiti. You were the son of an affluent French planter and your name was Patrice Beaumont. Your second life will take you from Ireland immediately following the Great Famine in the mid 1800's to New York. In that life, your name was Patrick Allen, and in both lives, you were involved with the important issues of the time. By the way, you were always called Patrick. Patrice is the French version of your name."

"Interesting. I've always been Patrick and always screwed things up at particular points in my life. So these do-overs are kind of my chance at perfecting Patrick. Appropriate, don't you think? One last question, though, how did you get me to come to The Boigen thinking I was meeting a date?"

Aunt Grace was so happy the mood had lightened and chuckled as she responded, "Oh my, Patrick. Do you think there is some mystery to the formula for getting you to respond to an online profile? Some tasteful pictures showing high fashion, then one showing a little skin, and then a little language about 'not looking for anything too serious.' Am I right?"

"You have me pegged!"

"All right then, when we wake up in the morning, we will be met with the challenge of one of these past lives. I will be with you in each one. We have always been together, although as I've said, the relationship has been different. When the adventure of each life is over, we will meet in the Reflektions Cafe for coffee."

Well, that didn't go too badly, Grace thought. *I might have let him down this last life, but now we can try again.* Success for him would also mean success for her. She hoped they would be up to the challenge.

PART II

Patrice

CHAPTER 4

St. Domingue

PATRICE PACED BACK and forth on the front porch of his ever-expanding home. His latest addition, an extension in the rear, would accommodate three of his house slaves. The house served as the centerpiece of the Beaumont Plantation and contained 20 rooms with a massive common area on the main floor designed for entertaining. Beaumont was located on the outskirts of the growing city of Jacmel in the southern region of St. Domingue, a French colony in the Caribbean. A recent report from the government identified St. Domingue as the wealthiest French colony in the Americas. The island supplied about half of all the sugar and coffee consumed in Europe, and the Beaumont Plantation had a long reputation as one of the biggest coffee producers.

Slave labor fueled the thriving economy. The latest estimates, published a year earlier in 1789, put the slave population at about 500,000 and the *blancs* (ruling whites) at only 32,000. The colony also included the largest and wealthiest free population of color (*gens de couleur*) in the Caribbean. This mixed-race community in St. Domingue numbered 25,000 in 1789, with many, like Patrice Beaumont, slave-owners themselves.

The geographical separation of the sprawling 1000-acre plantation from the rest of the colony gave Patrice the privacy he needed to practice a kinder version of slave ownership, which would be frowned upon by both the *blancs* as well as his fellow *gens de couleur*. He paused for a second to survey the tangible evidence of all he'd accomplished by the relatively young age of thirty-six. Granted, his wealthy white father gave him his start, but he had done well in the years since receiving the initial gift to arrive at his current station in life.

Despite the obvious role slave labor played in Patrice's success, every bone in his body told him the institution of slavery was wrong. Each of Patrice's acts of kindness and generosity eased, but never eradicated his guilt. Despite his misgivings, however, Patrice often found himself adding to his slave population of 350 in order to both satisfy the needs of his sprawling plantation, and support the rationalization he'd adopted years before: any slave would lead a better life at Beaumont than at any other plantation in the colony.

Patrice tried to remember that he had much in common with his slaves. If not for the generosity of his father, his life would have been radically different. He appreciated what he had, but like many of the other free blacks on the Caribbean island of St. Domingue, he also believed change was in the air. The French Revolution had created a more welcoming society for mixed race landowners and one of the first actions of the new National Assembly was the passage of the Declaration of the Rights of Man and of the Citizen. The *gens de couleur* interpreted this groundbreaking declaration to mean free men of color would be able to vote and fully participate in society. One of the leaders of the free blacks in St. Domingue, Vincent Ogé, recently met with the colonial governor to press the issue, and Patrice expected to hear the good news any day.

Patrice hoped things would change for the 350 slaves on his plantation, but recognized that this might not be their time. Vincent Ogé's appeals to the governor were only on behalf of the *gens de couleur*, not the slave class. As long as slavery existed, Patrice planned to be as fair and kind as possible, although he appreciated that many of his fellow free blacks would frown on this approach. Several of his mixed race brethren were regarded as being among the most brutal slave owners on the island, despite their partially shared heritage with their unfortunate "property."

The island's class system was firmly in place: the ruling *grands blancs*, who owned most of the largest plantations, were in charge in all respects. The *petits blancs*--lower class whites who worked as artisans, shopkeepers or overseers— came next in terms of political clout, and then the *gens de couleur*, who had full economic rights, but limited basic civil liberties. The *grands blancs* resisted the rule of France and envisioned St. Domingue breaking off from the mother country much like the American colonies did a few years earlier. They liked the

American model of an independent nation in which slavery continued to be lawful. The *petits blancs* were more loyal to France and pro-slavery. The *gens de couleur* wished to gain full rights as citizens within the framework of French rule and held different opinions regarding slavery depending mostly on whether or not they owned any. While each group had held these positions and beliefs over a long period of time, change was in the air in October of 1790.

Grace began to speak as she observed the scene from above with her nephew. "Patrick, the gentleman who is pacing on the porch is you, my dear. The year is 1790 and you are a mixed-race slave owner by the name of Patrice Beaumont. Your life was going very well at this point and you've displayed great charity and kindness to your slaves. During this period, slave owners were particularly brutal and slaves would often die after a few years only to be replaced by other new arrivals from Africa—but not on your plantation. Your slaves thrived because you treated them more like valued employees than property. While they would have preferred freedom, they knew they were better off with you than just about any other slave owner on the island, especially the other mixed-race slaveholders, who were more brutal than the whites. This is something you never understood, but an issue with which you needed to be careful. You often found yourself talking tough when in the company of another mixed-race slave owner, but acting in a much different way while in the privacy of your large plantation. Your wife, also mixed-race, died during childbirth several years ago. A slave named Gabrielle is your current partner. You have one child with Gabrielle by the name of Christophe—he is five, and another child—Claude--from your deceased wife. He just turned six. So those are the basic facts. Once we finish this chat, we will assume our old identities. Here I am walking out onto the porch."

"Monsieur Beaumont, dinner is ready."

"Merci, Camille. I don't know what I would do without you," Patrice responded to his lifelong house slave who, more than anyone else, had raised him as a child.

"You be just fine, Monsieur. Just fine." Camille enjoyed the freedom with which she spoke to Patrice while in the house. In her early years, Camille had been exposed to a brutal slave owner, and she celebrated the day Patrice's father, Guillame Beaumont, purchased her from a neighboring plantation to be his nanny. Now in her fifties, an unheard of age for a slave in St. Domingue, Camille was still able to do many things around the big plantation house. Making sure Patrice ate properly was her most important role, and she enjoyed the daily ritual of summoning him for dinner. His standard response to her announcement of the evening meal, "I don't know what I would do without you," made her smile.

Chantal Archambeau, who owned the café in town that catered to the mixed-race population, had dined at the Beaumont Plantation at least twice a week for the past several years. She thought of Patrice as a younger brother and made every effort to keep him grounded. Whenever he seemed especially proud of some kindness he provided one of his slaves, she uttered her favorite saying, "Being the best of the worst is nothing to celebrate." Slavery was wrong— Chantal knew it, and she never failed to remind Patrice of that fact because he had the ability to do something about it as the unofficial head of the *gens de couleur* in southern St. Domingue. He could effect change and had the makings of a great leader. In her assessment, all he needed was a push, and she was happy to be of service.

A guest was expected later that evening, a merchant from the town of Aux Cayes by the name of Abraham Julian. Given the short half-day's ride and the favorable weather, Monsieur Julian might be early. Even without an expected guest, however, Patrice always insisted on privacy and closed the curtains of the dining room windows so no one could look in from the outside. The head of the table was reserved for Patrice. The seats to his right and left were for Gabrielle and Claude. Christophe sat next to his mother with Chantal across from him. Patrice nodded to Camille and she removed her apron and sat at the other head. In the privacy of his home, and within the sanctity of his dinner table, he wanted the people closest to him to understand they were full partners in his life. Two seats remained empty on either side of Camille; one for the rare guest, and the other for Camille's son, Andre, who was an overseer of sorts at the Beaumont Plantation. Andre never joined the family for dinner, but Patrice left the seat unoccupied in the hope that one day he would.

"*Mon pere! Mon pere!*"

"Yes, Claude. What is it?"

"Father, can Christophe and I go to town with you tomorrow?"

"Why yes, Claude, I think that will be fine. But do you think you understand the rules well enough so we will not have any problems?"

"Yes, sir. We won't wander off or try to play with any of the white children
and we'll act like we don't want to play with the black children."

"Good boys, we'll see if we can work it out."

Camille smiled as she realized that at such a young age, the two boys grasped
the essentials of St. Domingue society.

Gabrielle, looking lovely as always in her long white dress, became lost in
a momentary daydream and wondered if she would ever be Patrice's legitimate
wife. At first, marriage appeared to be an achievable dream, but of late, it seemed
like pure fantasy. The memory of Patrice's dead wife still held more value for
him than the real life, present-day love and comfort she provided. The funda-
mental difference in status: Patrice, a wealthy *gens de couleur* plantation owner, and
she, just a slave, also presented a major obstacle. Gabrielle was tempted to ask if
she could also go to town, but had tremendous difficulty tolerating the distant
and cold way Patrice treated her in public. She tried to be content with the fantasy of her "marriage" and the daily life she enjoyed within the confines of the
plantation. "Don't let these boys talk you into buying any candy," she offered.

The boys pouted at that, but perked up right away when Patrice managed a
little wink, which meant they needn't worry. Aunt Chantal then flashed a matching smirk, which suggested there would be more goodies waiting for them at her
café. Two house slaves, Elise and Henriette, entered the room to serve the ap-
petizer just as the gallop of a horse could be heard in the distance. Camille was
barely able to get out of her seat and put on her apron before Jacob Bernard burst
through the door exclaiming, "Patrice! Patrice! It's happening!"

Chapter 5

Word Spreads

"Jacob, what is the meaning of this? How dare you burst into my home in this fashion?"

Jacob tried to regain his composure as he said, "*Mon ami*, I'm sorry for the intrusion, but this is urgent. We must speak."

Patrice excused himself and his trusted advisor, Chantal, from the dinner table and led Jacob Bernard to the parlor. Despite his efforts to control himself, Jacob was still trembling. Patrice also had problems maintaining his own composure on occasion and often his heart throbbed whenever he found himself in a stressful situation. This wasn't good for him, and he tried to take his mind off of the problem at hand by taking in the details of his surroundings. This little game put him at ease. The parlor offered so many things to choose from, but Patrice's eyes initially settled where they normally did, the chandelier in the center of the room. This elegant fixture was imported from France and given as a gift by his father. The elder Beaumont suggested that Patrice consider it a symbol of the better things in life and a daily reminder never to settle for mediocrity.

Two layers of drapes, the first white and the second gold, adorned the large windows along the front wall of the parlor. A *petit blanc* had painted a mural of a metal gate around the border of this main window in order to create an even more distinguished look. Patrice frowned as he remembered the parting message offered by the painter after accepting payment and a compliment for his excellent work. The artisan said he couldn't believe all of this opulence was being wasted on a bunch of slaves. Patrice's heart had also thumped at that moment as he required every ounce of his self-control to prevent himself from beating the artisan to a pulp. Unfortunately, mixed-race people in St. Domingue were often confronted with such remarks. Whenever Patrice saw the mural, he tried his best to focus on the excellent quality of the work, but once the memory of the comment returned, his heart again started to pound. He realized his mind game wasn't relaxing him and looked elsewhere for relief.

Patrice turned his attention to the three beautifully framed portraits on the other side of the parlor. His portrait, positioned in the center, was flanked by paintings of his deceased wife, Marie, and father, Guillame. When Patrice felt lost or lonely, gazing into Marie's loving eyes healed him and reminded him of what it meant to love unconditionally. Whenever he faced a difficult decision, staring into his father's experienced eyes brought him back to the dozens of parlor discussions during which father taught son the ways of the world and the principles upon which sound decisions could be made. Today, the news from Jacob Bernard had to be either extraordinarily good or bad, and Patrice began a consultation with his father as he walked toward the portrait. He might not have received any specific advice, but he did get what he needed and his heartbeat slowed, which would enable him to understand, process, and react appropriately to Jacob Bernard's news.

Patrice's family, too disturbed to return to dinner, dispersed throughout the house. Camille went to the kitchen and found her son, Andre, and two servants, Elise and Henriette, gathered around the table discussing the surprise visitor. Andre had grown up with Patrice and many people thought they could pass for brothers—both had relatively light skin, were well-built, and unusually tall at a height of almost six feet. They did act like brothers growing up, but their current relationship was both complicated and strained.

Despite his special privileges on the plantation, Andre resented Patrice and couldn't understand why he'd not been given the greatest privilege of all—freedom. When they were boys, Patrice had promised to make Andre a free man on Andre's 13th birthday. He said this would be a very special birthday present Andre would receive when they were older and the time was right. Patrice repeated this promise for the next few years with each new birthday celebration, but when the elder Beaumont became ill, and Patrice began to assume the day-to-day management of the plantation in his mid-twenties, the promise had morphed from freedom into special privileges. Patrice, the man, appeared to have no intention of keeping his adolescent pledge. As a result, Andre had grown bitter and confrontational, but only in private. He knew to mind his behavior when others were around.

Patrice had a formal education and taught Andre, who boasted of the fact that he'd read every book and pamphlet in Patrice's library. Much of what he read either informed or entertained him, but the only document that ever fascinated him was the one Patrice did not freely offer. Andre had found it two weeks earlier, tucked in the back of Patrice's desk drawer, while searching for an old ledger sheet. Dated just a few months back, this Declaration of the Rights of Man and of the Citizen, gave Andre hope because it implied that the end of slavery was near. Jacob Bernard might have news related to an uprising or emancipation, but in order for Andre to hear it, he first needed to get his mother out of the kitchen.

"*Ma mére*, you look tired. The visitor must have upset you. Why don't you go to your room and I will bring you a plate of food?"

Camille was exhausted–she had gained a lot of weight over the last few years and she often had a good deal of swelling in her ankles. By dinnertime walking became difficult. Camille realized she must look as tired as she felt, because Andre was not usually sensitive to the needs of others. She smiled, took her son's advice and headed for her room. Before Andre prepared the plate for his mother, however, he decided to sweep the area just outside the parlor so he would be within earshot of their surprise visitor. Elise whispered to Henriette, "Since when does he sweep?" Henriette just shrugged her shoulders, because she would never question Andre, who had a kind of power and authority which came as a package with his special status at Beaumont. While he couldn't be formally called the overseer—a slave could never hold that position—Andre did run things as Patrice's right hand. All of the slaves did what he said without question.

Jacob Bernard finally started to speak, "Patrice. The governor turned him down. The governor turned down the petition for full rights. Vincent Ogé is forming an army of *gens de couleur* and we need to go into town tomorrow night to talk about joining his ranks. The *grands blancs* are together with the *petits blancs* in this and we do not want to be discovered, so we must be careful. Our day is coming, Patrice, but we are going to have to fight for it. Why would the *grands blancs* deny us these rights afforded to us by the Declaration? Don't they understand that without us, they will never be able to control the 500,000 slaves on the island? Even with us, the slaves outnumber us ten to one."

Chantal responded before Patrice. "You may use my café for your meeting. I will say I am closed for a private party." Patrice agreed, "We will meet at the café tomorrow night, but please be more discrete. Charging in here like you did tonight isn't good for either the cause or us. Let's not draw any unnecessary attention. Agreed?"

"Agreed."

Andre was excited, confused, and upset by what he had just heard. He knew that Patrice professed to have a distaste for slavery and promised he would advocate for its abolishment once the time was right. In Andre's estimation, that time had arrived but Patrice didn't seem to be honoring his word. First, he chose to hide the Declaration, which arrived months before, and his current talk of banding together with the *grands blancs* to keep the slaves in their place, did not support an anti-slavery position. The fact that slaves outnumbered the white and mixed race population to such a great extent gave Andre even more to consider. Others needed to know—his mother's plate of food would have to wait. Andre headed out to the slaves' quarters.

He moved much faster than he normally did and approached three slaves who were heading to their quarters after a long day in the fields. Andre leaned in and whispered in Creole, *"Lè nou rive. Lafwans libere nou men la gens de couleur Et grands blancs vle kenbe nou. Yo sont traçage kont nou nan vil demen swa, men yo peple sont plus pase nou panse.* Our time has come. France freed us but the *gens de couleur* and *grands blancs* want to hold us down. They are plotting against us in town tomorrow night, but their numbers are smaller than we think."

The three slaves scattered in different directions and within minutes they had passed the message on to a dozen more. Those slaves then gave the message to others. Within thirty minutes the entire slave population at the Beaumont Plantation received the message. One brave slave snuck away from the plantation and ran to a nearby maroon camp. The maroons, who were all runaway slaves, served as an inspiration to those still in captivity. Despite their outlaw status, they did move around and communicate with slaves from many plantations. Andre's message had been passed too many times and as a result, the content had mutated. The Beaumont Plantation slave ran up to the houngan, a voodou priest, who was the leader of this band of maroons and screamed, "*Lè nou rive. Lafwans libere nou men la gens de couleur Et grands blancs vle kenbe nou. Pifò ont s' nan zòn nan deja pou anpil moun yo pa piti. Nou ap atake nan vil demen swa. Libète ou touye!* Our time has come. France freed us but the *gens de couleur* and *grands blancs* want to hold us down. Most have fled the area already so their numbers are small. We attack in town tomorrow night. Liberty or death!"

By nightfall the entire slave population had been informed and Jacmel was like a powder keg waiting to ignite.

CHAPTER 6

Baako's Return

A FEW PLANTATIONS in the north—near the major port of Le Cap Francois—might make a claim of superiority in some respects, but in the Jacmel area Bel Air set the standard. The owner of Bel Air, Henri Baptiste, was known as both a shrewd businessman and a ruthless slave owner, but his brutality was not of a perverse nature. He only administered punishment when rules were broken, but he made sure the vicious nature of its delivery created the best possible deterrent against future transgressions.

As the leader of the *grands blancs* in the southern part of the colony, Henri Baptiste tried to set a good example for other plantation owners in terms of slave management. He considered himself to be a man of reason and spoke of business strategies which maximized his human resource investment. The foundation of his approach: slaves and horse carriages had similar useful lives—about five years. Most died or broke down at that point and needed to be replaced. A few lasted longer or shorter, but the average tended to be about five years. Monsieur Baptiste's slave management program consisted of four guiding principles, which had to be applied without fail during the typical five-year life of a slave:

1. Work them hard.
2. Make punishment immediate for even minor violations of rules.
3. Offer a handsome reward, if they run.
4. Publicly administer severe punishment to runaways upon their return.

He believed in his four-part program, and many of the other *grands blancs* and *gens de couleur* plantation owners followed his lead. Nobody, however, offered a reward even remotely close to what Henri Baptiste paid for the return of his human property. As such, finding a runaway slave with the Bel Air brand became cause for celebration. One of the local carpenters, Jean Claude Guilar, thought about his potential reward money as he waited with his prize catch, an oversized Mandinkha slave, who he believed ran from the Bel Air Plantation.

"*Bonjour* Jean Claude. You may be a fine carpenter, but you're an even better slave tracker. *Vous permettez?*"

"*Appres vous*, Monsieur Baptiste. Of course, please have a look."

"Where did you find this one?"

"Same place I find most of them. They come into town and think they can pass for *gens de couleur.* To me they all look the same, but this one stood out. He appeared to be a foot taller and 50 pounds heavier than any I've ever seen. I thought he might be a runaway, so I checked for the brand. Three of us needed to hold him down to uncover the 'BA.' Take a look, you'll see he tried to scratch it out, but I'd know the classic 'BA' of the Bel Air Plantation anywhere. After we grabbed him and brought him back to my shop, he got away for a moment, and swung at me with a hammer."

Jean Claude paused as he pulled his bandaged hand out of his pocket. "That's right, he crushed my thumb with my own hammer and should be punished accordingly."

"Believe me, Jean Claude, he'll be punished. I know this was no *petit marronge*—he's been gone a long time. I haven't seen him for years and although I own 1000 slaves, I do remember this one. My God, he must be 6' 3" and close to 240 pounds. My overseer is checking his records. The punishment will be severe, especially since he's injured such a prominent tradesmen as yourself. If you're able to manage with that injured finger, you and your assistants may secure him to that post."

"I think I can," Jean Claude responded with a smile as he marched the bare-chested slave to the wall. The slave, a young man of about 17 years, was a *bossale*—which meant he'd been born in Africa. Most of the African born slaves were not as submissive as the creoles, who were born in captivity. This *bossale* knew he was doomed because he'd run three times. All he could do is hope for a merciful death. When he arrived three years earlier, he worked in the *grand ateliers*, the work group for the strongest slaves–a highly unusual placement for a slave who was only 14 years old. Like many of his fellow Mandinkha, he developed physically at a young age and grew to be a strapping man. Despite Jean Claude's large size, he wouldn't have been able to detain this slave by himself. A group of three *petits blancs*: a black-smith, a tailor, and the carpenter, Jean Claude, put the odds in their favor.

Jean Claude whistled as he took the hammer out of his belt while his assis-tants held the slave to the wall. He used just two nails. The slave, nailed to the post though his earlobe, screamed in agony as each nail pierced the skin. All three men laughed, but Henri Baptiste remained serious. He was anxious to get the three buffoons–these low class *petits blancs*–off his plantation.

The overseer arrived with the logbook–a very thick journal used to maintain records on all of the slaves at Bel Air. At any given time, 1,000 slaves worked the large 3000-acre plantation. New arrivals replaced the 200 who died every year. Henri Baptiste loved the math and felt it proved his useful life theory. Replacing 200 slaves each year in an inventory of 1000 did, in fact, suggest a useful life of five years. It was cheaper to treat slaves poorly, have them die in five years and then pay for a replacement, rather than treat them reasonably and have them age and present other problems. Again, just like horse carriages, there's a point when repairs are too costly and functional value has decreased below an acceptable level. Sound economics. Henri prided himself on his deep, elevated thinking.

The overseer was Gilbert Kildew, a man in his late thirties with a beard as long and unkempt as his hair. He whispered a brief summary of the checkered past of this slave into his employer's ear. His name was Baako, and this was the third time he had been returned as a runaway. The first time had been classi-fied as a *petit marronge*—Baako returned in five days. The punishment—a whip-ping—then back to the *grand atelier*. When he ran the second time and returned after two months, Kildew knew he would continue to be a problem so he cut Baako's right hamstring. This explained the pronounced limp this otherwise excellent specimen displayed. This time, he'd been gone for two years and also injured a white man. Even though Jean Claude was just a *petit blanc*, violence against whites could not be tolerated, and his two-year run as a maroon also had to be severely punished. The overseer suggested the most extreme punishment, and Henri Baptiste nodded in agreement, but thought it a shame he wouldn't be able to get a few more years of service out of this strong slave. Baako's limited three-year run with gaps would have an effect on his average useful life calculation. Henri walked over to the slave and addressed him in Creole.

"Baako, ou te ale twò lontan. Sa te fè ou twazyèm fwa kouri ak li m' ap disparèt ou. Baako, you've been gone too long. This was your third time running and it will be your last."

Henri Baptiste turned his back to his slave as he addressed his overseer, "Mr. Kildew, remove Baako from the wall, and let him remain bound in position awaiting his fate."

Jean Claude and his two helpers struggled to control their excitement. They had such hatred for both the slaves and the *gens de couleur.* They understood what the punishment likely would be, but wanted confirmation.

"Does this mean he'll be broken at the wheel?"

Baako obviously understood more than just Creole and reacted when he heard "broken at the wheel," by ripping himself off the post, and charging Henri Baptiste. The four men struggled to protect the plantation owner. Ultimately, a clean blow to the temple from Jean Claude's hammer rendered Baako unconscious.

Jean Claude and his colleagues assisted the overseer in carrying the hulking slave to his place of execution. It wasn't a tree from which he would be hung, or a wall against which he would be shot, it was the large spare wheel of a carriage to which he was bound with his limbs positioned in such a way that they rested in the gaps between the radial spokes. This would allow his bones to remain stationary targets for a large sledgehammer as they were broken in multiple locations. Some slaves were shown mercy when being "broken at the wheel" and received a *coups de grace*—a fatal blow—before each major bone in their body was then systematically shattered. No such mercy would be afforded to Baako, because after running three times, injuring a white man, and attempting to attack his master, Baako's death needed to be an example to all of the other slaves of the consequences of certain actions. The four white men left the condemned slave attached to his wheel of death and began making preparations for the spectacle to come.

CHAPTER 7

Arch Your Back

CHANTAL ARCHAMBEAU SAT in the back of the carriage and inhaled deeply, enjoying the fresh evening air as she headed home. Patrice often spoiled her by sending a driver when she went out to Beaumont, and she had to admit she liked the special treatment. Not the most verbal of men, Patrice showed he cared by arranging for the carriage. He had become family—the little brother she never had.

In the past, the return rides from the Beaumont Plantation had been even more enjoyable with her mother, Giselle, by her side. Their lively discussions often caused the driver to turn his head and check on them, which made them laugh. People sometimes thought the mother and daughter judged the winner of their numerous battles by measuring the volume of their voices rather than the strength of their arguments. Tonight, they would have so much to discuss. Chantal couldn't wait to run up to her mother's bedroom to tell her about the *gens de couleur* meeting at the café. This meeting marked the beginning, and neither of the strong Archambeau women would rest until they saw the end—the end of slavery.

Chantal and Patrice met when he'd just become a teenager. Already a young woman in her twenties, Chantal soon took note of Patrice's potential. Both Giselle and Chantal heard thirteen year-old Patrice promise freedom to Andre—nothing short of majestic, in Chantal's opinion. When she submitted to her mother that Patrice should have delivered on this promise long ago, Giselle disagreed and suggested he would never renege. The time had to be right. Patrice was destined to do great things in his life, and this would be one of them. Chantal never wanted to argue that point.

Deep in thought as the carriage started down the final stretch of road, Chantal asked herself, *would Patrice seize this opportunity and realize the potential he had to be a great leader?* While he had broken new ground in terms of the humane treatment of slaves at Beaumont, he had done nothing of late. All of his changes had taken place within a few years of assuming control of the plantation. Little brother needed to get back on track and just needed a little prompting.

She was also concerned with Patrice's insistence on being secretive about his forward-thinking practices. *What good would it do to have nothing more than one plantation where a kinder and gentler form of slavery was practiced?* Patrice had to be an example, in order to make others change. Chantal hoped he would embrace the idea that it was not good enough to be the best of the worst. Time for Patrice to grow up. No more discussion of potential. As the most influential *gens de couleur* plantation owner in Southern St. Domingue, Patrice Beaumont had the ability to bring about change. He just required advice from time to time, and an occasional push. The carriage pulled up to the café and Chantal headed straight up the stairs to her mother's bedroom.

Conversations between the two Archambeau ladies were explosive—both were head bobbers and finger pointers. As the intensity increased, anyone might assume they were embroiled in a bitter fight, but the astute observer would take note of the little side smiles offered in response to particularly strong points. Chantal explained the evening's events to her mother and surprisingly, no argument ensued—Chantal's report ended with a hug. Giselle wished she had been part of the evening's activities, but she'd finally lost her battle with chronic lower back pain, a condition which plagued her from her early twenties and limited her mobility. She knew Chantal would offer the right encouragement to Patrice at each of the appropriate moments. *So shrewd, my Chantal, making sure the meeting took place at the café. There would have been no other way to insert a woman into the proceedings. Smart girl, just like her mother!*

A natural beauty as a young woman, Giselle was born a slave and served as the concubine of one of the most forbidding *grand blanc* plantation owners. Her dark, smooth skin shone in the strong Caribbean sun and when she graced those in her presence with a smile, she lit up the room. The master took note of Giselle when she turned twenty and moved her into the plantation house. While assigned some duties in the kitchen, her real job involved tending to the needs of the master. Phillipe Archambeau visited her most evenings and often became enraged when he had difficulty maintaining a strong erection. Whenever his body failed him, he took it out on Giselle by choking, punching, paddling, or kicking her. Even on a good night, there was nothing tender about intimacy with the master. The head of the kitchen staff stopped by Giselle's room each morning to determine if her appearance and condition would permit her to work. Many days, she did not meet the standard. The last night she spent with her master provided a lasting memory.

"Turn around, God damn it! I can't stand to look at your ugly face."

Giselle scurried off her back, and dropped to her knees on the edge of the bed. She needed to be exactly at the right level for her diminutive master—her eyes level with the windowsill. As she raised her head to make sure she lined up properly, Giselle spotted a striking red bird perched on a branch of a tree, which pressed up against the house. The bird's hunched posture and downward pointing tail made it unusual, but the black coloring around its eyes commanded most of Giselle's attention as she became lost in its gaze. In the end, however, the beautiful bird proved to be a distraction, and Giselle realized her mistake when Master Archambeau administered the first strike of the paddle; she'd forgotten to arch her lower back.

"God damn stupid whore. Can't you do anything right!"

The force of the paddle drove her stomach to the bed and she quickly got back on her knees and arched her back, but her eyes were still above the windowsill. The paddle again provided feedback. When Giselle assumed the position for the third time, she got it exactly right, but her master's erection failed him. The next five shots from the paddle told her who was to blame. Her masked friend couldn't bear to watch any more, turned its back, and flew away as the beating continued. Eventually, Giselle felt him inside her and then, thankfully, it was over with a few quick thrusts.

The next morning, Philippe Archambeau told Giselle she was not aging well and her unattractive 21-year-old body had to be the source of his erectile troubles. Dismissed from her duties in the house and sent back to the fields, Giselle paused as she departed and passed the full-length mirror at the end of the hallway.

Something wasn't right. She adjusted her clothes, hair, and tried to straighten up, but resumed her slouch in response to shooting pains in her lower back. Giselle's formerly smooth, dark skin was covered with bruises, and her smile, which featured gaps from lost teeth, no longer lit up the room. She agreed with the master and had to admit she had aged very badly during her period of personal service. The pretty young girl who entered the house one year earlier was gone.

Life in the fields was a miserable experience of a different sort. The sun, brutal, the hours, extreme, and the overseers ever present and ready with the whip. Giselle was taunted by the head overseer who joked that she might be too ugly for the master, but seemed just fine to him. The abuse was about to begin again.

Thankfully, Philippe Archambeau died a sudden and unexpected death when he choked on a chicken bone. The funeral attendance reflected the amount of grief generated by his passing—just his older sister, Chantal, and a few of the other plantation owners paid their respects. Everyone agreed—the world was a better place without Philippe Archambeau.

Chantal Archambeau, as sole heir, received all of the proceeds of the estate and had no interest in running a plantation or staying in St. Domingue. Paris seemed like a more fitting place for a single woman of means such as herself. When it became apparent Giselle was pregnant with her brother's child, Chantal moved her back into the house and she experienced the first real peace of her adult life.

The plantation sold before Giselle gave birth and the new owner purchased all of the property with the exception of four slaves who were either close to Chantal or who received the most brutal punishment at the hands of her brother. Chantal gave each of these slaves their freedom and a sum of money to begin their new lives.

For herself, Giselle assumed the only last name she knew, Archambeau, and for her daughter, she thought it fitting to use the first name of the woman who set her free. Her daughter's name, therefore, became Chantal Archambeau. Giselle's goal in life was to make sure her daughter would never be subjected to the same brutal treatment she received as a young woman. Status as a *gens de couleur* business owner provided an excellent starting point, but Giselle continued to push her child to be a fighter—someone who could stand up for herself. She did a good job.

CHAPTER 8

Abraham

ABRAHAM JULIAN NOTICED his prized horse, Champion, had a slight limp during the final approach to the Beaumont Plantation, so he decided to walk next to his friend for the last mile. *So much for my grand entrance*, Abraham chuckled. He seemed tall in the saddle with Champion, and loved the expressions of surprise when he dismounted. Abraham was barely five feet tall.

Given the hours spent training Champion, Abraham never needed to hold the reins or pull and tug. He merely motioned in a direction with his riding crop and the horse obeyed. If he tapped the crop on the ground, Champion attempted a crouch, and if he held it high, the horse would stand on his hind legs. This, however, was not the time for tricks. Abraham suspected Champion had stepped on something because he'd developed a slight hitch in his walk. Once inside the confines of the plantation, Abraham tied Champion to the railing outside the barn, and whispered, "So sorry to treat you like a horse, old friend, but we must keep up appearances."

Abraham strolled toward the main house and continued to be optimistic about his visit. He understood Patrice Beaumont had all of the right connections in Jacmel, and was looking forward to being introduced by him to the *gens de couleur* community. The Julians were established merchants in Aux Cayes, another port city to the west. They were seeking an expansion of their business to new locations.

Time for one more rehearsal—Abraham practiced his self-introduction to Patrice Beaumont, whom he assumed to be a man much older than his 30 years. He often forgot to use the new treatment of his last name. The Portuguese

Juliao, had become a more Anglicized, Julian. Abraham had no love for the Portuguese, who had persecuted Sephardic Jews like the Juliaos for hundreds of years. Changing the last name was an attempt to distance the family from that unpleasant history, but Abraham still found the new last name to be odd. He practiced one last time.

A young man about Abraham's age approached and he assumed it must be one of Patrice's children. When the gentleman opened with, "*Je m'appelle Patrice Beaumont*," Abraham was surprised by the both the youth and vitality of his host—he was sure they would hit it off. Abraham extended his hand, and said, "Monsieur Beaumont, my name is Abraham Julian, and I thank you so much for extending your hospitality to me." Patrice was taken aback by the warm and firm embrace offered by his guest. White men typically did not express such affection toward someone of mixed race, even in matters of business. Race took precedence over everything else in St. Domingue. The multiple handshakes and sincere persona of this merchant were a welcome change.

Patrice had learned of the developing Jewish community in St. Domingue some months before. The Jews were considered to be talented businessmen and Patrice hoped to profit from his dealings with Abraham Julian. He didn't understand much else about the Jews, but assumed he would learn a lot over the next few hours as the men became acquainted.

Patrice suggested they sit in the parlor and have a drink as they discussed their plans for the morning. The timing of Abraham's visit with the organizational meeting for a *gens de couleur* army the next evening was a concern, but Patrice thought he would be able to finish with his guest before the meeting commenced. Abraham found the trappings of the parlor impressive and paid particular attention to both the chandelier and painting of the railings, which framed the window so well.

"Very impressive craftsmanship. Actually, the whole room is remarkable. You are a man with excellent taste."

"*Merci*, Monsieur Julian. I do appreciate the compliment. I try my best to live comfortably in the Beaumont house. I have a nice room set up for you upstairs, but let's take some time to get acquainted."

Gabrielle came into the room with Claude and Christophe to greet their late night guest. She dreaded these situations because introductions could be so awkward, especially in the parlor. While a great man in many respects, Patrice could be odd and insensitive in others. In Gabrielle's mind, the purpose of the large oversized portrait of Marie was to enable Patrice to spend time with his dead wife. She always wondered whom he would introduce first.

"Abraham, I would like you to meet my two sons, Claude and Christophe. My oldest, Claude, is six years old, and this is a beautiful portrait of his mother, Marie, who passed away during childbirth—she was a wonderful woman." Patrice paused as he lost his train of thought and stared into the eyes of his beloved deceased wife. Gabrielle was dying during every moment of this awkward silence.

"And this is my youngest son, Christophe—five years old, and his mother Gabrielle. Come say hello to Monsieur Julian, boys."

Insulted, yet again—always an afterthought. Gabrielle offered a meek smile to Abraham who seemed to understand her frustration at that particular moment. After properly greeting each of the boys, Abraham mercifully turned to Gabrielle, and said, "Madam, I can only assume this wonderful home is the result of your fine attention to detail and superb sense of style. Congratulations on creating what must be the finest mansion in southern St. Domingue."

Gabrielle smiled and appreciated the acknowledgement, but it was all lost on Patrice, who again seemed content to stare into his dead wife's eyes.

Abraham saw that his new friend did not pick up these signals from Gabrielle, but it would have been inappropriate for him to point this out, even in private, because of the newness of their relationship. The two men settled into their chairs, and Abraham started to tell the story of how his family wound up in the Caribbean.

"My family was originally from the Portuguese town of Oporto. I can trace them back to that city in the 1500's. Sizeable numbers of Sephardic Jews lived in Portugal at that time. Years later, most of the Jews left Portugal and headed for Amsterdam, a more welcoming city to people of the Jewish faith. Then a large group, which included the Julians, travelled to the colony of Brazil when the Dutch took control, and a considerable Jewish community began to grow in the town of Recife. Unfortunately, the Portuguese regained control, which forced the Jews to leave with many, including my family, migrating to Curacao in the Caribbean. This is where I grew up. About ten years ago, I learned of a growing Jewish community in St. Domingue and I came here as a young man, took a wonderful wife, Rachel, and we have one son, Moses. I'm just as proud of Moses as you are of Claude and Christophe."

Patrice enjoyed the story and Abraham realized he'd already built a strong bond with his host. The conversation moved seamlessly from important issues of the day to funny anecdotes where the only response was a deep laugh. Soon, humor outpaced the serious matters. Abraham was on a roll. People who met him admired his business sense, but loved his stories and jokes. Things were going so well, Abraham decided to tread into dangerous territory when he caught a glimpse of Gabrielle in the outer area of the parlor. He waited for the right moment and said, "You know, Patrice, I'm quite sure you're as proud of Gabrielle as I am of my wife, Rachel." Patrice thought it an odd comment, but one worthy of reply, and said, "Why yes, she is simply wonderful. I don't know what I would do without her."

"Yes, I know what you mean exactly. I've realized though, at least with my wife, I need to tell her how I feel from time to time. There is something about hearing the words that makes all the difference."

"We seem to be similar in many ways, Abraham, but unlike you, I do have difficulty saying those types of things, but she understands me. Of that I'm sure."

"Yes, I'm sure you're right, my new friend. Quite sure."

Abraham hoped she heard the exchange. Thankfully, she did and Gabrielle sat for a moment to compose herself. Tears of joy streamed down her face. She wasn't just a slave who warmed the master's bed and cared for his children–he loved her. She hadn't understood, but due to this odd little visitor, she now did.

As the two men continued their conversation, they realized the similarities between the *gens de couleur* and Sephardic Jews. The Code Noir, the loose law governing the proper treatment of slaves in French controlled territories, actually had a section related to Jews. Like the *gens de couleur*, they were second-class in terms of liberties, but first-class citizens when it came to business. After a few hours of conversation, Abraham bid Patrice good night with a friendly hug around the shoulder. The last white man who showed Patrice this kind of affection looked down on the scene from his framed perch on the wall. Patrice wondered if his father would have been impressed with or suspicious of the warmth and sincerity of his special guest. While he was unsure of his father's position on the matter, his stance was clear. Abraham Julian's friendship provided an agreeable end to a difficult and tumultuous day.

CHAPTER 9

Celebrating The Catch

FEELING THE EFFECTS of the liberal amounts of rum he and his fellow slave catch-
ers had consumed, Jean Claude Guilar reflected on the evening's festivities.
Baako was a prize catch, but not so much because of his size. The true cause for
celebration: the extraordinary bounty paid by Henri Baptiste. The idea of drinking a toast to each bone in Baako's body, which would likely be broken the following morning, seemed brilliant at the time. The group started with the arms,
and at the point they got to the toes, Jean Claude was physically drunk from the
rum and emotionally intoxicated from the glorious vision of Baako screaming
in agony. *What a spectacle it will be!* Jean Claude thought, giddy with excitement.

Approaching his shop in downtown Jacmel, the carpenter took note of a
piece of paper nailed to his door as well as some townspeople across the street
looking his way. A document on his door was something out of the ordinary,
and Jean Claude's curiosity got the better of him. He picked up his pace. Given
his condition, however, moving faster proved to be a bad decision and Jean
Claude stumbled, falling face-first into the dirt in front of his shop door. The
group across the street started to laugh.

"Sleep it off you big drunk fool and pay your bills like a decent citizen."

Jean Claude heard the remark and tried to rise to defend his honor. As he
did, he fell again—this time falling backward. The group had a final laugh and
moved on. Much more intoxicated than he'd thought, Jean Claude took a moment while on his back to regroup.

His head started to clear as he peeked across the street. Thankfully, no one
was left to pass any additional humiliating remarks. Jean Claude laughed; he

knew he looked a fool. He also knew he wasn't in a position to waste money on rum or other excesses because he had trouble meeting his basic expenses. The expected bounty from Henri Baptiste would enable him to barely survive yet another month in this otherwise thriving French colony. St. Domingue never seemed so booming to Jean Claude. Perhaps he should have settled in New Orleans with his older brother, who told tales of the fabulous life he led with his beautiful wife and two children. Jean Claude often thought of making his way to New Orleans, but understood his brother, also a carpenter by trade, might also be struggling. Jean Claude couldn't write, but always responded to his brother's correspondence by dictating letters to a drinking friend who wrote on his behalf. One of these letters described his grand life in Jacmel and Jean Claude's scribe told him he didn't realize he'd be writing fiction. Perhaps his brother lied as well about his financial fortunes in New Orleans. If that were the case, the only thing worse than their actual circumstances would be the realization they were both failures living a fantasy.

Jean Claude got on all fours, scanned to his left and right to verify the group across the street had not come back, slowly stood up, and started to make his way to the paper posted on his door. *Probably a bill of some kind.* While he couldn't read, he did understand numbers and basic phrases. The bandage on his thumb made it difficult, however, to remove the notice from the door. He wobbled, almost fell backward, and then concluded the rum might also have something to do with his problems with coordination. Still, the bandage on his thumb had to go, and Jean Claude once again checked the immediate vicinity before he removed it. He smiled as he flexed his perfectly healthy thumb—Baako never attacked him at all. The claim of serious injury to a white man by a slave was sheer creative genius and ensured severe punishment regardless of the amount of time the slave had been a runaway. As it turns out, it wasn't necessary—Baako had been gone two years and the punishment would have been severe even without the false claim. Finally, Jean Claude turned his attention to the paper he'd just removed from his door and made a mental note of the number and the date—two months behind on his rent with three days to pay it. Another chuckle emerged from the drunken mouth of this very unsuccessful carpenter. At just two months behind, he was in better shape with his rent than most of his other bills.

The bounty for Baako would give him some temporary financial relief. A more permanent improvement could only come from greater success as a carpenter and he needed more business from *grands blancs* like Henri Baptiste in order to begin to move forward in that regard. Jean Claude knew what Henri and most of the other white plantation owners had to say about him behind his back and none of it was flattering. He wondered though, if Henri was sincere earlier that day when he referred to him as a "fine tradesman," because if he really thought of him that way, there was hope. Regular carpentry work at the Bel Air Plantation would make a tremendous difference for his business. Once Henri Baptiste gave him work, other *grands blancs* would as well. They always followed his lead.

One carpenter in Jacmel did well because he accepted work from the growing *gens de couleur* class. That was where Jean Claude drew the line, and while a mistake in terms of business, he couldn't bring himself to be subservient to these black dogs–they were all the same. The only difference–the *gens de couleur* had the luck of being fathered by a wealthy white man. Had there been more white women available for the *grands blancs*, Jean Claude reasoned, this entire mixed race class might not even exist. Jean Claude enjoyed insulting the *gens de couleur* by referring to them as "slaves in a suit." While hatred is what he officially espoused, jealousy was more the source of Jean Claude's animosity for the *gens de couleur*, who in comparison to most of the *petits blancs*, lived like kings.

Jean Claude went upstairs to his bedroom and collapsed on his bed. He had so much to worry about, but also reason to be hopeful because he was certain the French Revolution would improve the station of working class whites. After all, artisans like Jean Claude were the ones who made France into the greatest country in the world. He understood an important law called something like the The Rights of The White Man and of the Citizen had been passed in France, and once implemented, white tradesmen would more fully participate in the tremendous wealth being created in the colonies. Surely, this reaffirmation of white rights would mean an end to the *gens de couleur*, and would finally take the suits off these black dogs and put them back with the slaves. With change just around the corner, Jean Claude smiled as he collapsed on his bed still dressed in his street clothes.

CHAPTER 10

The Maroons

THE RITUAL HAD just begun in the maroon camp in the hills north of Jacmel and Mambo Variola needed to invoke Papa Legba, perhaps the most important loa, or spirit. His permission had to be sought before other loas could be summoned. This ceremony took place whenever a newborn child died. The loa who would be called upon after Papa Legba, was Marassa—the sacred twins of Vodou, who represent family, love, justice, the purity of children, and the mystery of conception. The Marassa are male and female and adhere to a notion that one plus one equals three—representing the fact that one female and one male can join to create a third through the wonder of childbirth. The assembled maroons began to sing the Song for Marassa in an endless loop.

"Marassa nou nan nwa e
Marassa Ginen nou nan nwa devan bondye
Dossou Marassa pote chandel pou klere nou

Marassa we are in the dark
Marassa from Guinea we are in the dark in front of God
Dossou Marassa bring the lamp to shine upon us"

The maroons actively practiced Vodou, a mixture of old African religious beliefs and Christianity. Prayers were directed to loas like Papa Legba or Marassa, because the supreme being, Bondye, was unreachable. When slaves arrived from Africa, forced conversions to Catholicism were common, but the practice of Vodou secretly continued when the slaves began using the images of the Catholic saints to represent the different loa. So while the slave owners assumed prayers were being directed toward Christian saints, the slaves were actually praying to a particular loa. The Vodou concept of heaven was a return to "Guinea," a generic term used for West Africa. The houngans and mambos—male and female priests—led all of the religious rituals.

This sprawling community of maroons numbered in excess of 2,000 runaway slaves with leadership concentrated among the houngans and mambos. Over the hill from the location of the religious ceremony, a small group of three houngans sat together to strategize about the confrontation, which would take place the next evening in Jacmel.

The de facto head of the camp, Houngan Alanso, had been a house slave to Henri Baptiste for a number of years before escaping. Literate and more considered in his approach to matters than most of the other leaders, Alanso was respected without doubt as the religious authority, and also exerted significant influence over many aspects of maroon life. The other priests and priestesses, with one notable exception, deferred to his views on most topics. His one problem child had always been the volatile Houngan Baturu, who seemed distracted and agitated at this particular moment. Alanso needed Baturu's support. A maroon community was not a military organization, and Alanso was concerned about his ability to direct the actions of the maroons in the upcoming conflict. Typically, the masses were more receptive to the dramatic and radical pleas of someone like Baturu, rather than the simple voice of reason, which was Alanso's standard offering. The leaders knew the events of the next evening might mark the end of slavery in St. Domingue and also offer them the opportunity for revenge against their long-time captors. Houngan Alanso was the first to speak.

"*Nou pa te resevwa nouvèl enpòtan sa a de twa diferan sous, Et sa ap difisil nèt pou pa remake diferans nan vèsyon yo. Reyalite a se sa nou konnen ke yon bagay k ap pase nan Jakmèl demen swa Et li kapab yon révolte, oubyen li kapab yon bagay anpil mwens ke sa.* We have received this important news from three different sources, and it is hard not to notice the difference in the versions. Something is going on in Jacmel tomorrow night and it may be a revolt, or it may be something much less than that."

Alanso paused for a moment and Houngan Suma nodded in agreement, while Baturu rose to his feet and began to pace. Alanso continued.

"Se tou tout posib ke la grands blancs o kouran de sa e yo planifye pou rankontre nou gen gwo kout. Nou bezwen pou yo toujou pare pou fè, si sa ki dwat devan Bondye, nou dwe jwenn kèk fason pou kontwole tèt nou, si kòrèk desiz yon an, se pou retire kò l tounen ret tann pou yon opòtinite pi bon. Mwen panse ke nou pwal kapab pou detèmine sa pou nou fè, men mwen menm ki konsène ke nou p'ap ka pou kontwole yon pil nou. It is also possible the *grands blancs* are aware of this and plan to meet us there with tremendous force. We need to be ready to act, if the time is right, and we must find some way to control ourselves, if the correct decision is to pull back and wait for a better opportunity. I think we will be able to determine the right thing to do, but I am worried we will not be able to control our masses."

Houngan Suma, who tended to be similar to Alanso in ideology and temperament, chimed in, *"Mwen dako. Nou ta dwe eseye pou plis pase yon militè òganizasyon Et dw nan ti gwoup ki te kontwole pa chak nan nou.* I agree. We should try to be more of a military organization and divide into smaller groups controlled by each of us."

Baturu's pacing suddenly stopped and he raised his voice, as he countered, *"De kisa w ap pale? Denmen, nou goumen yo, ak soit nou genyen, Et abattage kaptire yo a nou ou nou bon mouri tounen al jwenn Guinee. Yon bagay sa inaseptab. M pral pa tande yon lòt bagay. Mwen konnen sa nou gen pou fè ak mwen pral bay ouf a.* What are you talking about? Tomorrow we fight, and either we win and slaughter our captors or we die a good death and go back to Guinea. Anything short of that is unacceptable. I will not hear anything else. I know what we have to do and I will provide the inspiration."

Baturu rushed away from the meeting of the leaders and headed over to the area where the religious ceremony just ended. Alanso had failed yet again to get through to the volatile young priest. Even with his help, Alanso doubted if the large group of maroons would take direction to any extent, but without his cooperation, it was certainly impossible. Suma raised his eyebrows at Alanso in a request for guidance. Alanso lowered his head in response. Neither man had anything to say.

Word spread that Baturu was about to channel the spirits. A large crowd of maroons gathered and formed a circle around the houngan who started to writhe and tremble on the ground as the skies opened up. Within a few moments, thunder clapped in the distance. Baturu's convulsions increased in proportion to the thunder and lightening, which appeared to be moving closer to the ceremony. Rain started to pour in buckets. The loa of Kalfu was being channeled. Once Kalfu was present, the assembled group became silent because they were in the presence of evil. Baturu's eyes blackened and his muscles started to swell. An elderly maroon, who often assisted with religious rituals, walked a squealing black pig toward the possessed houngan being careful to keep the pig between himself and the convulsing priest. A tremendous bolt of lightening provided Baturu with his cue, and he slit the pig's throat while crying out, *"Lanmò pou nou kaptire yo demen swa rekòt kafe/zaboka libète ou touye!* Death to our captors tomorrow night…liberty or death."

Whipped into a frenzy, the throng of maroons who gathered to see the spirited houngan deliver his message, sat and drank the blood of the pig as they continued crying into the night, *"Libète ou touye!* Liberty or death."

Houngan Alanso viewed the ritual from above the hill as he grasped the magnitude of Baturu's mistake. There would be no self-control in Jacmel. No thought or coordinated action. Throughout the day, the chant of "liberty or death" summarized the two possible outcomes of the unfolding conflict. Due to Baturu's error in judgment, however, "death" was a much more likely outcome than "liberty."

CHAPTER 11

Why, Master, Why?

NAKED, BLOODY, AND terrified—Henriette burst through the kitchen door in the back of the Beaumont Plantation house. Her only thought, putting as much distance between her and the main house as possible. This wasn't the first time. Numerous bruises on her back chronicled previous episodes of abuse. Blood dripped from her lip as she ran toward the slaves' quarters passing Abraham Julian, who had decided to enjoy a smoke in the cool evening air. Henriette barely noticed the little man as she dashed past his position behind the house.

While sex with slaves was not at all uncommon in St. Domingue or anywhere else in the world, Abraham found himself shocked as he processed the image of the fleeing house servant. When he met Patrice and his strikingly beautiful partner, Gabrielle, he didn't think the man had either the disposition or the need for such abuse. *What a shame, I thought he was more enlightened in that regard.*

Abraham became lost in his thoughts and realized the hypocrisy of classifying anything related to the institution of slavery as being enlightened. In Abraham's mind, the goal of his personal participation in its practice was to avoid two distinct disadvantages. First, if he did not own slaves, those who did would have a natural distrust of him, and as a Jew, trust issues were always a concern. Second, cheap labor provided a significant business advantage, and Abraham considered himself to be a shrewd businessman. Once slavery became outlawed and wages started to be paid to everyone, prices would adjust for the increased costs, and competition would again be level. Until then, however, it was hard to compete without some assistance from cheap slave labor. *What absolute nonsense*, he told himself after rationalizing with this two-part argument, yet again. Slavery was wrong, and sexually or physically abusing your slaves, exponentially worse.

As Abraham decided whether he should stay the night or make an excuse and leave in the morning, he heard the voices from inside the house. Camille, the head housekeeper, who Abraham caught a glimpse of earlier, appeared to be chastising Patrice for his transgression. *What nerve!* Abraham thought. This could easily escalate into a terrible scene. Patrice was shirtless, and Abraham became disgusted by the bloodstains, which were splattered all over his back. *The woman must have fought. How foolish of her! It probably made him abuse her even more.*

Camille picked up a rolling pin and started to hit Patrice. *This is not going to end well. Time to head back to Aux Cayes.* First, he needed to collect his belongings from inside the house. As he headed toward the door, Patrice turned and glanced in his direction. *Thank God, it's not him.* The shirtless man with the bloodstains on his back was the overseer, Andre—Camille's son–who could have been Patrice's double from a distance.

Abraham quickly circled around to the front of the house so as not to get involved in this family matter and left the mother and son alone to deal with the unfortunate incident.

"What wrong with you, Andre! How you treat Henriette like this? I know she ain't only one. You got three babies already here with three women. How you like it this happen me? You say you want freedom outside, but look what you do with it inside at Beaumont. You just bad, plain bad, through and through. Don't know why Patrice puts up with you. How you do this to her, how you do this me, and how you do this to Patrice? Tell me, Andre. How?"

She hit him with the rolling pin to punctuate her thoughts. "Tell me how." another blow, "How you do this? How?" Camille, in a state of exhaustion, started to lose her footing. Her son let her fall to the floor.

"I hope you're done, because I'm done. We grew up like brothers and he promised me my freedom, but I'm still nothing but a slave. Yes, I'm angry, and you better stay out of my way. Things are about to change, and he thinks he can treat me like this? I'll treat him the same way when the tables turn, and they are turning, that much I promise you."

Andre left, and Elise, another house servant who hid behind the closed door in the adjoining room, came in and helped Camille to her feet. After thanking Elise for her help, Camille straightened her clothing, and sat alone in the kitchen with her thoughts. Camille was so concerned for her son Andre, who had good left in him, and also Patrice, who didn't deserve this kind of thanks. Change did seem to be in the air. On that point, Andre might be right. The slaves had been whispering all night, but most didn't confide in her because of her closeness with the master.

Camille got up from her seat at the table and decided to sit in the parlor in front of the portrait of Patrice's father, Guillame. The rendering of the elder Beaumont seemed even more severe when illuminated by candlelight. She settled in for a conversation—Patrice was not the only person in the house who spoke to the portraits. "Master Guillame, look what you done. Why? You no see this coming? Why, Master, why?" Once again, the master had nothing to say. Camille always wished the answer would be offered one day, and based on what Andre implied, she hoped it wouldn't be one day too late.

CHAPTER 12

The Old Barn

THE OLD BARN was constructed on the highest point of elevation at the Beaumont Plantation and was no longer in active use. When Patrice took over the plantation from his father, he questioned its location. With so much flat space where a more accessible structure might be built, Patrice never understood his father's rationale for building on top of a steep hill. Once he was in charge, building a new barn had become Patrice's first project.

The old barn still had its uses, however, because of the elevation as well as its unusual construction. The tall structure had two staircases--one in the front and one in the back--which led to railed rooftop decks. The decks, separated by a wall upon which a large bell was mounted, provided an unfettered view for miles. During the day, guests approaching Beaumont could be spotted well before they ever reached the property from the front deck. At night, the back deck was the best place in Southern St. Domingue to star gaze or admire the big boats, which appeared as shadows because of the odd combination of moonlight and industrial lanterns mounted on their decks.

Patrice and Andre started walking up to the barn every evening as teenage boys. They did everything together during those years: trips to town, chores around the plantation, and late night stargazing. The back deck became their favorite spot to sit, legs dangling, while they held onto the rail and dreamt of sailing away on one of the ships silhouetted in the harbor. Andre would have been happy to leave and never return, but Patrice classified all of their imaginary voyages as brief adventures. His life was at Beaumont and soon his education as a man would commence. According to Patrice's father, he'd been granted sixteen years of foolishness, during which his job was to be a well-behaved son and a good student. Once he turned seventeen, however, his apprenticeship with his father would begin and he would learn the rules of business and society.

Patrice remembered his last night of childhood—the day before his apprenticeship began.

"Look at the boat anchored just off the shore. What a fabulous ship. A good one for our trip. Maybe we should go to Marseilles and spend time with fancy French ladies?" Patrice's suggestion caused both boys to smile, giggle, and take a momentary break from their conversation. He continued, "Then when we come back, we can see how the St. Domingue girls compare. What an adventure! Do you want to do it, Andre? Or do you want to go somewhere else?"

"France would be an excellent choice, but why do we have to come back? Let's get out of St. Domingue and be men of the world. Just you and I. We're a team."

"I know we are, but we're also kind of like brothers. We'll really be a team once I give you your freedom and we run Beaumont together. We'll be the best team ever."

"When will you make me a free man?"

"I can't do it until I'm in charge. Father runs things now and he says it shouldn't be done and he won't do it. Once I'm making the decisions, I'll make sure it happens. My training starts tomorrow, so we can't go to town like we normally do. Father says you're also starting in the morning, even though your birthday is a few weeks away. He says it is time for both of us to be men. Meet me up here tomorrow night and we'll talk about our training."

The sun barely rose the following morning. No rain fell, but dark clouds covered the sky. Guillame Beaumont was finishing up with Andre behind the big house.

"Andre, you'll be treated fairly, and I will always give you some special privileges, but you must come to grips with the fact you are a man—a black man who is a slave. You had a carefree childhood and I'm happy I did that for you, but you and Patrice have different places in society. If you continue to behave properly, you will lead a good life, but not the same kind of life as Patrice. He is a free man and he will be your master when I pass on. It is time for the two of you to forget the foolishness of childhood. I want you to move from your mother's room in the big house to the slave quarters. The overseer, Mr. Johnson, will first teach you how to be a good field hand and then he will put you in charge of a group of slaves. It will be good honest work, Andre. This is your life. Embrace it. Do you understand?"

"What did I do wrong, Master Beaumont? Patrice and I always do everything together. Why am I being sent out to the fields? I don't understand?"

"Listen, boy. I let this go too far. You were good company for my son growing up, but that's over. Get your things out of my house, report to Mr. Johnson, and learn how to do the work of a slave. I'm being very generous in arranging for you to only be in the fields for a short time. After you're trained, you'll be Johnson's assistant, and it will be a decent life. Go on. Get your stuff and go."

Andre ran right by Patrice as he entered the house with tears streaming from his eyes. His mother was nowhere to be found–arrangements had been made for Camille to be on an early morning trip into town. Guillame Beaumont followed behind Andre intent on preventing any interaction of any kind between the boys.

Andre accepted his fate, walked over to the slave quarters, settled into his new home, and sought out Mr. Johnson. He'd gone from being an optimistic boy with hopes for the future to a young man who understood his whole life had been a lie. He had never belonged in that house. The master made that clear. His only consolation was that all of this would change when Patrice was in charge.

"Patrice, let's go to the parlor. It is time to begin."

Father and son retreated to the parlor for a two-hour lesson. Every weekday morning for the next year would begin this way. The father soon realized his son had a natural sense for business. He had difficulty, however, with the rules of society. This was a concern for the elder Beaumont because no matter how shrewd you were in business, if you didn't adapt to the norms of society, you would not survive.

A year into Patrice's education, his father asked him to provide a description of St. Domingue society based on what he had learned in his early morning lessons. Patrice began:

"White men should marry white women, but when they are not available, a free colored woman is an acceptable substitute—the lighter the skin, the better. When the white man and *gens de couleur* woman conceive, the offspring should be lighter than the mother. After years of careful planning, each generation should be more white, and eventually, the purity should be such that the presence of color is almost undetectable. I am the product of a white man and a *gens de couleur* woman, and I will seek a light skinned woman to marry and be the mother of my children. If I make the mistake of mating with a slave, I can choose to either recognize the child or not. As a *gens de couleur* plantation owner, I will have absolute authority on my property, and if I hire any white workers, they must do as I say, but when I leave the plantation, I must understand my lower standing in life."

Patrice hated this when he heard it for the first time. He did his best, however, to spit it back without emotion. In essence, his father told him he'd be the king at Beaumont, but a peasant anywhere else, and he knew he had to accept that fact because as his father always said, you have to go along to get along.

A few days after the boys' orientations, Guillame Beaumont permitted them to walk together to town for supplies. It was intended as a test of whether their relationship could evolve into something more appropriate. That trip, however, was a disaster, and after that interaction, Andre and Patrice had little regular contact. Camille detected the change in her formerly happy boy, who was becoming a bitter man. Eventually, Mr. Johnson left Beaumont for another opportunity, and Andre started filling in temporarily as the acting overseer although a black man could never truly be in that position. In time, the slaves grew to hate Andre, and Guillame Beaumont was pleased to see that he inspired as much fear as any white overseer would have.

Patrice did find a beautiful light skinned *gens de couleur* woman named Marie. Their attraction was immediate, and their courtship, brief; Patrice was married before his 30th birthday, but became a widower before his 31st. One night in a drunken moment of weakness soon after the death of his wife, Patrice invited Gabrielle to his bed, and even though it was much too soon and somewhat disrespectful to the memory of his beloved wife, he needed a mother to his newborn child, and Gabrielle was a natural. Initially, Patrice could not feel deep love for Gabrielle because he continued to mourn Marie. When Gabrielle became pregnant, he realized this child would be a step lower in the class system than his first son, Claude, but celebrated the birth of Christophe and made a point of never flaunting the fact he had a slave as his mother. Luckily, Christophe had the same skin color as Claude–perhaps he would get by.

Guillame Beaumont passed away after Christophe's birth and Patrice was finally in total charge of the plantation. One evening, he needed a place to think and decided to go up to the old barn. He noticed Andre's legs dangling from the back deck and Patrice assumed he had his eyes trained on the big ship in the harbor and was enjoying a grand adventure in his mind. Joining his childhood friend to reminisce or share a simple "How was your day?" discussion was not an option–they no longer enjoyed that type of relationship. After climbing the staircase to the front deck and comfortably situating himself on a crate, Patrice became lost in his own thoughts as he admired the view of Jacmel.

Andre's visions continued to take him far away from St. Domingue never to return, and Patrice's thoughts started to do the same, as he questioned so many of the rules of society, but the dreams of the two men were individual fantasies– they were no longer a team. In time, they developed an understanding of who would walk up first and come down last, and Patrice ceded the harbor side of the barn to Andre. The two men continued their daily nocturnal visits for many years, never acknowledging each other, and always maintaining the separation appropriate between a master and his slave.

CHAPTER 13

Broken at the Wheel

"Drink this Baako. It help speed trip to Guinea. This help. Drink fast. No slow death, Baako. Guinea calling."

The woman, captured with Baako three years earlier in West Africa, always had a liking for him, and wanted to make his death more merciful. The special formula for this drink, passed down verbally for generations in her village, required herbs, which luckily grew in abundance in St. Domingue. After the initial reduction of pain, Baako would hallucinate, and then experience terrible cramps followed by death. She scurried away before the guard returned. It was almost daylight.

The roosters signaled the morning sun and the slave quarters began to show signs of life. Normally, it would be straight out to the fields, but today there would be a late start, because Henri Baptiste wanted a full crowd to witness the execution. He lined up the *grands ateliers*, the work group containing the strongest workers, closest to the execution. These slaves represented the greatest value to the master and needed to be so close, they could almost feel the pain. Henri Baptiste thought the pace of runaways would slow after the spectacle of seeing Baako broken at the wheel.

Despite his heavy drinking the previous night, Jean Claude arrived a few minutes before Henri Baptiste and Gilbert Kildew. The overseer began to strategically place thirty-five armed men throughout the crowd of about 400 slaves who would witness the execution. The *petits ateliers*, the work group with the weaker or slightly incapacitated slaves, took up the rear.

Jean Claude did his best to act calm, but his hatred convinced him that being broken at the wheel was fair punishment for the crime of running away. The fact he'd enjoy it so much—an added bonus. The overseer motioned for Jean Claude to pick up the sledgehammer in order to act as the executioner. Henri winked as he whispered to the flattered carpenter, "Do you think you can manage with that injured thumb?" The pretense of the bandage no longer necessary, Jean Claude smiled as he removed it from his thumb, and started to take some practice swings with the sledgehammer.

The effect of the herbs took Baako's mind thousands of miles away to Africa where as a young boy he received his rite of passage. At the age of thirteen, all Mandinkha boys and girls were sent from the main village to the bush for a ritual cutting of the genitals. For boys, it amounted to a rough circumcision. While in the bush healing, the boys and girls were instructed by selected elders in the proper way for men and women to interact in Mandinkha society. The bond formed with others who participated in the same ritual was lifelong and the woman who gave Baako his deadly herb cocktail had shared this experience with him four years ago. He remembered the cut, the pain, and then the joy in knowing he'd become a man. Baako also recalled the agony experienced by the girls and the compassion he had for them. Years later, the memory of the pain faded but the sense of relief and celebration remained. He recalled returning to the village and being welcomed back as a man.

Henri Baptiste addressed the crowd, but to Baako, it sounded like background noise. He was still back in Africa listening to his mentor instructing him in the joys of manhood. The wisdom of the words and the sincerity of the advice made Baako smile. *This is what it means to be a man.* The walk back to his village provided time for reflection. It was a triumphant return—his life as a man was about to start. As Baako smiled again in a moment of celebration, the assembled Bel Air Plantation slaves did not know what to make of his apparent good spirits. His courage, however, was emboldening.

Baako was still tied to the large wagon wheel, arms and legs positioned between the radial spokes. On occasion, the brutality of being broken at the wheel was lessened by slitting the throat of the victim before the systematic breaking of bones commenced. If the executioner had less mercy in his heart, he broke one or two bones and then provided a *coups de grace* of a different variety, a fatal blow to the chest. All of the other bones would still be broken for the purpose of the spectacle, but at least the suffering would be over.

The question of mercy never occurred to Jean Claude, who planned to enjoy each and every broken bone. Compassion also did not factor into the thoughts of Henri Baptiste, who wanted the kind of brutal display that would deter other slaves from running. Jean Claude started his work. The first blow connected with Baako's big right arm. Whack!!!! The sound of breaking bones filled the air, and Baako simply winced, but remained quiet. Without the anticipated scream, Jean Claude's drunken dream of unbearable agony went unfulfilled.

Baako smiled once more, and Henri Baptiste offered a sneer to Jean Claude, who was determined to produce a better result with his next blow. The carpenter, no stranger to a sledgehammer, took a step back to widen his arc and grunted as he swung with all of his might—whack!!!!!—the left arm shattered and hung lifeless from the wheel. Baako's reaction…a small grunt, still no screaming, just another smile. The houngans and mambos in the maroon camp had prepared him with the knowledge that death would bring him back to Guinea. Baako smiled with his widest grin of the day. The crowd roared in reaction to his courage.

When Jean Claude broke Baako's right leg, the crack of the bones was so loud, the slaves in the front row screamed. Incredibly, Baako started to chant:

"O Legba! Commandé
Vié Legba! Commandé
Commandé-yo.

O Legba! Give Orders
Old Legba! Give Orders
Give them orders."

The other slaves could not believe Baako had the strength to chant. His volume low at first with his body slumped, but later with both his head and voice raised higher by the encouragement of the crowd. Baako appealed to the important loa or spirit, Papa Legba, to give orders to the imprisoned slaves. The *grands ateliers* joined first, followed by the rest, and many started banging on the barn and stomping their feet to create a punctuated rhythm as they joined the chant. Again, Baako's mind took him home to his village after becoming a man in the woods and he remembered the release and celebration of the cut. The cramps started as Jean Claude swung the sledgehammer to break Baako's left leg. Whack!!!! It was done. Baako experienced the same release as when he'd become a man back home in Guinea. The deadly herb concoction had run its course. The crowd realized this, gripped their arms together, and rocked back and forth with their eyes closed as they continued to chant:

"O Legba! Commandé
Vié Legba! Commandé
Commandé-yo."

Henri Baptiste had the dead runaway removed from the wheel. His initial plan, to leave Baako to die slowly, while the slaves walked by him twice a day on their way to and from the fields, would not work. The brutal exhibition did not have the desired effect and leaving Baako on display for any additional time would further incite the Bel Air slaves. Instead of being deterred from running, they were more determined than ever to make the most of their opportunity to rise up against their captors later that night. One slave whispered to another that Papa Legba had given orders, and the message was passed down the line. Within minutes, the entire group of assembled slaves stared menacingly at Henri Baptiste, Gilbert Kildew, and Jean Claude Guilar, and then looked past them to the three carriage wheels mounted on the wall behind them. The orders from Papa Legba were clear: one wheel would be for the carpenter, another for the overseer, and the last for the master himself. This final act of indignity and cruelty would not go unanswered for long.

CHAPTER 14

The Minuet

"FATHER, WHY DO I have to go to this ball? I'm too busy. I don't have time for this."

"I'm surprised you would ask such a question. You're always telling me that I'm old fashioned and not open to new ways. Don't you think a social function where *grands blancs* are willing to mingle with *gens de couleur* is important? It may not be the biggest event of the year, but over twenty people should be in attendance, and it is being held at Beaumont. So don't be foolish, Patrice, this is something you must attend."

"As you wish, father."

Guillame Beaumont worried about Patrice, who at the age of 29 had no prospects for marriage. Three of the most desirable and unmarried *gens de couleur* women would be at the ball. Hopeful one of these beauties would catch his son's eye, Guillame needed Patrice to be ready to impress.

"Patrice, time for your dance lesson," Chantal Archambeau called up the stairs of the Beaumont mansion. The large common room on the ground floor had been transformed, the rug rolled and removed to another part of the house, and the wooden floors polished and ready to celebrate. With all of the furniture pushed out to the perimeter, the center of the room became the dance floor, and a single violin player, seated in a chair in the corner by the entrance, took her position. Chantal and her mother, Giselle, prepared to demonstrate a minuet for Patrice.

"Good afternoon, Chantal. Good afternoon, Mademoiselle Archambeau. Thank you so much for helping me in my time of personal need."

"Yes, we understand you've never received a proper dancing lesson. My daughter and I plan to correct that mistake. Chantal, please come here. Helene, begin Bach's Minuet in G Minor."

"Mother, I will lead."

"Why should you lead? I am the mother, you are the daughter. Respect your elders."

"Well, if it's logic we're using, how about—I am the dancer, and you are not!"

"How dare you!"

Even though he knew it was their habit to spar, it made him uneasy. Patrice rushed over and inserted himself before the conversation escalated further. "Ladies, ladies, ladies. Please, let's all get along. Chantal, why don't you let your mother lead the first dance? Helene, please begin whenever you are ready."

The lively 3/4 rhythm and soft melody transformed the mood of the mother and daughter as they began their dance. Giselle offered instructions.

"Pay attention, Patrice. It is simple. Watch my feet. Right, together, left, right, left, together…right, together, left, right, left, together. That is the basic step. You step in for me, and give it a try."

Giselle continued her verbal instructions as Patrice took her place and continued the dance, "Yes—right, together, left, right, left, together—again— right, together, left, right, left, together—excellent!"

Little hops and arm movements were inserted at appropriate points in the highly punctuated dance. While not a master by any means, after an hour with the Archambeaus, Patrice had confidence he would get by.

⇥═◑ ◐═⇤

Thank God for the wine. Social pleasantries—always difficult for Patrice—became easier with each passing glass. He and his father had to greet every guest as they arrived. While everyone was welcomed, the few *grands blancs* who agreed to grace the ball with their presence were exalted. Guillame Beaumont was quite obvious with his introductions of the eligible women, and two of the three to whom he hoped Patrice might be partial had already arrived—his son, however, did not seem so impressed.

"Thank you for joining us. Patrice, I'm sure you remember Monsieur and Madame Gastineau. This is their beautiful daughter, Marie. She recently moved to St. Domingue from Marseilles."

Patrice greeted the father and mother first and then turned to Marie, who had her head tilted slightly downward. As Patrice took her hand, she looked up, and he became mesmerized by her beautiful smile, which presented the most remarkable dimples at the peak of its expression. Patrice had to admit the candlelight from the chandelier might have been of some assistance, but she could have lit up the room all on her own. *After all these years, I finally met my first fancy French lady*, Patrice thought to himself as he remembered his discussions with Andre at the barn. He bent to kiss her hand, and she giggled, which caused him to do the same. Guillame Beaumont smiled.

"A pleasure to meet you, Mademoiselle Gastineau. Welcome to Beaumont. I would be honored to share a dance with you later this evening. Perhaps the minuet, if you are so inclined?"

"Thank you so much for the wonderful welcome, Monsieur Beaumont. I've always loved minuets."

Giselle and Chantal smiled at each other as they surveyed what appeared to be a highly successful social event. Although the balance could have been better: twelve women and eight men, of whom two men made it clear they had no interest in dancing, they already had a work around in mind to keep the dance floor active. The Archambeaus always got a good result and tonight was no exception.

Giselle carefully reviewed the order of the dances. The first two would be the warm-ups to the popular minuet. They began with a sarabande, followed by a courante. By the third dance, Giselle hoped all able and interested dancers would then make their way to the dance floor for the minuet.

The sarabande concluded with little participation or fanfare. Most of the guests were concentrating on the wine and delicious appetizers. Then a young *grand blanc* man walked across the room, and asked one of the single *gens de couleur* women to join him for the courante; the *grands blancs* and the *gens de couleur* enjoyed a rare moment of camaraderie. The dance floor filled, but Patrice was still on the sidelines multi-tasking—practicing the minuet in his mind, while keeping an eye on the whereabouts of Marie.

The time had arrived for the third dance and Giselle nodded to Patrice before signaling to the musicians. Patrice found Marie just as he heard the announcement for Bach's Minuet in G Minor. Patrice and Marie took their positions. The music began...

La—lo-lo-lo-lo-li—dum-dum
La— lo-lo-lo-lo-ti--dum-dum,
Da—di-da-ta-da-du—-di-da-ta-da-du
do-da-di-da-do—dum-dum

Most eyes focused on Marie, who was not only a beauty, but a natural dancer as she glided around the floor. Chantal and Giselle, however, admired their dance student who appeared so much more advanced as he served as the straight man for Marie's theatrical embellishments of the basic steps. Marie punctuated each bar of music with a hop and a smile; the hops entertained the crowd, and the smiles melted Patrice's heart. Marie laughed as she overheard her partner quietly whisper instructions to himself as he took each step:

"Right, together, left, right, left, together
Right, together, left, right, left, together."

The minuet ended on the last "together"—and that's what Patrice and Marie were from that point forward. They saw no reason for a long courtship and began living life passionately. Many tender embraces in the privacy of Patrice's bedroom soon followed their first social embrace on the dance floor. Marie never thought she would give herself to a man before marriage, but this was not any man, this was Patrice. They were one. They found each other and their love was the kind about which most could only read. Life at Beaumont was going to be more than Patrice ever thought possible, but only for a very brief time; Marie died giving birth to their son, Claude. Patrice was heartbroken.

CHAPTER 15

Slaves in a Suit

THE ROAD FROM the Beaumont Plantation to Jacmel was more of a well-marked path than a true thoroughfare. The little traveling party, led by Patrice on his horse, needed to pass through adjoining properties on the way into town and he was concerned about the noise being made by his companions. The carriage, driven by Andre with Claude and Christophe in the back seat, appeared to be the source of the commotion. As Patrice turned to admonish his children, he realized they were playing a game with Abraham Julian, who was riding beside the carriage. Abraham's horse, Champion, contorted his face whenever the boys made a high pitched whistling sound. Each new whistle generated another contortion by Champion and raucous laughter from Claude and Christophe. Abraham Julian's broad smile, clearly evident beneath his scraggly beard, was accompanied by a deep boisterous laugh the boys found almost as humorous as Champion's antics. Patrice smiled; his new acquaintance had become a good friend of the family.

When the group reached the peak of a hill, which provided an unobstructed view of the surrounding area, Patrice became concerned as he discovered a large group of maroons in the distance travelling conspicuously.

"Andre, where do you think they are headed? I'm worried about Beaumont. "

"They're going the other way. No reason to worry," Andre responded while turning and muttering under his breath, "At least not now." Patrice didn't hear this final comment, but Abraham did, and it caused him to have a look for himself. The maroons, who were brandishing machetes, did appear to be looking for trouble and Abraham surmised from the mischievous smile on Andre's face, he understood the nature of that trouble.

Realizing his comment might have been overheard, Andre scrutinized Abraham's facial expressions to determine if he had reason for concern. The odd little man seemed oblivious to everything and continued to play his game with the horse and the boys. Andre settled back into his role as the driver and made the final turn off the makeshift path, which would lead to the town.

Andre had made this trip to Jacmel hundreds of times over the years. Whenever he reached this last turn, his mind always thought back to the one trip that scarred him for life—the time he went to town with Patrice a few days after their disturbing orientations into manhood.

"Patrice, you won't beat me again!"

Andre began his sprint of the last mile, which would bring the two teenage boys to the finish line--the signpost which marked the entrance to the town of Jacmel. This race had become their ritual every time they travelled to town. As seventeen year-old men, the races were true athletic contests. People in town often took a moment to watch the final stretch leading up to the signpost, and many complimented them on their speed after they caught their breath and began to run errands in town.

Given the physical similarities of the boys, their races were always competitive, but Patrice had won the last two, and Andre was determined that his winning streak would not extend to three. Off to a great start after a few hundred yards, Andre didn't realize Patrice had tripped at the beginning of the race, conceded, and was strolling into town happy his best friend would not have to endure yet another loss.

The signpost was within view—100 yards to go, and less than half of that if he cut behind Madame Archambeau's Café. While this shortcut might be considered cheating, given that Patrice would never know it seemed like an excellent idea. As he dashed through the small alley leading to the path behind the café, Andre felt the rope at his feet, and then fell forward--face first. A group of three teenage white boys quickly surrounded him.

"Oh look, the cheater tripped. Here, let me help you up," the tallest boy offered as he extended his hand to Andre.

"I can get up by myself," Andre responded.

"Are you talking back to me boy? You better be careful or we'll tell your master how you cheated and teach you a lesson."

Andre decided not to say anything else and tried to scramble to his feet. The tall boy kicked him in the stomach and he fell back down.

"Oh, my God! I cheated too! Not so sure my kick helped much. Maybe my friends can do better. Let's try again."

Andre could have overpowered any one of them and possibly even faired well against two, but fighting was not an option. The safest course of action—stay on the ground. The other two boys became impatient and kicked Andre a few times just to participate in the fun. Andre couldn't understand why Patrice had not yet arrived. He desperately needed his help.

Patrice also opted for the shortcut behind Madame Archambeau's Café and the moment he entered the alley he saw Andre on the ground. The *petits blancs* boys realized they'd taken their little amusement as far as possible. They would always be able to physically abuse a slave without any repercussions and they enjoyed abusing Andre, in particular, because of his size and connection to Patrice, who was the most wealthy *gens de couleur* boy.

Patrice helped Andre to his feet. "Enough! Leave him alone. Enough!"

The tallest boy decided to push a little further. "You think you're a free man, Patrice? Well, we think you're nothing but a slave in a suit! If you're a free man like us, you understand slaves must always know their place. Are you a free man, Patrice, or are you just a slave in a suit? Which is it? Which is it?"

Four more boys arrived on the scene. Patrice understood the class structure well—these *petits blancs* were nothing but trash who liked to take advantage of their skin color and bully both the slaves and the *gens de couleur*. Patrice needed to make sure this incident did not escalate, however, because physical violence against whites had to be avoided at all costs.

"We are leaving. Step aside." Patrice commanded.

"I asked you a question, and you're not leaving until I get an answer."

The white boys tightened their circle, and Patrice took a deep breath. "I am a free man just like you."

"No. I don't think so. Because if you were, you would tell this slave he has no business being by himself in town and cheating in your race by cutting through the alley. He's nothing but a cheating dog and I spit on cheating dogs! We all spit on cheating dogs. Let's show him, boys!"

All seven boys took turns spitting on Andre—mostly on his face and a bit in his hair. Andre may have closed his eyes, but did not flinch. He stood perfectly erect and took the abuse. The last boy pulled the shirt away from his body and spit down his back. Andre knew he couldn't respond, but Patrice would not let this treatment go unanswered. The rules and priorities were clear—he could not initiate any action against these boys, but once Patrice did, he would defend his best friend, no matter the consequence. The signal to spring into action never came, however; Patrice had his head down with his body frozen in place.

Spit hung from various parts of Andre's face and the *petits blancs* boys admired their work. The leader turned to Patrice and said, "We hope we've taught you how to properly treat your slaves. Let us know if you need any more lessons." The boys laughed at the sarcastic remark, which prompted the leader to take the game a little further.

"We'll let the two of you leave as soon as you call him the cheating dog he is and spit on him like any free man would."

Patrice hoped his momentary glance at Andre would be interpreted as, "I'm so sorry to do this to you, but I have no choice." The spit emerged before the words, and while Andre's shoe may have been the target, his heart received the direct hit. Things were never the same between Andre and Patrice after that. Later that evening, Guillame Beaumont congratulated his son on his handling of the matter, and punished Andre for entering the alley--because that, after all, was the only error of the day and the only punishable offense.

Andre came out of the memory as they entered the town, and he and Abraham went to secure the carriage and horses while Patrice walked toward the General Store with the boys. By then, Andre had dismissed Abraham as nothing more than a buffoon—certainly not a threat. Andre exchanged some words with the slave who was assisting with the horses. They spoke softly and in Creole, but Abraham, who had a gift for languages, heard the exchange and understood.

"Nou ranmase nan ti mòn pi wo pase vil la jis anvan solèy kouche. Liberty ou touye! We gather in the hills above the city just before the sun goes down. Liberty or death!"

Andre responded, *"Liberty ou touye!"*

Abraham was certain things would erupt in Jacmel that evening and while he had a good sense of the factions in this conflict, he had to determine with whom he would be aligned. He knew the slaves were the ones with "right" on their side. Unfortunately, he also recognized the slaves were also the group with whom he had the smallest chance of being able to reason, and that is what Abraham needed to do. Abraham had picked the wrong day to pay a visit to the sleepy little town of Jacmel, which would be anything but sleepy that night.

CHAPTER 16

How Do You Like Your Candy?

PATRICE'S PLAN FOR the afternoon, complicated by the presence of Claude and Christophe, was to make the general store the first stop. The boys would get their candy while Patrice introduced Abraham to the shopkeeper. Lunch at Madame Archambeau's Café, the *gens de couleur* restaurant, would be the next and final stop for the boys. It might be odd for a white man to be with them in this segregated café, but the likable Abraham Julian did not have any problem with the idea. *Certainly Chantal will like him as much as I do*, Patrice thought, and she would know how best to explain his presence. Patrice learned so much from Abraham during their chat and found Abraham's analysis of the similarities between the *gens de couleur* and the Jews in St. Domingue to be fascinating.

Patrice had not understood that Jews had the same limited rights as *gens de couleur*. They could be full economic participants in society and even own slaves, but they were not the equals of the Christian whites. Abraham went as far as to say they were brothers in some way, but Patrice had not informed him of the *gens de couleur* meeting, and assumed Abraham would not extend his analogy to "brothers in arms." The plan was to have Andre take the boys back to Beaumont after lunch while Abraham had one final meeting with a local lawyer, before heading home to Aux Cayes. If everything went according to plan, Patrice would be on his own for the meeting at five o'clock.

Patrice stopped for a moment on the road in front of the store to chat with another plantation owner. A group of white teenagers standing in front started pointing and laughing at the boys. Christophe thought they might want to play and Claude knew they were trouble. Soon the *petits blancs* boys dispersed, except for one who walked into the general store. Finally, Patrice checked to make sure there were no carriages or horses headed their way, and nodded to his children. After dashing across the road, Claude and Christophe stopped on the other side, gathered themselves, and entered the store like gentlemen—just like their father taught them.

Once inside, Claude pointed to the candy counter located in the back next to the rear exit, and then grabbed Christophe by his arm.

"Christophe, remember what Daddy said. The white boy is looking at the candy. Let him finish before we go over there."

"But Claude, there are only two more pieces of licorice in the bowl. Licorice is my favorite. Maybe he won't mind if I go over there and take those—he seems friendly. He's not looking at the licorice. He must want the cookies. Claude, he smiled at us!"

Claude suspected the older boy, who was pointing toward the bowl with a big grin on his face, had bad intentions.

"Claude, he isn't like the rest of them. He wants to know if the licorice is what I want. See, I told you. It's okay, Claude, it's okay. Daddy won't mind. He won't mind at all."

"No, Christophe, I don't think he's different. We need to stay away from him."

Claude spotted his father entering the store, and lost his concentration. When he turned his head, he released his younger brother's arm, and Christophe ran toward the candy. Claude tripped as he went to chase his brother, and went head first into one of the counters. By the time Claude scrambled to his feet, there was no sign of Christophe. The back door was wide open and Claude ran through it first, followed by his father. They found Christophe seated in a pile of horse manure, which covered both his clothing and his face. The boys were all running away laughing as they screamed, "How do you like your candy?"

Claude tried to help his brother, who was not badly hurt, just upset and embarrassed. He slipped as he reached out to Christophe and he too became covered in horse manure.

Patrice took control of the situation. "Christophe, are you okay? What did those boys do to you?"

"Daddy, he smiled at me. I thought he wanted to be my friend. He dragged me out here and they all called me a slave in a suit. Look what they did to me, Daddy. Look at what they did!" Christophe showed his father the big bruise on his arm and his torn, manure-covered clothing.

"Christophe, I warned you about this. I told you the rules. Claude, I hold you responsible for this. You were supposed to take care of your little brother. I'm very disappointed in you."

"Daddy. I tried to tell him, but I let go of his arm just for one second. I'm sorry Daddy. I'm sorry."

Chantal Archambeau witnessed the incident from the window of her apartment above the café and ran over to help. "Patrice, I have some clothing that should fit the boys well. *Vous permettex* to take Claude and Christophe back to my apartment to clean them up? I think I might even have a little candy for them, which should make them feel better."

Chantal Archambeau had one of those maternal voices that did make things better. She couldn't undo what the rough white boys had done to these innocent young men, but she could provide the kind of healing comfort they needed.

"*Merci*, Chantal, that would be fine, and I do thank you for your help."

"*Je vous en prie*. We must all stick together, Patrice, and I want you to remember that later tonight. We are counting on you to do the right thing. Let me take Christophe and Claude to my place for some candy and a bath."

Christophe showed a hint of a smile beneath his manure-covered face, and he walked obediently behind Aunt Chantal. Patrice turned to Andre, who was also on the scene, and said, "I want you to get the boys home right after lunch. Don't stop for any reason. This is upsetting and I want to get them back to the safety of Beaumont." Remembering the day he was similarly humiliated a few feet from where they stood, Andre nodded to his master. He was sorry Claude and Christophe had to endure this as well as what he had planned for them after lunch. Andre had no intention of taking the boys back to the plantation. He had other plans for them and special plans for their lying father.

CHAPTER 17

The Stage Was Set

ABRAHAM HAD ONE more appointment at 3:30 PM with the local attorney before he headed home to Aux Cayes, and Patrice told him he could not host him beyond that time. The whole town was aware of the *gens de couleur* meeting, and Abraham wondered how Patrice could still consider it to be a well-guarded secret. Abraham used the excuse of checking on Champion's injured hoof, and told Patrice he wanted to take him for a short ride. In reality, Abraham wanted to investigate the rustling in the trees outside of town, which became more noticeable as the day progressed.

"Nice and easy, boy. Easy, boy. We don't want to have any problems later if we need to move quickly. I hope they took good care of you. Yes, yes. I know... treated you like a horse. Highly insulting. I will have a word with them. Let's circle around town, so we can check on all of this movement in the hills. Okay, my friend?"

Abraham waited for the horse to make any movement that might broadly classify as a nod of agreement, and then responded, "Good, boy. We have our plan. Off we go!"

→⊨◎ ◎⊨←

Over the course of the last hour, at least another one hundred slaves from surrounding plantations had joined the maroons. The word was out...the revolt would take place in the evening. Some slaves were content to take a wait and see approach, but many wanted to join the fight. The larger their numbers, the better their chance of success. Houngan Alanso, the leader of the maroons, had done his best to establish some type of control system because without a coordinated effort, the maroons would be doomed despite their large numbers. As always, his challenge would be the unpredictable Houngan Baturu, who had already stirred up most of his followers to the point where they simply craved blood. To Alanso this was much bigger than that–he wanted to succeed. He needed Baturu to appreciate the magnitude of the evening's events, along with the potential for victory.

"Baturu. Please sit. We need to talk. We have a lot at stake here."

Baturu stayed on his feet, pacing. "Time for talking and sitting is over. Time to kill. Our turn. Tonight, we swim in the blood of our captors, and if we die–it will be a good death."

"We don't have to die, Baturu. We can actually win. Our numbers are strong, but we must be together and have control."

"Control?" Baturu chuckled, "You say, control? This not about control. We've been controlled too long. Tonight we lose control, tonight we get revenge."

"Baturu, remember when you joined us last year, I realized immediately you were a leader of men, and you can show control if you try. I need you to be with me and not fight me as we organize for tonight."

Baturu stopped. Surprised to hear Alanso thought he was not "with him," Baturu took a seat next to his elder, whom he did respect without question–he worried, however, that Alanso, was no longer in touch with the undeniable need for revenge which permeated the camp. Revenge for the killing of loved ones, revenge for the torture, revenge for the rapes, revenge for the deplorable living conditions–the list went on and on. Many of Baturu's followers felt their lives would be meaningful and complete if they could kill even one of these brutal slave owners before they met their own end. Freedom did not seem achievable, but revenge did. Baturu knew Alanso considered him to be a crazy man without rational thought, but to Baturu, pursuing the realistic goal of revenge was more rational than chasing the elusive dream of freedom. Baturu appreciated Alanso's intelligence, however; perhaps there was a greater chance of success than Baturu realized.

"Alanso, I will listen, but we're not an army. No rank, and no rules—what we have is anger and hatred. Not afraid to die—may be time to go back to Guinea. I'm not sure you're right, but Baturu respects Alanso. I will listen."

"Thank you," Alanso took Baturu's forearms and looked him full in the face. "Baturu, we must be together in this, because we need to wait until the time is right to strike. First, we'll divide into three groups. You will head one of them, but you must wait until I give the signal. Our people in town will let us know the size of our enemy's forces, and if the numbers are in our favor—and they should be—we will strike from three different directions and not only have revenge, but also victory. Are you with me, Baturu?"

"I am."

⤛⬛ ⬛⤜

The meeting at the Bel Air plantation had just ended. Ten of the wealthiest *grands blancs* in the southern part of St. Domingue assembled at Henri Baptiste's request to discuss the events of the evening. The white plantation owners learned of the *gens de couleur* meeting in town and planned to greet them with a show of force. The *gens de couleur* had a role, but needed to stay in their place. At least one hundred heavily armed men along with a few of the other plantation owners would be accompanying Henri Baptiste to teach the *gens de couleur* a lesson they would not soon forget. A more troubling piece of news, a large band of maroons had been spotted heading toward the town as well. Some of the *grands blancs* thought these maroons might be joining the mixed race plantation owners in a plot to overthrow the whites. Henri Baptiste dismissed this suggestion as nonsense. He had a good understanding of the *gens de couleur*—they were as pro-slavery as the *grands blancs*, and he assumed the governor's refusal of Vincent Ogé's request for full rights would be their topic of discussion at Madame Archambeau's Café.

A decision was made toward the end of the meeting to increase the firepower to one hundred fifty men. After the brief show of force with the *gens de couleur*, the men would be dispatched into the surrounding area to find and kill as many of the runaway slaves as possible. The *gens de couleur* would be put in their place, and dozens of maroons would be killed—both of these events making a much needed statement. Many plantation owners had noted increased levels of disobedience among the slave population. Henri Baptiste sought a return to proper order in Jacmel.

—⊷ ⊶—

Jean Claude Guilar observed it first from the second floor window in his apartment. Then the tailor saw it when he went to the stream just outside of town. The other white tradesmen took note of it at some point in the afternoon. At 3:30 PM, all had temporarily closed their businesses or left their jobs and assembled in Jean Claude's shop to discuss their plan of action. Jean Claude had a bad reputation in business, but was held in the highest esteem when it came to tracking and capturing runaway slaves. He stood front and center as the obvious leader of this meeting to discuss the tremendous opportunity at hand—a few dozen runaway slaves in the hills surrounding Jacmel.

Jean Claude could only imagine the sums of money he would earn from the capture of these maroons. His plan called for all the *petits blancs* to stay together so they would have the advantage of numbers and split the proceeds. He readied himself to pitch his plan to the group.

"Gather around. I want to do this quickly so we can get ready to go into the hills before we lose daylight. There are a few dozen maroons outside of town—maybe as many as fifty. Why they are here? The damn fools are probably starving and plan to steal food. We're going to be smart, though, and not wait for them to raid the town at night—we'll take the fight to them and take as many as we can by surprise. I say we work together and split all of the proceeds evenly. While we hope there will be many of Henri Baptiste's slaves in the group, most of the plantation owners pay fairly well. This will be a profitable day for us. I figure with each of us and our older boys, we'll probably have a group of about twenty armed men—they won't know what hit them. Do you agree with my plan?"

"Yes!" They shouted in unison as they agreed to meet at the edge of town at 5:00 PM. In his mind, Jean Claude had already counted and spent his reward money.

Patrice said goodbye to Claude and Christophe who were being driven back to the Beaumont Plantation by Andre—the final piece of Patrice's complicated plan for the day. He wanted the boys to be out of the way well before the meeting took place. Andre insisted each boy consume a special beverage, which was waiting for them in the back of the carriage. The Mambo who gave the drink to Andre said it might take up to an hour to set in, but, probably due to their small size, Claude and Christophe were already feeling a little sick and drowsy in the rear carriage seat.

Andre thought he was being quite magnanimous with the boys by sparing them the sight of seeing their father brutally killed during the revolt. He circled back to the shed behind Madame Archambeau's Café, tied Claude and Christophe together on the floor, closed the door, and then nailed it shut from the outside. Confident that they were not going anywhere, Andre walked into the hills to join the maroons who were positioned throughout the woods and would be easy to find.

4:30 PM. Patrice bid Abraham farewell at the café. In the hills, Alanso, Suma, and Baturu, were having surprising success at controlling their "troops." All three maroon groups were awaiting the signal, which would only be given by Alanso. They had been tempted to spring into action when a large group of armed white men became visible on the road into town, but the signal never came, and the maroons reluctantly stayed hidden in the trees.

Jean Claude was the first to arrive at the meeting place for the band of twenty *petits blancs* who were about to go maroon hunting thinking they had numbers in their favor. Claude and Christophe were still sound asleep in the shed behind Madame Archambeau's Café. Inside the café, Patrice sat with five other *gens de couleur* who had arrived early for the meeting. The stage was set. This final few minutes of calm would soon give way to chaos. Jacmel would never be the same.

CHAPTER 18

Nothin Thicker 'n Blood

"CHANTAL, THANK YOU for your help today. My sons needed the steady hand of a woman at the moment you arrived."

"There's no need to thank me. Remember, I'm their aunt. I wanted to speak with you about the meeting, but there's one last surprise you'll need to deal with before we can talk. "

"What surprise?"

"Camille arrived a few minutes ago at my backdoor and is upstairs in my parlor. She is upset and asked to speak to you privately."

Chantal walked her little brother upstairs and hoped whatever Camille had to say would not distract Patrice from the important *gens de couleur* meeting. She left Patrice sitting with Camille in her parlor, while she went next door to her mother's bedroom. Giselle Archambeau understood they needed to be quiet in order to hear the conversation next door and positioned two chairs next to the wall. Mother and daughter took their seats and sat quietly, perhaps for the first time in their lives.

⌖ ⌖

Claude woke up in the dark shed and resisted the urge to cry. He couldn't move and there was something in his mouth--a bit of cloth, tied on, that kept him from calling out. The last thing he remembered was being in the carriage with Andre and the bitter drink that he could still taste. *I'm the big brother,* Claude thought. *I have to take care of Christophe. I have to make a plan.*

Realizing he and Christophe were tied together, he started to think. *I can be brave. Christophe is little. He will be more scared than me. But he has to wake up and help. Maybe if we work together, we'll be able to untie ourselves.* First, he had to wake up Christophe. He tried shaking them both back and forth, but it didn't help. He knew he wasn't supposed to kick his brother, but he decided this was important even if he got in trouble. He gritted his teeth and drove his knee into his brother's stomach. As Christophe started to wiggle and cry, Claude struggled to remove his brother's gag with his teeth. Claude had to wait until Christophe stopped screaming to press his own gag into Christophe's teeth. Finally, they could talk.

"What happened, Claude? Where is Papa? I want Papa!" Christophe started crying again. Claude tried to think what to do. He thought of Aunt Chantal. She always got them to stop crying. "Christophe, we will see Papa soon. I'm your big brother and you have to listen to me. Okay, Christophe? Can you listen to me?"

Christophe started to cry hysterically and screamed, "I want my father. Where is Papa? Where is Papa?" *We will never get free this way,* Claude thought. *I need his help.* He kneed his brother again. The screaming stopped.

"Stop kicking me! Stop! I'm going to tell Papa! Stop!"

"Okay, but you need to be quiet and listen to me. Okay? Tell me it is okay, Christophe. Okay?"

"Okay, Claude."

"We must figure out where we are and how we can get out of here."

Both boys started to frantically scan the shed—they were in the center of the small structure, tied together at the waist, chest to chest, with their heads resting on each other's shoulders. Claude faced the front of the shed and he tilted his head downward in order to look through the little gap between the floorboard and the door. He strained to see anything at all and saw something familiar—the distinctive hooves of Champion, which were decorated with a small red fabric. He had an idea.

"Christophe, do you remember the game we played with Mr. Julian's horse, Champion?"

"Yes, I do."

"We whistled like this…" Claude made the whistling sound, "And Champion made his funny face. Can you whistle together with me?"

Both boys started to make the whistling sound as loudly as they could. Outside the shed, Champion's ears pricked up and he started to perform. Two of the early arrivals for the meeting stepped out of the backdoor of the café, saw it, and started to laugh. After a few minutes they called others over to witness the spectacle. The crowd around the horse grew.

⋅→▣ ▣←⋅

Abraham Julian had circled back to Jacmel, left his horse in the back of the restaurant, and taken a walk in the surrounding area to get a sense of what was going on in the town. If something was about to happen, he thought he might be better off in town with others rather than out on the road alone. He heard the commotion in the general area where he left Champion and headed back to the cafe. Once he saw the group surrounding his prized horse, he ran over to dismiss the onlookers.

"Quite an amusing horse, sir," one of the men remarked.

"Yes. He often is the center of attention. I don't think he is feeling well, though. Please gentlemen, give him some space." The crowd dispersed slowly.

Abraham understood what Champion was doing, but couldn't hear the whistling himself. As soon as everyone was gone he untied Champion, and said, "Tell me where boy. Tell me where." Champion walked straight for the shed and touched his nose to the door. As Abraham got closer to the shed, he detected the whistling himself and asked, "Who is in there?"

"Christophe, that's Mr. Julian! Mr. Julian, it's Claude and Christophe! Claude and Christophe!" Both boys kept screaming their names.

Abraham took note of the nail in the door, removed it with a rock, untied the boys, settled on a bench outside with Christophe in his lap and Claude beside him, dried their tears and asked, "What happened?"

⋅→▣ ▣←⋅

"Mwen jis te kouri de la Plantation Beaumont Et mwen vle pou jwenn ak batay. I ran from the Beaumont Plantation and I want to join the fight."

The four maroons who came across Andre in the woods consulted with each other before they responded.

"M konnen l. Li se esklav pwensipal kay la nan Beaumont. Anpil moun isit la ki vle pou menm pwen yo avè l. Li gen pwivilèj espesyal. Guide autour tankou se li rele chèf la. Te gen jan l' ak anpil fanm. M pa kwè nou ka kwè l. I know him. He is the main house slave at Beaumont. Lots of people here want to get even with him. He has special privileges. Walks around like he is the boss. Has his way with lots of the women. I don't think we can trust him."

The four maroons circled Andre, overpowered him, bound his arms behind his back with vines, and led him to their group leader, Baturu.

"Non. Ou genyen li mal. Mwen isit la pou jwenn ak ou, pa batay ou. Mwen se yonn nan nou. No. You've got it wrong. I'm here to join you, not fight you. I'm one of you."

"Mwen konnen ki ou. Ou kwè ou pi bon pase nou. Ou pa santi w yonn nan nou. Lè pou peye pou peche yo te fè mèt Andre. I know who you are. You think you're better than us. You're not even one of us. Time to pay for your sins, Master Andre."

⋅⊷⊷⊷⊶⊶⊶⋅

"This is the chance we've been waiting for. With twenty of us together and armed, we can overpower these maroons even if they prove to be double our numbers. If we do this right, today will be a big payday for all of us. Let's fan out in a straight line with each of us about 15 feet apart and march straight into the forest. Scream if you come across any maroons and we'll all gather around our catch. That's right, gentlemen, our catch...we're going maroon hunting!"

The group formed their line, marched into the woods, and couldn't have been more conspicuous if they tried. Alanso observed them from the hilltop and put a plan into action. An advance group of four maroons headed toward the marching *petits blancs.*

One of the white tradesmen screamed, "Whooo hooo, I've got four of them here!" The twenty *petits blancs* circled the four maroons and started to celebrate.

Just as they tried to secure their catch, one of the runaway slaves pointed over Jean Claude's shoulder. The carpenter turned and his jaw dropped. The maroons formed a circle of their own, but their circle was five deep. The first row flung their machetes at the legs of the white men. Several of the machetes missed their mark entirely, some hit the intended target with the wooden portion of the weapon, and a few connected with the blade–mostly in the area of the legs. One man, the tailor, caught the blade in his chest. He fell to the ground immediately. The maroons pounced on the *petits blancs*, took their weapons, secured their hands, and marched the bloodied prisoners back to camp.

Houngan Alanso prepared to inspect his first prisoners of war and admired the amazing discipline and restraint of his followers. He appreciated, however, that this was more due to Baturu's influence and cooperation than his leadership and authority. Alanso whispered to Suma and Baturu to make sure the men who took the muskets and other weapons from the *petits blancs* understood how to use them. There was a bit of squabbling over that point, but soon twenty, somewhat trained, armed maroons were guarding the captured tradesmen.

When Alanso approached the prisoners, Baturu called him aside and motioned to another group of men in the distance and explained, "Two special prisoners. One is a traitor. His name is Andre and he says he wants to join us, but he is nothing but a spy from Beaumont. Then there's the large white man who we caught with the others. He is the one who broke Baako at the wheel today. We will do the same to him when we celebrate later."

Alanso enjoyed the cooperation he was receiving from Baturu and had no reason to disagree with his assessment or recommendations. The fate of these two special prisoners was certain, but Alanso was unsure as to what to do with the rest—starting any large-scale violence might be a mistake. If things went the wrong way for the maroons, they could still retreat to the hills without the fear of unusual repercussions, but if they killed all twenty men and did not win the day, the retribution from the whites would be too much to handle at this point in their resistance. There was some grumbling at this announcement of the uncertain fate of the majority of the prisoners, but the maroons had become more of a military force and appeared to accept the decision of their leader.

⊶⊜ ⊜⊷

"Camille, why are you here? You shouldn't have left Beaumont. What is the meaning of this?"

"Master Patrice. Waited too long. Should've done this many years ago. Too much time, too many problems between you two. You in trouble–slave revolt tonight. Andre says you liar for not freeing him. He's set on killing his Master. You in danger, Master. You in danger!"

"Camille, you're wrong. There is no revolt tonight, only a peaceful meeting of *gens de couleur* plantation owners. It is about to start. Andre left hours ago with Claude and Christophe. This is nonsense."

"No nonsense, Master. This for real. Claude and Christophe never come home. Didn't pass them on road. Something bad happening tonight. I waited too long, Master. I'm so sorry, too long."

"Waited too long for what, Camille? What are you talking about?"

"I waited too long to tell you truth–you and Andre. Gonna tell you. You gots to know. Waited too long, Master. Waited too long."

"What do I have to know, Camille? Tell me what you need to tell me."

"Always said you and Andre look so alike you could be brothers, but never said it in front of your daddy. Fact is—you half-brothers. Need you to know, need Andre to know–nothing thicker'n blood. Remember that—nothin thicker'n blood. You and Andre are blood."

Patrice sat down slowly. "Camille, how could that be? I must go downstairs for an important meeting. Please explain quickly."

"Life funny that way. I took so long to tell, now have to rush--guess that's life, Master. I'll do my best to splain. I was a pretty li'l girl and I met your daddy when I just fifteen. Master Beaumont came over to the Gaspard Plantation. He young man–maybe 25–and drink too much. They all drink too much and then Master Gaspard ask pretty slaves come round. My first time as pretty girl–didn't know what to spect. All the other girls got picked 'n just me 'n your daddy left. All his friends makin fun cause he didn't want do nothing–they laugh at him, and he drank too much–way too much. He pologized when we done and asked me if I was pretty girl before. I said no, and he didn't like that. Your daddy came back two days later and bought me to come back to Beaumont as nanny. Master Beaumont never touch me again. A few months later, I with child. Andre born when you one month old–you was free, cause your mom *gens de couleur,* and Andre is a slave– cause that's all I ever was. Your daddy said, never tell you 'n never tell Andre cause it better leave things way they sposed to be—no need to mess things up. I waited too long. Gots to remember–nothin thicker'n blood. Remember that, Master Patrice. Remember."

"My brother? He was my brother all of these years and you never told me? My father never told me either. Why?"

"I'm sorry, Master, but your father said I can't say nothin. The two of you like brothers anyway. Didn't seem to matter so much until it did. Should've told you sooner. So sorry, Master, so sorry."

It was so much to process, but given the similarities between himself and Andre, Patrice had to admit it did explain a lot. He didn't have time to fully digest it, however, because he had to get downstairs for his meeting. On the other side of the wall, the mother and daughter were surprised, but not shocked–such was life in St. Domingue.

⇥ ⇤

Henri Baptiste turned to his overseer and asked, "Monsieur Kildew. Any maroon sightings yet? I would like to pick up at least a few on the way into Jacmel so we can make a display of them."

"Yes, sir. A small group of our men went into the woods. They'll blow their horn once they find something and we'll head their way."

"Well, I hope the horn blows soon, because I want to arrive at the *gens de couleur* meeting early before they get carried away with themselves."

"Yes, sir. Hopefully, it will be soon."

A few minutes later, the horn sounded and the large contingent of armed men headed in the direction of the sound. The same scenario played out as with the *petits blancs.* The white men surrounded a few of the runaways. They, in turn, became surrounded by hundreds of maroons. Alanso was on the hill waiting to give the signal to attack, but instead he held his hand in a signal to wait, when he saw Henri Baptiste and the rest of the armed contingent arrive on the scene.

Alanso gazed down at his former master and delivered a confident nod. Henri Baptiste looked up and offered much the same. They both understood that running scared at this moment would be an admission of weakness. Alanso had to be concerned with what appeared to be well over 100 trained and armed men, and Henri Baptiste became worried about the overwhelming number of maroons and the disturbing fact that at least a few of them had muskets. Both sides retreated—the maroons back into the hills for a senior level discussion, and Henri Baptiste at a much faster pace toward the town of Jacmel. His agenda, however, had changed.

CHAPTER 19

The Meeting

THE TWENTY GENS *de couleur* plantation owners fidgeted in their seats. As much as they all wanted to get started, a meeting like this would not begin until the most important plantation owner in their ranks, Patrice Beaumont, arrived. Each owner brought four or five additional armed men from their plantations and this security force, which numbered about seventy-five, was positioned outside of Madame Archambeau's Café.

Chantal decided it was time to speak with Patrice. She knocked on the parlor door and asked Camille if she wouldn't mind keeping her mother company in the bedroom; as Camille left, Chantal sat opposite Patrice in the parlor. When Camille entered the bedroom, the two chairs had been repositioned to their normal places and Giselle was sitting upright in bed. Giselle planned to console Camille while Chantal advised Patrice.

"Patrice. I heard everything and I'm sorry for eavesdropping, but this was too important. What Camille told you epitomizes what tonight is about. You and Andre were like brothers and your father drove a wedge between the two of you based on race and status. Now, you know you were actually brothers all along. This separation has got to end Patrice, Camille is right, Andre is your blood–you must remember that. Go downstairs and be the man you're destined to be. Go ahead, they're all waiting."

The conversations died out as Patrice descended the stairs. Chantal Archambeau moved a chair to the top of the staircase so she wouldn't miss a word and sat silently for the second time that day–she was starting to get used to it.

Patrice headed for the lone unoccupied seat, located prominently at the head of the table and Jacob Bernard took the liberty of pointing out the obvious. "Patrice, it is no coincidence we've reserved that seat for you. We need your leadership and guidance as we discuss what we will do because the wrong move could be the end of us, and the right move might mean we become full French citizens."

Patrice was honored but not surprised by their request. He provided leadership and counsel to his fellow *gens de couleur* on many an occasion and understood what to say and how to finesse things for a good outcome. Often he hid his personal feelings and beliefs in order to develop rapport with adversaries and friends alike. While not always personally fulfilling, this approach served him well in business and within the mixed-race community. Patrice settled into his chair and called the meeting to order.

"Gentleman, we're here to discuss the refusal of the governor to accept Vincent Ogé's demand for full rights for the *gens de couleur*. Let's begin with a report from Jacob Bernard, who appears to be well informed of all recent developments. Jacob?"

Before Jacob stood to begin his report, the back door burst open and Abraham Julian rushed into the cafe with Claude and Christophe. He considered waiting until the meeting concluded, but felt a kinship with the *gens de couleur* and the boys were his ticket inside.

The boys ran to their father immediately. Patrice looked at Abraham Julian. "What is the meaning of this? This is not a meeting for children."

"Monsieur Beaumont, I found your two boys bound together in the shed out back. The last thing they remember is your man, Andre, giving them something to drink as they headed out for the return trip to Beaumont."

"Andre did this to you? Claude, was it Andre?"

"I don't know Papa, I can't remember," Claude responded. Christophe chimed in, "Maybe it was those boys again. Why do they hate us so?"

Chantal had heard enough and moved her chair from the top of the staircase in order to be ready to receive the boys. Patrice didn't understand what had happened to his children, but was relieved they were safe—there would be plenty of time to investigate later. As Patrice excused himself for a moment to escort Claude and Christophe upstairs, Abraham Julian seized the opportunity and began to speak.

"*Je m'appelle* Abraham Julian, and I am a Jewish merchant from the town of Aux Cayes. Monsieur Beaumont has been my host here in Jacmel. I mention that I am Jewish because it puts me in a similar class with the *gens de couleur* here in St. Domingue. I can be successful in business–even own slaves–but I have limited civic liberties. Fighting for your rights is the topic of discussion tonight, but you must realize this private meeting of yours is not as secret as you think. Hundreds of maroons are in the woods outside of town and I am certain their activities are connected in some way to your meeting here tonight."

One of the men quickly asked, "Hundreds of maroons in the hills? How did you learn this?"

Another plantation owner responded before Abraham had a chance to do so and said, "I noticed them as well. A large group. I was going to bring it up once we got started. Thank God for the dozens of armed men we have outside."

As Patrice made his way back to the head of the table, the door burst open again. This time, the surprise guest was none other than Henri Baptiste, whose initial plan was to disband the meeting through a show of force. He now realized the *gens de couleur* needed to be confederates, at least in the short term. Their security detail along with his 150 men, created a sizable force to repel the maroons.

"Monsieur Beaumont, I am sorry to interrupt your meeting, but there are well over a thousand maroons in the woods waiting to descend on this town. Some are armed and I would imagine all free people in Jacmel, regardless of color, are at risk. We must band together and turn back this group. I am here with 150 heavily armed men and you also have men outside. What additional forces can you muster from within your ranks?"

The room erupted with confusion and passion...

"Over a thousand maroons!"

"You are here with 150 heavily armed men?"

"How did you know we were here?"

Patrice reached for the heavy wooden spoon, which rested in front of him on the table, and used it as a gavel to try and restore order. He was uncharacteristically stern as he spoke.

"Gentlemen, silence! Monsieur Baptiste. Tell me why you have arrived in Jacmel at the moment we began our meeting, and tell me why you are here with 150 armed men. What is the purpose of your business here this evening?"

Henri Baptiste could not believe a lowly *gens de couleur* like Patrice Beaumont would dare question him in this fashion. *He'd better learn his place.* It took all of his self-control to resist the temptation to put this black dog down. Gilbert Kildew seemed equally shocked, and without exchanging any words, both men agreed the truth would not serve them. The overseer started to spin a tale. "I heard reports of the maroons in the hills and assembled this force to capture them or at least drive them away. Monsieur Baptiste is here to supervise the operation and we only came into Madame Archambeau's when we saw your men outside. We did not know about your meeting tonight."

The old Patrice would have accepted this explanation at face value because running the risk of insulting a man like Henri Baptiste was not something done lightly. The old Patrice said all of the right things to all of the right people. Subservient to the *grands blancs*, mindful of the *petits blancs*, Patrice understood how to navigate society well, as his father had taught him. He didn't even voice his objection when his fellow mixed-race slave owners bragged of the brutal ways in which they disciplined their slaves. While he never told similar stories, his silence was interpreted as a tacit endorsement. Patrice felt like a coward at times—unable to marshal the courage to say what he truly thought. In his heart, he knew right from wrong, but publicly his father's old advice–go along to get along–provided the guidance. This approach had served him well in business, but was tearing him apart inside.

Never one to provoke, Patrice surprised himself with his terse response, "With all due respect, Monsieur Baptiste, I believe you intentionally came here today at the exact moment we planned to meet in private because you mean to intimidate us." Patrice never thought he would utter such strong words to the most influential *grand blanc*, but something triggered an assertiveness he'd previously not possessed. He realized Henri Baptiste had left the Bel Air Plantation that day intent on inflicting pain on the *gens de couleur*, and offered an alliance of temporary convenience. The *grands blancs* needed them, and Patrice was determined to enjoy this rare leverage, even if it proved to be fleeting.

The gruff Gilbert Kildew took offense, "Careful, Monsieur Beaumont, re-member your place, and remember who has 150 armed men right outside these doors. How dare you question my truthfulness!"

Abraham Julian had stayed on the sidelines for most of his life. He learned how to work the middle— deferring to the *blancs* who simultaneously tolerated Jews for their business acumen and demeaned them both publicly and privately. He wasn't at all sure why he chose this moment to take a stand, but he did sense a kinship with the plight of the mixed race plantation owners, and despite the brief time they'd known each other, Abraham had a tremendous bond with Patrice Beaumont, which was unusually empowering.

"Sir, I am Abraham Julian, and I am here as a guest of Patrice Beaumont. I do believe he has every right to question your motives. You came here to teach the *gens de couleur* a lesson."

Henri Baptiste lost his composure, "Yes, I know of you, you're nothing but a dirty Jew merchant, and a tiny one at that. The kind of person we tolerate as a means to an end. Be careful. I guess you think you are stronger because you are here with these dogs of a different color. Just understand, you exist because we let you, and that can change. Believe me. That can change in an instant. Yes, we came here to teach you a lesson, and while you may not learn it tonight, believe me you will in the near future." Henri Baptiste and Gilbert Kildew turned and left the café in a fit of anger, swearing to themselves that the treatment they had just received would not go unpunished.

Many of the *gens de couleur* plantation owners who had readily accepted Patrice's leadership just a few moments earlier now questioned their decision. Those in the room who realized they were only willing to talk about organizing an army left the café with Henri Baptiste as a sign of respect and allegiance to the wealthy white plantation owner. Patrice was not surprised because he'd done the same thing so many times in the past. This time was different. Patrice spoke his mind. "Enough of the going along to get along, gentlemen. Time for change."

While impressed with the courage of his new friend who had come to his defense, Patrice wondered if Abraham Julian had made a terrible error in judg-ment. They did convene that evening to discuss the possibility of forming an army of *gens de couleur* to stand up to both the *grands blancs* and the *petits blancs*, but the maroons in the woods provided an odd twist to the dialogue. The result, however, was similar. In a way, Patrice and Abraham had just declared war against Henri Baptiste, and by proxy, the *grands blancs*. Alliances were shifting fast. A mixed-race plantation owner and a Jewish merchant could not speak that way to the most powerful *grand blanc* without repercussions.

Within the last few minutes, Patrice had learned the lessons of a lifetime about brotherhood. He had discovered that the quasi-brother of his childhood was an actual blood brother...who was intent on killing him. He had also un-earthed an assertiveness he hadn't known he possessed, and as a result many of his mixed-race brothers, who were so anxious to nominate him as their leader a few moments earlier, might no longer stand with him. The most surprising thing, however, was his new acquaintance, this Jew from Aux Cayes with the trick horse, who might prove to be the most trusted brother of all.

CHAPTER 20

The Beat of the Drum

HOUNGANS ALANSO, BATURU, and Suma convened at the top of the highest hilltop in the nearby forest. The three men stood on a wide tree trunk, which provided an exceptional view of the outskirts of the town of Jacmel. Their authority did not flow from elections or any other formal process, but the power to act or not clearly rested with them. Suma never questioned Alanso's judgment and experience, and both Alanso and Suma had great respect for Baturu's ability to stir the masses. Once Baturu came around to Alanso's way of thinking, the leadership became both strong and unified.

In order to finalize their plans, the size of the enemy force had to be estimated. The maroons numbered approximately fifteen hundred. Many had machetes, but only twenty had muskets—the ones taken from their *petits blancs* prisoners. Some had nothing more than their fists and the fury of an enslaved people. Alanso estimated the maroon ranks had increased by well over 100 over the last few hours, as recently escaped slaves joined the group in anticipation of the evening's assault.

Despite their growing numbers, the maroons needed more weapons to stand a chance. If they attacked with limited firepower, casualties would be too severe. Reports of another 100 armed *gens de couleur* in town concerned the three houngans. The math was simple: if the mixed race plantation owners banded together with the *grands blancs*—estimated at more than 200–their combined force would inflict too many casualties to make the attack worthwhile. If that was the case, Alanso planned to recommend they hold off their assault and raid area plantations instead, to build a larger stock of weapons for future attacks. Suma offered to get as close as possible to the town to gather intelligence.

The captured *petits blancs*, bleeding from the cuts inflicted by the maroons' machetes, sat gagged and bound in a circle. The two special prisoners, Jean Claude and Andre, were held apart from the rest. One of their guards held up a sledgehammer and motioned toward Jean Claude, which caused all of the maroons in the area to cheer as they imagined the sight of breaking both of these men at the wheel during their victory celebration. While Alanso and Baturu toured the camp, Suma selected the group who would accompany him on his reconnaissance mission, and headed toward Jacmel.

Outside the café, Henri Baptiste's men surrounded the armed *gens de couleur* security. Several of the mixed race plantation owners came out and told their men to lower their weapons. In the event that Henri Baptiste developed a "good" and a "bad" *gens de couleur* list, they hoped this would save them. Sensing the imminent eruption, townspeople stayed off the streets with shutters and doors securely closed. Despite what was about to transpire, the group assembled at the cafe had no choice but to wait nervously for something to spark the conflict. Patrice's heart began to pound—he desperately needed to relax and hoped his little mind game would do the trick. With nothing in the room catching his eye, he decided to step outside the back door to find something of interest.

The moment Patrice left the cafe, he saw the spot where Christophe was humiliated and thought of how traumatized his youngest son must have been. Patrice was sorry he had yelled at Claude who had done his best to protect his brother. Sometimes doing your best isn't enough to fix the problem, but it should be enough to clear your conscience. Blaming Claude for not watching out for his little brother denied him that small dignity. Claude tried to help Christophe and he should be able to take some solace from that.

Christophe's humiliating incident reminded Patrice of that day in the alley with Andre when they were young and the memories came flooding back. *How hard did I try to help Andre? Shouldn't I have supported Andre and subjected myself to some abuse simply because it was the right thing to do? Is this policy of going along to get along, fundamentally flawed? If no one ever stands up for what is right, will things ever change?* Patrice kept asking himself the hard questions because throughout his life he'd been choosing easy answers. But Claude had done for Christophe what one brother is expected to do for another. Even though Patrice had just found out Andre was his actual brother, they couldn't have been closer at the time of the incident–Patrice understood that he let Andre down.

After that incident in the alley, everything between Patrice and Andre had changed for the worse. Andre had taken the wrong path in recent years, but Patrice pushed him down it. Patrice noticed that he hadn't played his mind game. Instead, he actually analyzed his past behaviors and plotted a course for the immediate future, which cleared his conscience. It had a deeply calming effect. The next few hours would be difficult, but Patrice could now face them with a cool and calm demeanor because he planned to do the right thing.

⋅→▶ ◀◼⋅

Suma, within viewing distance, noticed the obvious tension between the *grands blancs* and *gens de couleur.* He instructed each of his men to throw several rocks across from their position, and took note of both groups of men shooting together in that general direction. Suma's assessment: they might not be together in a broad sense, but they were united against the maroons. While this was bad news, Suma also verified their previous conclusion–the maroons had an overwhelming superiority in numbers. He headed back to report to Alanso and Baturu who were waiting on the outskirts of the camp in anticipation of his return. United in their decision, the three men began marching the entire army of maroons along with their prisoners toward the town of Jacmel.

It took some time for the group to arrive, because many had to circle around to approach from the far side. The leaders considered the "encircling" tactic to be the right choice given their superiority in numbers. Standing closely together also hid the fact that most of the maroons had no weapons whatsoever. Those with machetes and the few with muskets were all staged to be in the front row. The beat of a drum would be the signal for the entire army to step out from the woods and surround Madame Archambeau's Café. The *gens de couleur* inside the café organized their personal firearms and stepped outside as an additional show of force.

The streets of Jacmel were empty and the strong wind, which had blown for most of the day, retreated. Even the birds, whose song typically emanated from the woods, either fled the scene or held their tongues. But the uneasy calm did not last long; Alanso gave the signal with a single beat of the drum and 1500 maroons stepped out from the cover of woods like a highly disciplined military force.

The armed men outside the café could not believe the sheer size of the maroon force and Henri Baptiste was concerned about their ability to stay calm and follow directions. He whispered to Gilbert Kildew, "Tell the men to hold their fire. I think my old slave Alanso, may want to have a word."

Alanso emerged from the side of the circle directly facing the front of the café and walked forward with five of the captured *petits blancs*. He shouted, "I have 15 more prisoners. Hold your fire and send out Henri Baptiste to talk."

Henri Baptiste and Gilbert Kildew took a step forward and although he was not invited, Patrice joined them. The three men met Alanso midway.

"It has been a long time, Alanso."

"Yes. It has, but don't insult me by addressing me like an old friend."

"Fair enough. We will not partake in small talk. What's on your mind?"

"I have a proposal for you, but I prefer to tell you alone."

Henri Baptiste and Alanso stepped to the side and began to whisper. Patrice decided not to try to join the private conversation given the tense circumstances of the moment and the fact Henri would need to immediately share the proposal with the broader group.

The two-man huddle over, Henri Baptiste walked back to the café with Patrice and Gilbert Kildew in tow. Alanso headed in the other direction and stopped as he neared the edge of the circle and released the five *petits blancs*, who scurried off to the perceived safety of the café, as a sign of good faith.

Henri Baptiste returned to the inside of the café and explained what had transpired. "My old house slave, Alanso, is their leader and he is willing to return all of the prisoners unharmed and walk away as long as we give him something to satisfy their need to spill blood tonight. He wants to retain two prisoners who have done special harm to the slave population in St. Domingue—Jean Claude Guilar, the carpenter and well-known slave catcher, and a house slave by the name of Andre, who they say is a spy from the Beaumont Plantation. We can't let them keep a white man, but I think I can convince them to settle for just the slave, Andre. I plan to accept his offer with that modification. It will be a good result, one slave is of no consequence."

They had an out—if they made the deal, the events of this tension filled evening would be over with a minimum of bloodshed. Henri Baptiste indicated he would pay Patrice the fair market value for his slave, despite the earlier insults, just to end this.

Patrice studied the faces in the room—overwhelming consensus. This was a small price to pay for a return to some semblance of normalcy. Abraham's body language told a different story—he opposed the decision, even though he knew of some of Andre's transgressions. Patrice thought of Camille and Chantal upstairs with her boys, and their advice that there was nothing more important than blood. Despite all of Andre's sins, Patrice knew that the broken promise of freedom was perhaps the main trigger for most of his misdeeds. Much to his own deep disappointment, Patrice seemed to be reverting to his old go along to get along philosophy, and his failure to object was taken as his personal approval of the deal. A note scribbled by Henri Baptiste was placed under a rock half way toward the edge of the circle. Patrice made no attempt to stop the note from being sent to the other side—he was frozen, much like that day in the alley so many years before. Alanso read the note, nodded to Henri, and gave instructions to Suma.

The *grands blancs* and *gens de couleur* began to smile realizing the conflict had ended. The front door of the café opened, and both Camille and Chantal emerged with looks of extreme disappointment. Patrice thought of their message to him, "There's nothing thicker'n blood."

Suma cut the vine that tied Andre to Jean Claude, in order to release the carpenter. At the same moment, Patrice stepped into the center of the circle with a look of determination and resolve. He wasn't sure he would be able to stop this, but was determined to do his best because this time, his conscience would be clear. Patrice Beaumont screamed the one word, which would trigger a chain reaction that would change his life, and the lives of everyone who was part of this standoff at Madame Archambeau's Café. The word was "No!"

CHAPTER 21

The Aftermath

PATRICE INTENDED FOR his "No" to resonate in the ears of those inside and out-side the circle, which defined the sides in this battle, but his defiance brought about an immediate shift in some of the tentative alliances. He intended to clarify his objection and proclaim Andre to be a person of consequence…he did matter and still had good in him. This was Patrice's plan and he would have executed it well, but his "No" proved to be the only word he would utter.

When the bullet hit Patrice, he assumed it came from one of the armed maroons. Later, however, Patrice understood he was shot in his back by either a *gens de couleur* or *grand blanc*. He fell to the ground immediately and then the melee began.

In the end, fifty white and mixed-race men survived, while hundreds of dead maroons were stacked around the same circle that formed their perimeter. Henri Baptiste escaped with his trusted aid, Gilbert Kildew, and most of the surviving maroons retreated to the hills happy with their partial victory. Jean Claude Guilar did end the day on the wheel. Many of the maroons wanted to leave him tied to it barely clinging to life for days until he finally died, but Baturu walked over at the end of the spectacle and provided the *coups de grace* by slitting his throat. He remarked to Alanso and Suma how unsatisfying it was to see a man, any man, die that way.

When Patrice screamed his "No," Andre and Jean Claude were being sep-arated. Jean Claude was immediately detained when the fighting began, but Andre escaped, made his way toward the café, and spent the balance of the short but furious fifteen minute battle as a human shield, protecting the fragile life of his fallen brother—the man who saved his life. Abraham Julian retreated to the café and protected the family.

Over the next few years, the maroons achieved greater victories and many of the wealthy *grands blancs* returned to France. The lives of the most brutal *gens de couleur* and white plantation owners who remained, fittingly came to violent ends. Patrice's one word objection catapulted him into the public eye. Years later, Alanso would say, in hindsight, Patrice's "No" in front of the cafe, provided more inspiration to the revolution than even the charismatic Baturu could have offered. Patrice went on to become one of the leaders of the new republic of Haiti from the comfort of his wooden wheelchair.

He would never again know the joy of taking a long walk on his fabulous Beaumont Plantation, but in many ways he enjoyed his day-to-day life even more. Curtains were no longer drawn during dinner, and all of the seats were taken as Andre assumed his rightful place at the other head of the table with his mother Camille by his side. Patrice still played mind games in the parlor, but did not stare into the eyes of his father for advice. He still found time to be in the company of his beloved Marie, but never in the presence of Gabrielle, who became his passion as well as his legal wife.

Every night, Andre pushed his brother's wheelchair up the hill to the Old Barn, and the men relived their childhood fantasies as they admired the silhouetted ships in the harbor. They still giggled at the talk of fancy women in France, but for both of them, their nautical adventures were short-lived, and always returned them home to Beaumont, where they belonged.

PART III

Patrick

CHAPTER 22

Lessons Learned

PATRICK ARRIVED AT the Reflektions Cafe before Aunt Grace, and placed their order—one coffee, one chamomile tea, and a small plate of oatmeal raisin cookies. A light kiss on the top of his head served as the hello. "We did it, didn't we!" Patrick turned to greet his aunt. They sat together in silence for a few minutes, and while no words were exchanged, they communicated on a higher plane. An important lesson had been learned and Patrick was surprised it involved race, which hadn't been a major issue in his current life. After further reflection, however, he realized he was always going along to get along.

Patrick admired the interior of the elegant Boigen Hotel once more, and this time recognized the chandelier as a duplicate of the one at Beaumont. *Of course it seemed familiar.* The same two groups congregated in the lobby. The lively one standing by the tulips, excited about beginning their new lives, and the calm and content group sitting off to the side door leading to 20th Street, all headed for their ultimate reward. This time, Patrick recognized a face in the second group, and realized the St. Domingue do-over involved someone else. *Congratulations, Andre, I'm happy it worked out for both of us.*

Patrick wondered what he and Andre did the first time around when things became tense at Madame Archambeau's Café. Aunt Grace followed Patrick's thoughts and responded, "No reason to wonder. This information is at your disposal. All you have to do is concentrate. Here, put your hands palms up on the table, and I will help."

Patrick wiped the cookie crumbs from the tips of his fingers and held out his hands. Once Aunt Grace's palms rested on top of Patrick's, he experienced the sensation of travel, but he wasn't driving—he was flying. She landed first on the branch of a tree outside the clearing leading to Madame Archambeau's Café. *What beautiful red feathers*, Patrick thought as Aunt Grace sat with her back slightly bent and her tail pointed downward. Patrick wondered if he had the same black feathers around his eyes, which gave the appearance of a mask, and he took his position next to his aunt on the tree branch.

Hordes of maroons milled around the outskirts of the tree line beneath them and Alanso finished reading the note sent by Henri Baptiste. Patrick looked across the clearing at Patrice. This was his moment. Patrick sensed Aunt Grace had control of the speed at which the story would unfold, and things were moving in slow motion. Airborne once more, the two birds landed closer to Patrice—Patrick again by his aunt's side. They both listened to Patrice's internal dialogue.

There's no one to blame but yourself, Andre. After all I've done for you, you tie my boys up like animals and then abandon them so you can run off to join the maroons? Well, I tried. I gave you more privileges than any other slave and nothing was good enough for you. Nothing I can do to help you. You did this to yourself.

Chantal Archambeau came out of the café and stood next to Abraham Julian. Both offered Patrice a most disappointing glare. Suma cut the vines securing Jean Claude Guilar to Andre. The carpenter made his way to the safety of the café as the maroons disappeared into the hills.

A few hours later, Andre was broken on the wheel, but Baturu recognized he was a lost soul, and offered the *coup de grace* by slitting his throat before the first bone shattered. This act of mercy was a great disappointment to the crowd who wanted vengeance, but Alanso considered it to be another big step in Baturu's development as a leader.

Later that night, Patrice stared at the portraits in the parlor, but found himself too embarrassed to admire his deceased wife's image, too disgusted to view his own, and unwilling to receive congratulations again from his father for going along to get along. Andre had deserved his help, but Patrice failed to act—again frozen in place, just like that day in the alley.

Camille partially blamed herself for her son's death—she should have told Patrice that Andre was his blood brother. As a result, Camille was more forgiving of Patrice than Chantal or Gabrielle, but she would never again treat him with the same level of respect and love. Always mindful of her place as a slave, Camille found subtle ways to express her displeasure. Another house slave began to summon Patrice for dinner and Camille took her meals alone in her room. Chantal's visits to Beaumont eventually came to an end because Patrice no longer felt like the brother she never had.

Every night Patrice walked up to the Old Barn, climbed the stairs to the harbor side deck, and studied the big silhouetted ships. He wished one of them would take him away. Anywhere at all would do.

Aunt Grace and Patrick, travelling again, found themselves back at their table in the Reflektions Cafe. When their hands separated, Aunt Grace offered her assessment of what they'd just witnessed. "We all blamed you, but Chantal and I knew you were capable of doing important things, if you had a push. Each of us has faults and challenges, dear Patrick, and 'needing a push' has always been yours. My failure to tell you what you needed to understand before that pivotal moment made me just as responsible for Andre's death as you. We both failed, Patrick, after being so close."

"It is true. I've always required a trusted advisor to coax me down the right path, and I thank you for being that person."

"At least the second time around," Aunt Grace said.

Patrick smiled as he responded, "Point taken. If you wouldn't mind, though, I think I would like to sit alone for a while before I head up to the room."

"As you wish my dear. I'll meet you up in Room 1010 when you're ready."

Patrick sat for a moment on the same lovely couch off the lobby where he had waited for his online date, puzzled as to whether he should consider this to be a few hours or a lifetime ago. He tried to remember the dozens of women he'd met online, but in Patrick's mind they all fused into one. So regimented with his first, second, third, and fourth date routine, he had tremendous difficulty differentiating between experiences. *How embarrassing*, Patrick thought, and then corrected himself, *how sad*. Time spent reflecting at The Boigen was supposed to be about things of importance, Patrick's online dates were not—he assumed this to be part of the reason for his poor recall.

One past relationship had mattered. Patrick had met her on the train and he recalled that meeting in full detail.

Lady, move your carriage a little bit, Patrick silently wished. He wanted to get another look at the remarkable woman he noticed as she entered the train—tall, perhaps six feet with her heels, and maybe in her late thirties. While he only caught a glimpse of her profile, her beauty was the type that took his breath away. Patrick became impatient and decided to move around the carriage.

He worked his way toward the rear, glanced in the beautiful woman's direction, and again noted her dark complexion, which at first made him think she might be Hispanic. Now that he was closer, she seemed to have more of an Indian look, but he couldn't be sure. *Ethnically ambiguous, yes, that's what she is.* There was nothing ambiguous, however, about her beauty and grace. She confidently sipped an open cup of coffee, while navigating the traffic in the aisle. As she turned slightly in response to the bumpy ride on the 4 Train, Patrick took note of her extraordinary cleavage. Oversized dangling earrings provided the final accents. Patrick liked taking it all in, but didn't want to get lost in one of his mind games—he wanted to meet her.

The seat next to his mystery lady was free, but so were many others—Patrick didn't want to be too obvious so he wandered over to the back part of the car, and then paused for a few moments at the pole immediately in front of her. He rubbed his back as if to indicate some muscle discomfort, and thought she might have flashed a dimple-loaded smile his way as he took a peek. When Patrick heard the announcement, "This stop 86th Street," he couldn't risk losing the empty seat next to her to someone else. One more rub to his back, and then the slightest bit of contact as he descended into the seat.

"So sorry miss, didn't mean to bump you."

"Don't worry, you've got to be a little tough to ride the 4 Train," she offered once again flashing her fabulous smile.

Patrick had his opportunity…her response begged for a comeback.

"Just what I thought—you give off a tough as nails kind of feeling," Patrick responded in an effort to be both charming and witty, always a difficult combination. He added, "My name is Patrick," as he extended his hand.

"Kasandra," she said. "You must be a good judge of people. You've got me pegged." Kasandra squeezed Patrick's hand as hard as she could to prove her point. The absurdity of her added effort caused her to giggle and tilt her head ever so slightly downward as she morphed her wide grin into a small mischievous smile and said, "And what about you, Patrick, are you a tough guy also?" Patrick took time to respond because at that moment, with her head still tilted downward and that silly smile on her face, she was the most charming and beautiful woman he'd ever met.

The flirting had worked. The newness of the first date had given way to the anticipation of the second, and then one year of smiles—nothing but fabulous third dates. Inevitably, the fourth date arrived and she asked the question. Patrick remembered the lead-up to the moment well—it happened at a comedy club where they made the mistake of sitting up front by the stage. The first comedian finished his set and the host came back out to work the crowd and introduce the next act. The couple seated next to Patrick made the fashion mistake of wearing shorts to the club, which appeared to be excellent fodder for the host and the audience had a big laugh at their expense. The host had been picking on everyone in the front row. Patrick and Kasandra suspected they were next.

"Oh my God, what do we have here? Do me a favor guys, and wave your hands for the audience." Patrick and Kasandra each tuned to face the crowd and waved their hands slightly over their heads.

"Ok, I've got two guesses. You are either a movie star with her accountant or a model with her agent, because it is hard to believe someone like this could be attracted to someone like that. Sorry, no offense, sir, but you're a little bit out of your league with this one!"

"Don't I know it!" Patrick offered as he put his right hand on his heart, and reached for Kasandra's hand with his left. He paused a moment to build more dramatic tension and then raised her hand to his lips and kissed it ever so softly. The crowd ate it up and showed their approval of Patrick's romantic gesture with a big round of applause. Patrick thought he'd handled himself well, but the comedian still had a few more minutes of time to kill on stage.

"I don't see a ring on her finger. Buddy, if I were you, I'd close this deal real fast! Thanks for being such good sports. I'd like to bring out our next act…"

Kasandra leaned into Patrick and whispered in his ear, "When are you closing this deal, buddy?"

That was the beginning of the end. Patrick and Kasandra saw each other a few more times, but they were all fourth dates and they drifted apart.

He settled into his chair at The Boigen and considered his terrible mistake with Kasandra. *Why do I have such trouble with commitment?* Patrick thought people were programmed in a certain way. Relationships never felt right to him and this was confirmed every time he verbally expressed his desire for "something more"–he knew he was lying the moment the words left his mouth. Deceit always seemed worse than ending things as he did.

It hit him all at once. Because he hadn't been able to come through for Andre, Patrick had labeled himself as someone who couldn't be counted on. He realized this was the reason he lost touch with his family and could not commit in any relationship. It suddenly all made sense, and he wondered if he'd ever get another chance to reconnect with his family or the lovely Kasandra. He probably should have expected to experience a true "Aha" moment at The Boigen, because that, after all, appeared to be the purpose of the place, but he was still surprised.

Patrick walked toward the reception desk on his way to the elevators, and noticed the same bearded elderly gentleman behind the counter. Well dressed as always in a different three-piece suit with the "P.S." monogram on his shirtsleeve, the clerk paused for a second, looked up, and gave Patrick a smile in recognition of his accomplishment. Patrick still did not understand who this man was, or even know his name, but knew he mattered at The Boigen. Patrick enjoyed the moment, and then turned to head up to Room 1010.

CHAPTER 23

Eleventh Avenue

PATRICK'S FLEETING MOMENT of celebration had turned into deep concern and he attempted to steady his trembling right hand with his left, in order to insert his keycard at Room 1010. Inside, he sank into the large cushioned chair by the window and offered the New York skyline a blank stare. Patrick realized he hadn't fully understood.

Aunt Grace rose from her place on the bed, and assumed the seat by his side. They trained their eyes on the world outside their window, but the skyline remained unimpressive. The lights of New York faded, much like Patrick's sense of optimism. Aunt Grace reached out and held his hand; the touch pulled him back to reality. He turned to his aunt, took a deep breath, and said, "You never told me about Eleventh Avenue."

"No. I didn't. You needed to experience it for yourself."

"A terrible thing. I saw it in his eyes."

"Yes, I know, Patrick."

"Will this happen to me?"

"Not if I can help it. We're in this together. Remember, if you fail, I fail, and if you succeed, I succeed. I don't plan to leave The Boigen through the Eleventh Avenue exit, and neither should you. Tell me what you saw."

Patrick settled into his seat, unable to shake his new sense of pessimism.

"The man arrived through the Tenth Avenue doors with a look of terror on his face. I noticed him immediately and sensed his fear. I read some of his thoughts and understood he'd blown his last opportunity to make things right. From what I could tell, he got greedy. I'm not sure with what, but greed was the issue. Security greeted and escorted him over to the elevator bank, where I stood waiting for a car. He smiled momentarily because he assumed he was headed back up to his room, but the elevators were all stuck in the basement. Nothing was moving."

Patrick paused for a second and swallowed hard before continuing, "The bearded front desk agent walked over and told the man he was so sorry, but he'd been given more than a fair chance to succeed. I could understand some of their thoughts, but then I was blocked and whatever the agent communicated to the man scared him beyond belief. He tried to run, but his legs wouldn't move. The two security officers grabbed him by either arm and dragged him to the back exit onto Eleventh Avenue. They literally pushed him through the door. At that moment, the elevators started to run, and the bearded front desk agent looked at me, but didn't say a word. I took it as a warning. The old man then had the nerve to wish me good luck as I got into the car. One thing is certain—he's not the polite and harmless senior citizen I thought him to be. He's a monster through and through. I'm truly petrified of whatever is lurking beyond the exit onto Eleventh Avenue. Why didn't you tell me about Eleventh Avenue? Aren't you my guide?"

"Patrick, I've done my best to tell you everything at the appropriate times. Most of what happens here is about positive reinforcement. You make a little progress with each life, reflect over coffee, peel a tulip petal, and try to do better the next time. If all goes according to plan, you're sitting calmly by the 20th Street exit waiting for the ultimate reward after a number of successful lifetimes. Occasionally, we have souls like you and I who get so close and screw things up at critical moments. Lots of souls do this, so this doesn't make us special, but there aren't so many who continue the bad pattern as we did. You were so screwed up as Patrick Walsh, you were destined for an Eleventh Avenue exit, and I would have been right by your side, but we still had potential and were given the opportunity for these do-overs, as we've been calling them. After some time, everyone at The Boigen understands an Eleventh Avenue exit is bad, but no one appreciates how bad until moments before they're escorted through those doors. The thought you were blocked from understanding was a description of what awaited that unfortunate soul."

Patrick tried to process all of this new information and offered his reaction, "So they downplay the negative, but eventually an unlucky few face the reality of what the penalty for failure actually is. I understand–we're both at that point, but why show me now, after the great success we just had?"

"Not for me to decide, Patrick. The Boigen works a certain way and I'm not in charge."

"What makes me so screwed up that I deserve whatever is waiting beyond the Eleventh Avenue exit?"

"Ok, Patrick. Time for you to understand. Come and hold my hands. We need to take a trip."

They landed on the branch of a tree on the side of a small house. Patrick needed a moment to recognize his surroundings, and the street sign confirmed it. He was at the house where his brother, Frank, lived ten years ago. The sun had already gone down, and Frank, seated in in a chair in one of the upstairs bedrooms, appeared to be having a good night talk with his eleven-year-old son, Brian. Grace assumed her slightly bent posture, tail down, and admired how Patrick's red feathers reflected the light from the nearby streetlamp.

"Brian, I know you're upset, but did he actually promise to go to your game?"

"I told him that you couldn't go to the father-son game. You always say that you played baseball and Uncle Patrick was really good at basketball. I've been bragging to my friends all week about him. I needed him to show up. The other kids laughed at me, Dad. They all laughed. Where was he, Dad?"

Frank consoled his son and whispered, "I can't say, Brian. Sometimes he's hard to pin down. I'm so sorry. Let's not ask him to get involved any more. Next time, I'll be there for you, even if I have to miss work. Did I ever tell you about my killer three-point shot?" Frank jumped up and took an imaginary shot and then fell back into his chair. "It might need some work!" He tried, but nothing Frank said or did improved his son's mood. Frank turned off the lights, and took down the picture of himself as a teen in a baseball uniform standing next to Patrick holding a basketball, which had always been proudly displayed next to Brian's mirror. Once in the hallway, he placed it in the closet, and then headed for bed shaking his head.

A chill jolted Patrick's spine when Frank touched the frame of the picture. Grace stated the obvious, "You let them down Patrick. They were counting on you."

"Do you think I don't understand that? I wanted to go, but it didn't feel right when I headed out and I turned back. I didn't know why."

Airborne again. This time, they landed on a mailbox in front of a suburban home. A beautiful bay window provided an excellent view of the dining room table. Patrick's sister, Diane, always hosted holiday dinners, and all of the seats were occupied, except for one.

"Yes, mother, of course I told Patrick what time to be here."

"Maybe he got the time wrong, he is such a busy man."

"Please mother, how is Patrick a busy man? He may live in the busiest city in the world, but he lives like a hermit. He just doesn't give a shit about us, especially me. He hasn't been to one of my Thanksgiving dinners for four years. Four years, mother! Do you think he gets the time wrong every year?" Diane picked up Patrick's plate and threw it against the wall and her mother, Gloria, started to cry.

Patrick became disoriented when the plate shattered against the wall, and he fluttered from his perch on the mailbox. The duo headed back to The Boigen. Grace and Patrick settled into their chairs in Room 1010 to discuss what they had just witnessed.

"For most souls, life isn't meant to be experienced alone—certainly not for you, Patrick. After being so close in your prior lives, this solitary existence became an affront to everyone who cared about you.

"But I always let everyone down. I thought it would be better if I was alone. Better for everyone."

"Haven't you realized yet it wasn't only you and I who were together in this last life? Think about the immediate connection you had with Abraham Julian and the tremendous assistance provided by Chantal Archambeau and her mother Giselle. This is our group, Patrick. We've always been together, but they've just done better than you and I, and are much more developed souls. They will be there to help us in the next life as well. Let's end the night on a positive note. Have another look at the computer screen. Remember, the upper right quadrant."

Patrick slowly walked over to the monitor and didn't quite understand how looking at himself incapacitated was going to help him, but he would not question Aunt Grace. He sat down in front of the screen, braced himself, and trained his eyes on the upper right hand quadrant. A smile broke out across his face. Still unconscious—no change there—but he had three family members standing around his bed—his mother, Gloria, his brother, Frank, and his sister, Diane. It was definitely an improvement and he appreciated both the magnitude of his predicament and the strength of the full team working on his behalf for a good outcome. Patrick smiled and touched his index finger to the screen in a symbolic hello to his people.

Aunt Grace thought she'd done a good job in restoring to Patrick some much needed confidence, but her smile morphed into a long yawn—a lot had happened that day. She knew Patrick would need his rest, too, and they both retired for the night determined to succeed in their final challenge, which would greet them in the morning.

PART IV

Pretty Paddy

CHAPTER 24

Ireland

PATRICK SCRUTINIZED HIS surroundings for the third time, but he could only see Aunt Grace, who stood a few feet away from him in the middle of a thick mist. *No need to worry,* Patrick thought, because he sensed this was where they needed to be. Aunt Grace answered the obvious question. "We're on the way to the life you had before you became Patrick Walsh. So sorry to disturb your rest by waking you this early, but I'm afraid you'll need some background and context to understand this old life."

"Why, what's so complicated about this life?"

"It takes a while for the details of a life to return to a soul during these do-overs, and I'm worried the initial assumptions you might make about your circumstances may be far off the mark. Most modern day Irish Americans do not appreciate the condition of the Irish over the last several hundred years. You'll need an appreciation of this to succeed in this life you are about to rejoin."

"Several hundred years? How much time are we going to take with this explanation? Remember, I'm hanging onto my life back at St. Lukes!"

Grace smiled. "Trust me. I'll be brief and only provide the highlights, but you need to understand a bit about Ireland as well as your parents—who are from Galbally, Limerick. Ireland and England have been at odds for many years, and some trace the problems back to the late 1600s when an Irish army backed the losing candidate for the English throne. The payback for the Catholic Irish, delivered immediately through legislation, prohibited them from voting, buying land, attending school, serving in an apprenticeship, possessing weapons, and practicing their religion."

Aunt Grace waved her hand to clear some of the mist away from her face before she continued. "Before these laws existed, Irish Catholics owned 80% of the land in Ireland. By 1778, they owned just 5%, with the majority controlled by wealthy Protestant absentee landlords and managed by their agents. Poor Irish Catholics, reduced to working small plots of land, turned to the potato, which was the only crop that could thrive on such tiny parcels, and this one vegetable became the foundation of the Irish diet. As long as the potato crop remained strong, the Irish didn't starve."

"As an Irish American, I'm embarrassed to say I didn't know any of this. I knew of the tension between the Irish and English, but never the underlying reason. The resentment of the English must have been extreme."

"Extreme is an understatement. Once news of the successful American and French Revolutions settled in the minds of the Irish, they also rebelled in 1798, but the English crushed the revolution and many of the rebels were hung as examples to others. After the rebellion, England permanently stationed a force 100,000 strong in Ireland to discourage any further misbehavior. Two years later, England passed the British Act of Union, which made Ireland a part of the United Kingdom. The act abolished the 500-year-old independent Irish parliament in Dublin."

"So after the rebellion, the Irish lost their own Parliament. That must have been the final insult."

"Yes, an insult, but unfortunately, not the final one. Things continued to get worse in Ireland, and by the mid-1830s, most Irish laborers had no regular work and begging became common. The British response was to establish workhouses for the destitute. Upon arrival at a workhouse, the head of the family needed to prove his family had absolutely no means. Despite two million Irish living in a state of poverty by the late 1830s, these workhouses were often empty because it meant the complete loss of dignity and freedom."

"So things were bad even before the Irish famine?"

"Yes, Ireland was one of the poorest places on earth, but by the early 1840s, a charismatic Catholic lawyer by the name of Daniel O'Connell, provided reason for hope as he led the movement for the repeal of the Act of Union, which featured "monster" rallies filled with O'Connell's fiery oratory. At one such rally in County Meis, nearly 750,000 people came together to hear his message. In 1843, the movement for independence peaked as O'Connell and half a million supporters attempted to gather near Dublin for another "monster" rally, and this is where your story begins. The mist is clearing. Look down below...your father, Patrick Allen, is in the center of the warehouse, and your mother, Grace, is standing in the street outside the front door. Grace is pregnant with you—the third and last Patrick to be born to them. The previous two were baptized, but did not survive infancy. Not an unusual occurrence in those days. Let's listen in."

Patrick Allen placed the last barrel perfectly in back of the wagon and stepped out of the way as two other men struggled together to accomplish the same task. The proprietor of the brewery smiled as he gawked at the enormous man, dubbed Pretty Paddy, who was anything but pretty. Patrick stood 6' 4", weighed in excess of 300 pounds, and had scars on his face and arms from fights in the back alleys of Dublin as a young man.

His boss called out, "Good job, Paddy. Your wife is outside waiting for you. I'll see you in the morning. We've got a big load to get out."

The supervisor knew he'd get no response; Patrick was a man of few words. Paddy's wife on the other hand, had lots to say. Also over-sized, Grace's smile and curly brown hair softened her otherwise severe and intimidating appearance. The supervisor remembered when Grace filled in for Paddy when he injured his arm and couldn't lift for a few weeks. While no match for him, she was easily as strong as most of the men on the job, and had a much better work ethic. Paddy headed out of the warehouse to meet his wife.

"Paddy, I'm sorry. The monster rally is off. The government sent in troops and ships. There will be bloodshed if Daniel O'Connell speaks his mind. O'Connell called it off, but he's a brilliant man. No rally tomorrow."

Paddy nodded and the couple began the slow walk home as people in the street got out of their way.

"My parents look like they were not to be messed with."

"Yes, but also quite intelligent. Your father, made a conscious decision to downplay his intellect. The laws of the day banned him from pursuing many professions and his unusually large size made him highly sought after as a laborer. Patrick thought he'd have an easier time being hired for manual labor if people assumed him to be a simple man in all respects. As such, he let his size and productivity speak for itself and earned a premium as a laborer, but never said much. In private moments with his wife, he shared his dream—to pursue a political career in a free Ireland. Grace often told him he'd have to say a few words to accomplish that and he always responded with a smile, 'There's a price to pay for anything worthwhile.' Your father hoped to speak to Daniel O'Connell at the monster rally the next day about his political ambitions. With the rally cancelled, his dream was deferred, but not dead by any means. There would be other opportunities."

Aunt Grace paused for a moment to make sure Patrick was following her narrative—she could see from his face that he was. She continued, "A few days after the postponed rally, O'Connell was imprisoned and the movement toward independence experienced a major setback. Times would get tough in Ireland over the next few years and the Irish people would have to navigate this difficult period without Daniel O'Connell."

Patrick jumped in, "I've definitely heard of Daniel O'Connell, but I didn't understand much about him. Did my father eventually become part of his inner circle?"

"I'm afraid not. In 1845, potato blight destroyed Ireland because of the total dependence on this one crop. People were starving, couldn't pay their rent, and many became dispossessed. Your parents moved back to their family farm in Galbally, Limerick. They didn't want the city life for you, and as unusually large your parents were, you showed the potential to be even bigger at an early age. As a four year-old, people thought you were a slow ten year-old. In the winter of 1847, your family finally exhausted all of their savings, except what your father called his "security"— a small amount of money he saved for the most dire of circumstances. By the end of 1847, the Allens' only source of income came from the Public Works programs set up by the government. Roads were being built—not so much because they were needed, but because the pay for this work provided some income for Irish peasants to buy food."

Patrick decided to add a touch of sarcasm, "So we worked on the roads. Not exactly the political career my father had in mind."

"True. Keeping your belly full will trump career ambitions any day. The Irish died in droves from hunger. When you don't have anything to eat, nothing else matters. Here you are with your parents working on the Public Works project outside of Galbally in the Winter of 1847 during a period referred to as The Killing Snows."

The wind cut through the workers like a knife. Without this financial relief, the peasants would starve, but in this snow and wind, many wondered if they would succumb from exposure first. Most looked like skeletons in rags. Despite the extreme temperatures, it was not uncommon to see exposed skin on the upper body with rags tied around feet as a creative substitute for shoes. The Allens, better off than most, dressed in many thin layers of clothing with proper shoes, which kept their feet dry. Paddy and Grace were pleased when the system changed from a flat daily rate to a piece rate system, because their ability to break and move rock was remarkable. Patrick and Grace alone could generate the same amount of work as any typical group of ten emaciated workers. Even their four-year old son would work an hour or two at a time and generate more income than the average adult based on this piece rate system. The Allens were good Catholics, however, and decided to give a portion of their proceeds to a different neighbor each day by quietly giving them some of their output. This made them well liked and Paddy thought he was responsible for generating more feelings of friendship than fear for the first time in his life.

"Daddy, Mr. Kilmore won't get up. I tried to wake him, but I think he's sleeping."

Paddy Allen walked over to his slumped neighbor, noticed the black marks on his face, and looked for signs of breathing—there were none, he had passed. *That damn typhus*, Paddy thought to himself. Most of those who died on the job at the Public Works were left on the side of the road, where their bodies would be picked at by dogs and other stray animals. Paddy Allen wouldn't permit that fate to befall Mr. Kilmore, and took a break from his work in order to carry his neighbor's corpse on his shoulder to a clearing behind the worksite. He gave Mr. Kilmore a proper Christian burial.

"Patrick, it is important for you to understand this simple act of kindness proved to be fatal for your father. No one knew exactly how typhus spread and whether the germs were transmitted through the air or touch, but somehow ty-phus always became prevalent during periods of famine. Starving people tended to sleep in unsanitary places and generally struggled with their hygiene. Once body lice from someone who had the fever travelled to an uninfected person, it took just a few bites for the other person to be infected. Paddy noticed the body lice that night, and did his best to clean up and rid himself of them. It was these efforts that probably saved you and your mother, but he had already been bit-ten. Within weeks, your father checked himself into the Union Workhouse as a pauper in order to be admitted to one of the fever sheds to die."

"Oh my God, what a terrible ending."

"You're right, but your father endured that terrible ending so you and your mother could have a new beginning. He finally went into his "security" to buy passage for the two of you to travel to America. You actually travelled with some level of comfort because he had enough to pay for a proper berth on the ship. Most of the Irish completed their voyage huddled with the masses in the "holds" of large ships designed for materials, not people. These ships were a breeding ground for typhus and became known as "Coffin Ships," because more than half of the passengers died from the Black Fever during the crossing. You may have guessed I was your mother in this life. It is interesting to note how you've always been called Patrick, but this is the only other time I was called Grace."

"Yes, Patrick suits me, but this is a sad story and means I never got to know my father."

"That isn't true. You had some fond memories of him from when you were a child and in his last few days, he wrote a long letter to you, which he called Daddy's Rules. You grew up in New York learning to live by those rules."

"I like the sound of that, but I have no memory of any of this yet. When will things come back to me?"

"Just like your last life…once you assume your old identity. Believe me, you will be quite familiar with Daddy's Rules. It was a big thing in your life. Not to worry."

"Okay, Aunt Grace, or should I call you Mom?"

"We're not in that life yet, dear—Aunt Grace will be fine. As a single moth-er, I had a tough time when we arrived in New York City. The only work for the Irish was manual labor, which paid even less for women than men. I used my size and rough looks to my advantage and dressed in a masculine way to pass as a male laborer on the docks. The work was hard. It is 1863 and you are 20 years old. New York City is all abuzz with talk of the Draft that is about to be instituted to increase the size of the Union Army during the Civil War."

"Here we go, Patrick. As Irish in New York, we were better off than we would have been in Ireland, but on the low end of the social order in America. We took all of the menial jobs nobody else wanted—that is until the Blacks started coming into the city. Lots of tension existed between the Irish and the Blacks over jobs, which contributed to this week in the summer of 1863 when riots erupted in the city. This is it, Patrick, if we do well here, we will move on. I hope you're ready. I know I am."

CHAPTER 25

A Good Gosoon

Young Patrick Allen, a true Gemini with two distinct personalities layered over a wandering spirit, had made a promise to himself in his early teens–he would move out of the city by his 21st birthday, which was now only a year away. He wanted to say goodbye to tight places like his apartment on Tenth Avenue and planned to go out west for grand adventures in wide-open spaces. In some of his dreams, Patrick was a gold prospector, in others, a rough and tumble sheriff, and in a few, a cowboy out on the range. His fantasies came in different varieties, but just one size–they were all big. A mammoth man shouldn't be forced to live small–he couldn't even stretch out his arms; something was always in the way. Patrick wanted out and he often escaped though daydreams, which took him far away from cramped New York City and also calmed him down. He wouldn't allow himself to be stuck in the city for long.

Patrick started every day the same way. First, he got up and straightened the sheets on his small bed. He'd been managing with this outshot for years by sleeping in a curled up position. In the morning, however, the space had to be converted from a bedroom back into a kitchen. Patrick folded the outshot back into the wall, sat at the table, and began eating his first meal of the day with a book by his side.

An arrangement with a bookstore owner enabled him to borrow books in exchange for work. He concealed the books as he walked the streets of the city, however, because of Daddy's Rule #1; never let them know you have a brain. Given the physical size of the Allens, hiring managers at the docks often gave them preference, but these same managers might become nervous about an educated Irishman. As Patrick Senior said when he clarified Rule #1, "First and foremost we must eat, and never let anything get in the way of that." Nothing did stand in the way of Patrick Allen Jr. and his next meal—his huge appetite needed to be satisfied every few hours. Patrick heard rustling from the far corner of his tiny apartment as his mother sat up in bed.

Aunt Grace pointed down to the scene in the kitchen and turned to her nephew.

"You're a giant of a young man. 6'7" is large today, but almost unheard of in 1863. Back in those days, weightlifting as exercise didn't exist, but given all of your hard manual labor, you are solid muscle. As you already know, I'm your mother, Grace. The years have been tough on me. Working on the docks put food on our table and paid the rent. At this point, you are the major wage earner, but I can't understand how you make so much money. I suspect you're doing something I would not approve of." Grace smiled and squeezed his hand. "And now we assume our old lives."

"Morning. Going to be another hot one," Patrick offered as he displayed his shirt, which was already stained with perspiration at this early hour of the day.

"Morning, a ghrá. Hot indeed. Summer in New York—not like back home. This heat is too much. Put the book away and head over to the docks. All you'll have to do is show up to be picked because of your size, but you can't be late and arrive after they've done the picking. Go on. Get out of here."

"Yes, Ma, you tell me every time," He smiled, "but I hope you're not going also. Here." Patrick handed his mother a stash of bills—almost twenty dollars. "I did well last week. We've got the rent and food covered. Stay home, Ma."

"Do you think I'm an eejit? Where the Hell did you get that kind of money in one week. The Irish can't even make a dollar a day. This is almost a month's pay! What are you up to Patrick Allen? You best not bring shame down on this family! Your father didn't give his life for us to come to this country for you to become a criminal. I want you to do good, honest work. How'd ya get this money?"

"I worked second shifts for the storekeeper who loans me the books and I unloaded a bunch of deliveries for her. Normally a few guys do it, but since I did it all by myself, she paid me extra. Honest money, Ma. I promise. Believe me, I'm no criminal. As a matter of fact, I couldn't afford to go to jail–they don't serve enough food to support all of this." Patrick stood up with a wide grin and flexed his muscles. His mother tried to back away because she knew what was coming, but wasn't fast enough. Patrick quickly lifted his 200 pound mother like she was a little baby and cradled her in his arms. "See Ma, I'm no criminal, I'm just a boy who needs to eat to stay strong!"

Grace Allen couldn't stay mad at her behemoth of a son. He'd been able to lift her this way ever since he was fifteen. There was something about the ritual of the son lifting the mother that they both found entertaining and endearing. Grace still didn't understand how Patrick got all of this money, but was determined to find out. For now, she enjoyed this private moment with her boy, who'd been the sole focus of her life for the past twenty years.

"Put me down, you big bastard!"

"Is that any way for a proper Irish mother to speak to her adoring son?"

"You bet it is! Put me down, you lumper, and get down to those docks!"

Patrick carefully delivered his mother to her chair next to the table, while he poured her a cup of tea. She noted how gentle her otherwise rough son could be at times. Grace knew Patrick Jr. loved her and was fundamentally a good gossoon, but the Irish weren't paid like this, and he had to be up to something. She smiled, wished him a good day, and resigned herself to the fact that despite this mystery, the family had done well since coming to America–certainly when compared to what their lives would have been like had they stayed in Ireland. When assessed against other groups in New York, however, "doing well" was no longer the right conclusion; the Irish were looked down on by almost everyone else in the city. Grace was happy with her life anyway and while she missed some things about Ireland, she had absolutely no desire to return. The Allens had become New Yorkers, and New Yorkers they would remain.

CHAPTER 26

The Breakfast Club

PATRICK ALLEN OFTEN left his apartment on Tenth Avenue with the general intention of heading over to the West Side docks. Sometimes he hesitated at the first cross street, which would take him west toward the water, but on the morning of July 10th, he was past the point of hesitation. It had been several months since he'd worked at the docks, and now he had a different daily routine, which involved heading east toward Midtown. Patrick disliked the work on the docks and didn't want that to become his life, but knew his mother would never understand. He aspired to more than manual labor as a career, but appreciated how much he had to overcome in New York to be anything other than someone who lifted something up, walked some distance, and then put it down—the basic job description of an Irishman.

Mrs. Kilpatrick often left the front door open for Patrick early in the morning, and he noticed some cases of books, which hadn't been stacked properly. After straightening them up and walking toward the back of the store with a stack of newspapers, Patrick read the morning's headline, which announced the beginning of the Draft on Saturday, July 11, 1863. The article explained eligibility and exemptions--all male citizens at least 20 years of age were subject to the Draft and three basic exemptions had been established, two for wealthy whites and one for blacks. The affluent could either pay the government $300 to be excused or offer some poor soul a lesser amount to be their substitute. Blacks were exempted because they were not considered citizens. This combination of eligibility rules and exemptions guaranteed that the dirt poor Irish, who comprised almost half of the city's population, would be forced to serve. Margaret Kilpatrick came down the stairs with a cup of coffee and greeted her friend.

"Patrick, my smart young man. What is the headline?"

"The Draft is the top story, Mrs. Kilpatrick. Exemptions for the rich and the blacks—seems like the makings of an all-Irish army. Not going to go over well in my neighborhood."

"You may be right, Patrick. Let's see what my breakfast club has to say."

Mornings had always been the slow, boring part of the day, until Margaret Kilpatrick started her Friday Morning Breakfast Club a few years ago. Since then, she had had excitement at least one morning each week. Over the past two months, however, Patrick's daily visits made the early morning hours her favorite part of the day.

Margaret and Patrick hit it off right away because he reminded her of her son, whom she'd lost to the Black Fever in Ireland years before. The day she met Patrick, three large crates of books had greeted Margaret when she opened the doors and she was upset. At the age of 60, the more physical duties required of a shopkeeper had become a challenge, and she always carefully coordinated her deliveries with the hours of her part-time staff. This delivery, however, caught her by surprise. She decided to unpack each crate in the street and bring the books inside a few at a time. Patrick was walking by as she started to work on the first crate. Margaret recognized the large young man as someone who would often stop by her window to browse the book titles.

Patrick noticed her struggling with the first crate and offered to help. Before she had the opportunity to answer, he bent his knees, squatted, and stood up carrying all three crates at once. He wouldn't accept any money for helping, but asked if he might borrow a book, and wondered if she had anything to eat. As the days passed, Patrick started to come by most mornings. He did some work around the store, ate like a horse, and read an average of two books per week.

As the Breakfast Club began to arrive, Patrick and the shopkeeper headed to the rear of the store and greeted their esteemed guests at the back door. The professor brought the muffins, the editor took responsibility for a supply of cigars, and the merchant, who was quite wealthy but notoriously cheap, got off by saying he was always certain to bring his charming personality. Mrs. Kilpatrick provided the coffee and Patrick served.

Patrick had been there every Friday morning for the past two months and received the education of his life. At first, the older men were intrigued by his massive size and then were surprised to find he was also well read. The professor began tutoring Patrick on a regular basis and remarked at how he could be at the top of his class if he were a student at Columbia. In the beginning, he only served the coffee, but the "beginning" didn't last long. Patrick had a seat at the table and became accepted as one of the gang, although in this group he thought it wise to listen and absorb, and only offered his opinions if directly asked.

The Republican editor of the Tribune, Edward Simmons, who worked closely with their famous publisher, Horace Greely, loosened his necktie and fanned himself with his napkin as he asked, "When do we think we'll have a break from this oppressive heat?"

Jason Timbers, a Democratic professor of Political Science at Columbia College, responded, "If you think this is hot, wait until you and your friends begin the Draft. That will be true heat. Lincoln's got some nerve bringing the Draft to New York."

The successful merchant, Johnston Stewart, agreed. "You're damn right. Don't forget, Edward, New York could have left the Union a year ago. We should have followed the recommendation of our former mayor, Fernando Wood—a truly great man. He had it right. This is no war for New York City." The former mayor had led a movement to secede, and while some support existed, most never gave it such serious consideration. One of the major newspapers, The Daily News, backed the idea, but when even the most casual of observers peeked below the surface, the fact that the publisher of the Daily News was also the mayor's brother, substantially tainted this endorsement.

Edward Simmons offered his standard retort, "Do you say this because of your ideology or your wallet?" New York City was connected to the South economically. Most of the southern cotton crop was exported to Europe and the rest of the world through the ports of New York, and by recent accounts, southern plantation owners were indebted $200 million to New York merchants. Men like Johnston Stewart were afraid the Port of New Orleans would replace New York City as the hub for cotton exports.

The democratic professor chimed in next. "We don't need all of those poor Blacks heading up north to cities like New York. Let them stay in the South. We've got the Irish to deal with—same kind of thing. You can't have too many groups competing for the lowest jobs. It will lead to chaos." The professor glanced at Patrick after his somewhat questionable Irish remark as a reminder of the basic rule observed at the breakfast club—the dialogue needed to be free and could occasionally be sensational–all sensitivities, however, had to be left at the door.

The editor responded, "So we're supposed to continue enslaving a population because they'll be more competition for jobs at the docks? Is this your position, professor? What about a free, competitive economy? What about education to improve the lot of the Irish?"

"I'm trying to avoid unnecessary violence. Our local democratic government runs the city well without outside interference–we don't need problems like this war and Draft, which have only come about because of the Republicans–especially that damn Lincoln!" exclaimed Professor Timbers.

Johnston Stewart, who normally stayed out of this end of the ongoing disagreement between the publisher and professor, couldn't resist the opportunity to provide a little jab, and stared down Jason Timbers as he said, "Is it the Democratically elected government of New York City that makes it run, or is it William 'Boss' Tweed and the corrupt Tammany Hall that gets things done–all in exchange for a little piece of the pie?"

The professor jumped to his feet as he exclaimed, "How dare you!"

All three men started to laugh, and Patrick, who got caught up in the passion of the arguments, didn't immediately realize what had just happened. As a result of these regular breakfast meetings, the three men had become close friends, and realized that reasonable men needed to understand all sides of an argument. This was essential to develop a thoughtful personal opinion, but also to co-exist with people who espoused different points of view. When it became apparent they all shared this evolved approach to the issues of the day, they realized their discussions would not be as lively, so on occasion they each offered their official party line depending on their inclinations and had these heated debates. While the experience was much like acting in a play, hearing the passionate arguments in this setting helped them to handle them better in their real lives on the outside.

The reality was Edward Simmons did not share all of the Republican viewpoints of his newspaper, the Tribune. Edward still did a little writing on the side under a pen name, in which he exhibited some Democratic leanings. He always waved the Republican banner at work, however, because any other position would lead to the end of his 30+ years of employment.

The merchant, Johnston Stewart, did not believe in the secession argument for New York City and considered the former Mayor, Fernando Wood, to be an uncontrollable wild card. Johnston's business caused him to be aligned somewhat with southern interests, but his personal hatred for the institution of slavery put his affiliation firmly with the North.

The professor, Jason Timbers, was happy to present the local Democratic views through the eyes of Tammany Hall, but he was not a Tammany disciple. He understood they ran things in the city and respected the power of their leader, William "Boss" Tweed, but did not believe in inciting the Irish with the threat of southern Blacks coming up north to steal their jobs, and was no fan of the graft and corruption for which they were known. Jason Timbers had no reason to ever publicly adjust his views because he had no ambitions to be anything other than a college professor. He was known as a free and independent thinker with his students and found it amusing to act upset when someone questioned the integrity of Tammany Hall. He sometimes joked it didn't even seem right to use the word "integrity" in the same sentence as "Tammany."

Edward Simmons tapped his spoon on his coffee cup to call the group back to order, and then posed the question of the day, "Whether you like it or not, next week's Draft will take place. What do each of you think will happen? Johnston, let's assume, for argument's sake, you speak for the rich." Offering this somewhat obvious statement as anything other than fact, caused everyone in the room, including young Patrick, to chuckle. "Yes, assuming you speak for the rich, what will the well-heeled portion of our population think of the Draft?"

"We will be grateful to our President for not adding insult to injury by making us directly participate in this Godforsaken war and then we will happily pay the $300 to be exempted or provide a substitute for a lesser cost to serve in our stead. At least this will enable us to endure this war without having to lose our lives for a cause that is ruining our livelihoods."

"Thank you for that frank answer, Johnston."

The publisher turned his attention to the professor, "And what are your thoughts?"

The professor sat down and slowed his pace of speech as he spoke in somber tones, "I'm afraid of violence and bloodshed and I'm also afraid the repercussions will be so severe they will impact us all."

Johnston asked, "What do you mean by repercussions affecting us all?"

"I mean the Republicans and the Federal government will take the biggest hit because they are directly responsible. Lincoln, who is hated by the Irish because of his Emancipation Proclamation of a few months ago, will be the main source of animosity. As soon as the Irish heard about the proclamation, they feared losing their jobs to the freed Southern Blacks, who would relocate to the city and work for half the wages. Irishmen throughout the city will look to take out their anger against all representations of Lincoln and the Federal government, and God help those poor Blacks here in the city. Unfortunately, the Democrats will also be blamed because we appear to be in charge and we're somehow letting this happen. Don't think the Irish will forget how quickly we had them become citizens, which makes them subject to the Draft. This Conscription Act was written in a way that guarantees this will be an all-Irish war. The $300 to be exempted might as well be $300 million as far an Irishman is concerned. The Irish view is that they're being forced into a war where the goal is to free the same people who will take their jobs. Next week, gentleman, will go down in the history books. It will be ugly. Mark my words."

The professor's strong words gave the men food for thought. Despite the constant references to the dirt poor and uneducated Irish, Patrick knew not to get insulted, because it actually was true. He remembered Daddy's Rule #2, don't accept everything you hear as the truth, and Rule #3, don't reject a truth only because it is personally hard to accept. Patrick hadn't said much at the breakfast, but never did. He occasionally asked a question when he didn't understand, but he could never speak in a heated way to any of these men.

He understood they played their game and yelled at each other for sport, but Patrick couldn't be part of that. These gentlemen saw something in him that made them take an interest, and this Friday morning session along with his regular tutoring from the professor, provided Patrick with a remarkable education. The men finished their coffee and took one last bite of their muffins as they said their goodbyes and wondered what they would be discussing next Friday morning after the onset of the Draft.

CHAPTER 27

The Boss

"Boss, lots of shit going on today. We've got to figure out who's doing what."

"There's only one real boss and that's 'Boss' Tweed," John Sanderson responded to his long time staffer, Billy Conklin. "But I do like the sound of that, and after all, I am the Ward Boss. I'm headed down to Tammany Hall to get the update on the Draft bullshit later this morning, so I've only got a few minutes."

"Yeah, we need to figure out how we can make this go away. Some of the Irish are starting to blame us for this Republican shit. They say if we didn't get them their citizenship so quickly, they would have never even been in the Draft."

"Damn off the boat Irish. Don't they understand how much better we made things for them here in New York? They were all starving back in Ireland, and what about all of the jobs we arrange for them? Remember those signs–No Irish Need Apply? Now, they're all working—lots of them on the docks. We've done right by them, and all they have to do is vote early and often for whoever we want–a real good arrangement."

"I know boss, but they're afraid of the freed Blacks coming up from the South to take their jobs."

"We'd never let that happen. Tammany controls the jobs and Blacks aren't citizens—they can't vote for us and we have no reason to ever help them. Those damn abolitionists! Those damn Lincoln Republicans! They're messing everything up for us. What else is going on?"

"Well, we've got the fights tonight down in Five Points. Looks like there'll be lots of betting and a huge crowd. Two big fights. I'll be at the warehouse early and make sure the police don't interfere. Of course, I'll also make sure we're properly compensated for our efforts."

"Of course is right! Let me get out of here. Keep things calm. All this Draft bullshit has everyone on edge."

"Sure thing, boss."

The Ward Boss, John Sanderson, headed out to Tammany Hall. Billy Conklin, always happy to be the "boss" of the moment, unlocked the door. The line had already formed outside.

"All right, one at a time…"

Person after person streamed into the small Ward Office. The problems ranged from the lack of a job, issues with local gangs, and the biggest of all— every third person—the damn Draft. Everyone wanted to know how they could be expected to pay $300 to be exempted. Some of them joked that the government finally established the value of an Irishman's life at $300—slaves sold for $1,000; the difference in the price point did not go unnoticed. A few people saw the whole matter in reverse and wanted to offer their services to substitute for someone else for an amount less than $300. Most of those folks were in questionable shape, however, and Billy Conklin suspected these offers were scams—the plan being to take the money and run or a last ditch attempt by a dying man to make a couple of bucks for his family.

Billy made notes about everything—the people seeking jobs, the scammers, and the walking dead. Understanding a man's wants, needs, and problems created future opportunities for the organization. The local Ward Office was filled with lists of different categories of people, and they did, in fact, refer to these lists on a regular basis.

Boss Tweed stood in front of the group of ward bosses, listened to their reports, and offered suggestions on how to resolve some of their more pressing issues. These positions had been established to represent the Boss in each of the wards into which the city was divided. Tweed always considered the job of a Ward Boss to be the most important in his organization. In order to control votes, he first needed to create citizens who would then become voters, and this was done at the ward level. Many of his local staffers greeted immigrants as they staggered off the boats in the harbor, hungry and sick with promises of food, lodging, and employment. The Irish, who had been a godsend for Tammany Hall, did as instructed when it came to voting, and expected a certain level of employment and favors in return. Boss Tweed considered their expectations reasonable and he even over-delivered from time to time. This Draft mess was the one major problem Tammany had not been able to resolve.

Tweed's conversations with the Governor, also a Democrat, were all about the Draft these days. Governor Seymour, a "Peace Democrat," was absolutely opposed to the Draft and considered the quotas given to New York City, in particular, to be unreasonable. He worked on a plan to loan drafted men money to pay their subscription fee, and they were still secretly optimistic that the Draft, which was scheduled to start the next day, could somehow be averted.

Boss Tweed finished hearing all of the individual reports and thought the time had come to address the big issue. "Men, we are still optimistic we can stop this Draft, I'm working with the Governor on ways around it. What you have to do is make sure the people in your ward aren't blaming us. Talk about how we are fighting for them and how we would never support the Blacks over them. The Peace Democrats got them excited after the Emancipation Proclamation when they predicted the Irish would lose their jobs to the freed Blacks, and the idea of being drafted to free the people who will take their jobs is making them crazy. This makes us crazy as well, and that's what you tell them. Make sure they understand we think like them, and we are here to protect them. Not the Blacks, not the damn abolitionists, not the Republicans—especially that bastard, Lincoln. I think we can still avoid this thing and if the Draft does take place, there is talk of some organized resistance to shut it down fast. Just stay the course men. Stay the course."

Boss Tweed gave the most inspired speech he could muster, but admitted to himself, as well as his senior aides, that he did not have much of a basis for thinking the Draft might be stopped. The much more likely scenario was that the Draft would take place, and his loyal Ward Bosses would need to manage the messaging and control the fallout. He appreciated the strength of his crew and how they'd handle this important job, but they were certain to be tested in the coming week.

John Sanderson, always inspired after listening to the Boss speak, felt as empowered as ever about dealing with the Draft. Managing this issue well in the Sixth Ward would be a great feather in John's cap, because his ward had the largest population of Blacks in the city living side by side with the Irish. Tensions would be high. The Irish thought the world was against them and this notion was the basis of a longstanding joke that the wording of the Declaration of Independence had been formally changed to, "Life, liberty, and the Pursuit of Irishmen." John remembered his quick-witted retort when he heard this "joke" for the first time from someone in a group outside the Ward Office. He said, "It's not funny, it's not right, and it's definitely not happening here in the Sixth Ward!" The group outside the office gave him a round of applause. It was nothing more than bullshit grandstanding, but sometimes that was the most important tool at his disposal as Ward Boss.

CHAPTER 28

The Colored Orphan's Asylum

PATRICK SAID HIS goodbyes to Mrs. Kilpatrick and offered apologies for not being able to unload the afternoon delivery cart. Typically, Patrick would be happy to circle back, but today he had an evening obligation of some importance. Patrick continued his Friday morning schedule and headed further toward the East Side.

Outwardly cheery as he walked the streets, Patrick appeared to be a simple-minded giant–exactly the image he tried to project. Today, however, he couldn't shake the conversation about the Draft, and his heart raced as his smile began to fade. Patrick decided to play one of his mind games in an attempt to relax. He dedicated a small portion of his faculties to navigate the pedestrian and carriage traffic, while the rest of his mind transported him two thousand miles west–he was on horseback, riding into the sunset. The rhythm of his horse's gallop, slow and steady–bedump, bedump, bedump–what a ride! Nothing but Patrick, his horse, and the wide-open spaces. His heartbeat slowed.

Patrick's western adventure ended when he hit his head on an outdoor lantern, which was mounted too low for a man of his height. The people in the immediate vicinity started to laugh and snicker at the clumsy big fool of a boy. Patrick flashed his simple smile and headed into the building—The Colored Orphan's Asylum at 44th St. & Fifth Avenue.

An outgoing ten year-old child by the name of Charles ran over right away and asked, "Patrick, Patrick, what are you going to read to us today?"

"Anything you want, big man. Anything you want."

Charles loved being called big man by Patrick. Even at the tender age of ten, Charles understood size meant strength and respect. He'd never seen anyone as large as Patrick. Standing next to him was simply amazing, and then when he picked you up...nothing in the world could beat that!

"Patrick, Patrick, can you pick me up like yesterday and twirl me in the air?" Charles asked, excited as ever.

Four other children overheard the talk of twirling in the air and ran over to join in the fun. Charles hesitated as he crinkled his brow and pointed to the small prep table at the back of the lobby. Patrick took note of the concern in his eyes and bent down so the big man could whisper in his ear. Patrick nodded.

"Okay, kids. Give me a few minutes and I'll give everybody a ride. First, I have to do something with my friend Charles. Wait here for us." The children started jumping up and down in anticipation of their ride with the giant volunteer, while Patrick and Charles walked to the back of the lobby. Charles pulled away the long white tablecloth from the top of the prep table, and pointed to the small child, curled up in a ball on the floor.

"This is Carla, she got here a few days ago. This is her first day downstairs and she doesn't want to talk or play yet. I'm watching out for her, Patrick, because I'm big like you and I remember what you said, big people have to make sure bad things don't happen to good people. I think she's real good, Patrick."

"That's right, Charles, you keep an eye on her. Let's try to get her to say hello to us."

"She won't talk to anybody yet and might be afraid of two big guys like us. Could be scary." Charles smiled as he stood tall and puffed out his chest.

"Yeah, you might be right. Might be scary. Maybe we'll just wave and give her a chance to get used to us. Patrick and Charles turned to little Carla and waved. No reaction. The big men decided that a wave and a dance would come next and as the 300 pound man did his best Irish jig with Charles by his side, all of the children joined in—it was a Patrick Party—as it had been most mornings for the last month at the orphanage. Carla didn't join in, but Patrick noticed a twinkle in her eye and knew her first words and first smile were just a little below the surface.

The day manager, Joshua Redden, came over, greeted Patrick, and tried to calm down the children. Joshua liked how Patrick connected so well with the youngsters at the facility. "Children, please let Patrick get settled before you start pestering him. He'll do the best he can to make all of you happy, but please give him a chance."

Patrick didn't take long at all to settle and bent down to sit on the floor. All five children climbed on top of him. He made sure he either had a good grip on them or they had a good grip of their own, stood up, and started to gallop like a horse. The children laughed as they held on for dear life. Even the manager couldn't help but smile as this giant of a boy, the most popular volunteer at the facility, did his thing. The horse came to a rest and unloaded all of its passengers. Patrick looked at Joshua Redden and asked, "Where is she?"

"She's in the Great Hall getting ready to give her class, so you've only got ten minutes before she starts. Hurry up." Patrick galloped away to the amusement of his fan club and made his way to the Hall. Once inside, his eyes were drawn, as always, to the large dangling chandelier in the center of the room. There was something so regal about chandeliers, but this one, in particular, seemed special and caused Patrick to get lost in another daydream. This dream, however, didn't take him out west, and his mind's eye focused on a faint image of a majestic room with three portraits and fancy, ornamental furnishings. He had no idea when he'd been in such a room, but its image was always there, just a little under the surface, much like Carla's smile.

The rhythm of the horse returned–bedump, bedump, bedump—almost like the tapping of a drum. The sound became oddly mismatched with his image of the fancy room, and then Patrick realized the tapping was actually on his shoulder. He turned and saw his girl, Molly Morrison, a striking Irish lass from Dublin. Molly's natural beauty and extraordinary height intimidated many men, but not Patrick. Accustomed to bending down to receive the occasional kiss, she enjoyed the fact that with Patrick, he needed to drop to one knee for them to make a connection.

"You know what it means when a man gets down on one knee, don't ya?"

"Why, of course, it means I'm going to make an honest woman of ya!"

"Well, you've already asked me four times this week, so go ahead you big, handsome eejit!"

"Molly, my pretty wee lass, will you be my cook and housekeeper for life?"

"Cook and housekeeper! You lousy lumper! Let me get a frying pan to knock some sense into that thick skull of yours. How dare you!"

Patrick picked up his blond haired, blue-eyed fiancée and swirled her around in the air as if she truly was a "pretty wee lass." A few of the children rushed into the dining hall thinking the horsey game was commencing once again. Patrick was a charmer and loved by all in the orphanage, but one person in the vicinity was not amused by the popular volunteer. That person was Patrick's mother, Grace, who had decided to follow him and was peeking through the corner window of the large room observing her boy.

Grace needed to sit. She hadn't walked this much in a long while and knew her doctor would not have approved of this excursion, but she was so concerned about her son. Her fear that Patrick got involved with something illegal didn't appear to be true. If Patrick's day consisted of walking the streets as a simple fool, stopping in bookstores, playing with children, and courting some young girl in an orphanage, he wasn't breaking the law, but did appear to be lost. Grace had so many questions. *What kind of way is this for a grown man to pass his day?* Patrick's father was a worker, Grace was also a worker, and Patrick Junior started out as a worker at the age of four on the Public Works project back in Galbally. *What happened to his work ethic? Where did I go wrong with my Patrick? Is this what he's doing with his time? Doesn't he know how in demand he'd be at the docks? And where is he getting his money?* None of it seemed to matter, however. *Patrick,* she concluded, *was squandering his life away.*

CHAPTER 29

The Wall of Limerick

INITIALLY, MOLLY MORRISON was hired as part of the kitchen staff at the Colored Orphan's Asylum. In time, however, her personality and special skills enabled her to be promoted to work with the children as an aid, and for one hour each week, as their music and dance instructor. A friend of Molly's, Timothy Flynn, was scheduled to be the guest musician for today's lesson. He couldn't imagine why he'd been asked to play Irish music for a bunch of Black orphans.

"Children, this is my friend Timothy. He is going to play some music for us today while we all learn a special dance. Do any of you know what instrument Timothy is holding?"

"That's a violin, Ms. Molly! You had someone play a violin for us last month."

All of the children started chanting, "Violin! Violin! Violin!"

Molly knew from the enthusiastic response that she needed to get her students on the dance floor quickly. "Okay, children, excellent guess, quiet down now. You need to be able to hear my friend. A violin sounds like this…"

Timothy Flynn got up from his chair, buttoned his shirt, stood erect, and made a serious face as he began playing a baroque era piece composed by Antonio Vivaldi. He paused after the first five bars and sat back down in his chair.

"Today, however, this instrument is not a violin. Today, it's an Irish fiddle, which sounds like this…"

Timothy stood once more, but this time he unbuttoned the top few buttons of his shirt, pulled out his shirttails, offered a broad grin, and started stomping his feet as he began to play The Wall of Limerick. He again stopped after the first five bars and took his seat.

"What do we like better, children?"

"The Irish fiddle, Ms. Molly. The Irish fiddle!"

Molly broke into her heaviest Irish brogue as she offered, "All righty then, let's have ya on yer feet, and do as I do. All of the lasses line up here and all of the big strong gosoons across from them. Here we go."

The two lines were formed and the children began jumping up and down as the Irish fiddle came to life.

"First we'll learn to do Sevens. Do what I do while I call out the instructions." Molly stood at the head of the lines, jumped and moved to her side as she called out,

"Jump, 2, 3, 4, 5, 6, 7
Up, back, 2, 3, up, back, 2, 3
Jump, 2, 3, 4, 5, 6, 7
Up, back, 2, 3, up, back, 2,3"

The children caught on fast and Timothy Flynn smiled as he understood why Molly invited him to perform. Next, they practiced promenades, and moving diagonally between the lines. Finally, Molly explained about the arms. "We must all remember to keep our arms by our side like a well-behaved Irishman."

"Why does that make us well-behaved, Ms. Molly?"

"Well it helps us to fool the English. When they guarded us behind their walls, they didn't want us to dance, but they couldn't see our feet. Watch this." Molly went behind the massive serving counter in the Great Hall and continued to do a bit of an Irish jig, with the view of her lower body blocked by the large piece of furniture. "Can you tell I'm dancing?"

"No. You're sneaky. You're a well-behaved Irishman, Ms. Molly!"

"Thank you for the compliment. Let's all try." The whole group danced in place with their arms by their side. They were ready to perform the Wall of Limerick. Molly called out the instructions,

"Promenade forward for two
Promenade backward for two
Promenade forward for two
Promenade backward for two
Girls change places on a diagonal line
Set in place
Boys change places in a diagonal line
Set in place
Take right hands with partner-Do Sevens out
Set in place
Do Sevens back in together
Set in place"

Patrick tried to follow the steps on his own, and even though his Ma taught him about Sevens as a child, he had to admit he was not much of a dancer. When his feet came to a stop, his mind started to wander. Patrick remembered when he met Molly in front of a construction site not far from the orphanage.

"Hey, honey. How 'bout a little kiss for me?"

Molly jerked forward as the stranger pulled her toward him and fended off the unwelcome advance by slapping his hands. She jumped when another set of hands squeezed her buttocks from behind.

"If you don't want to kiss him, how 'bout me, sweetie?"

Her first suitor had his hands around her waist as he instructed his friend, "Okay, John, kiss her first, and then hold her for me."

It didn't take long. Within minutes, both men were tossed face first into the construction pit. Patrick helped Molly to regain her composure as the other construction workers tended to their rejected brethren.

"You're a big one, aren't ya?"

"That I am, and I'm happy to have been of service. My name is Patrick Allen, and what might be yours, my beautiful lady?"

That's when he experienced it for the first time. Molly looked up and offered him the most beautiful smile that was both new and oddly familiar. He could have stood and admired it forever. She responded, "Molly Morrison, and I'm pleased to meet you."

There was no response from Patrick who was still in the moment. Molly reached up and snapped her fingers in front of his face. "Are you okay, Patrick Allen? I thought I lost you there for a second." Patrick blinked and nodded. "I'll be late for work. My lunch break is almost over. Do you want to walk me?"

"Of course, my lady."

Patrick walked Molly back to work that day, and returned to the Colored Orphan's Asylum every day since. While he quickly began to enjoy the kids, he immediately fell in love with Molly.

"Okay children, that's enough for today. Let's thank Mr. Flynn. One, two, three..." They all screamed together, "Thank you Mr. Flynn." Timothy stood and said, "I've never had so much fun climbing the Wall of Limerick with such a fine group of well-behaved Irishmen."

Everyone laughed, which was Patrick's cue, "It's a Patrick Party! Bedump bedump, bedump. Horsey time." Five children piled on top of Patrick, and Molly was tempted to do so as well, but there was no rush...her ride with Patrick was just beginning.

CHAPTER 30

The Five Points

GRACE ALLEN HAD tremendous difficulty keeping up with her wandering son. The combination of a serious heart condition and the sweltering July heat had her at the point of exhaustion. The small piece of paper with her notes about each of Patrick's stops overflowed with information. As of 2 PM, he'd visited a bookstore, an orphanage, a library, and a museum, and eaten at least two more meals.

Mulberry Street, what the hell is this boy thinking! Surely, he didn't plan to go all the way to the end of Mulberry—*no, he couldn't be that stupid*—she thought. *He'll get himself robbed or worse.*

Five roads led to this part of the city: Mulberry Street, Anthony Street, Cross Street, Orange Street, and Little Water Street. Each of these five streets emptied into a plaza of sorts, hence the name Five Points. Gangs controlled many aspects of the Five Points, which had become the city center for prostitution, gambling, and crime, all taking place on a filthy, overcrowded stage. Grace had read a piece in the paper a few weeks earlier, which described the Five Points as the modern day "Gomorrah." *An excellent description*, she thought at the time.

Unfortunately, Patrick did walk to the end of Mulberry and headed into the Five Points. *Where the hell is he going?* Grace wondered how her innocent little boy would ever get out of this neighborhood alive. He did seem simple as he walked the streets of the city. When people gawked at him because of his size, Patrick offered an amiable blank stare in response. He just followed his father's advice…never let them know you have any brains. Appearing simple in the Five Points, however, could be a recipe for disaster.

144

With the end of Mulberry in sight, and the plaza within view, Grace noted a striking change. Patrick's lumbering, uncoordinated stroll gave way to a confident and determined stride. Grace caught a glimpse of his face and saw a manly stare, the likes of which Patrick Sr. would have been proud. Junior stepped into the plaza looking like he belonged in the Points. Grace, no longer so concerned for his welfare, shifted her worries to what business her son had in such a shady part of town.

People seemed to know him and stepped aside as he approached. One unfortunate soul, however, bumped Patrick, and found himself shoved into a brick wall. The man, who looked like he might have been drunk, quickly apologized, "I'm sorry, I didn't know it was you. I mean I didn't see you. Sorry. Won't happen again." Patrick scowled and continued his deliberate walk.

Grace nodded to herself. She hadn't raised a fool. Many pickpockets "bumped" people in the streets in order to ply their trade, but no one would be picking Patrick's pockets as long as he handled himself this way. The crowd gave Patrick even more room as he continued to make his way through the plaza, and he wasn't wandering anymore; he was headed to a very definite place. She realized her son actually had business in the Points. It had to be bad.

"Hey lady, over here. Over here. Lady, over here. Does an old broad like you need some of this?" asked an obviously drunken man who dropped his pants and waved his genitalia in her direction. "Maybe I do," she called back, as she pulled out the blade she kept in her bag for just such an occasion. "I'm in the mood to cut something. Come over here, sweetie." Grace Allen started walking toward the man, who quickly pulled up his pants and started running away yelling, "Crazy bitch! Crazy bitch!"

Despite her exhaustion, Grace had to act as if she could handle anything that came her way, but in dealing with the drunken idiot, she lost track of Patrick. Fortunately, he stood out in a crowd, and she spotted him just as he entered an abandoned warehouse off the plaza. Grace followed Patrick inside and down the stairs. She saw two men crouched behind some crates and tried to pick up her pace in order to warn Patrick. Unfortunately, her overheated and overtaxed body did not cooperate and Grace found herself face down on the stairs as she tripped over some debris and lost her footing.

The first attacker sprung out from under the staircase and swung a wooden chair with all of his might at Patrick's back. The second attacker stepped out from a doorway and swung a metal rod toward Patrick's chest. Instinctively, Patrick referred to Daddy's Rule #4: have total respect for a gun, substantial respect for a knife, some respect for a club, and little respect for anything else. Patrick allowed the chair to connect to his back, because he processed it as "anything else," and focused on blocking the metal rod, which to him was a type of "club" and worthy of more attention. Attacker #1 couldn't believe how little the crashing chair seemed to affect this monster, and Attacker #2 remained unconscious on the ground after being body slammed.

By the time Grace got down to the bottom level, Patrick was slowly advancing toward Attacker #1 with a menacing grimace. She thought, *he's just like his Da. Thank God!*

"Listen, Paddy. We're only doing a job. Nothing personal. Had to soften you up a bit. We weren't going to hurt you bad. We just needed to make it more of an even fight–change the odds a little bit."

"You're lucky I don't kill you. Get the fuck out of here. I'll give you a head start," Patrick exclaimed as he picked up the unconscious Attacker #2 and held him high above his head. He planned to toss him onto the staircase, but as he turned his body to throw the man with as much force as possible, he noticed his mother standing at the foot of the stairs. Patrick slammed the man straight back to the ground, which enabled Grace to read the poster on the wall behind her son.

Pretty Paddy vs. Thomas Johnson,
FRIDAY, JULY 10TH @ 7 PM
Five Points

So this is how he makes his money. Grace was less surprised at the fighting than she was at the name—his father had his share of fights—but she never used the nickname Pretty Paddy with her son. She considered it to be unflattering and mean, much like calling a grossly overweight man Slim. Grace shared stories of Patrick Senior with her son on a regular basis and took great pains to make sure Patrick Junior understood "Daddy's Rules," but rarely spoke of the nickname, Pretty Paddy—it was something to forget, not memorialize. It didn't serve Patrick to understand that, at times, his father was ridiculed. Grace knew the nickname always bothered his father and couldn't believe her son had resurrected it. She sighed and turned to her son. "So how long have you been fighting as Pretty Paddy?"

CHAPTER 31

The Ward Office

JOHN SANDERSON SAID his hellos as he passed the last few constituents waiting outside of the Ward Office. His assistant, Billy Conklin, seemed quite at ease at John's desk, which didn't go unnoticed. As much as Billy was willing to bandy about all of the "Boss" talk earlier that day, John thought he looked a little too comfortable in the big chair—time to set things straight.

"All right, Billy, so now you're the big boss? Is that right?"

Billy realized he shouldn't have allowed himself to get caught using the Boss' desk. "Sorry, I just needed something from your desk and sat for a moment. Won't happen again."

"You bet it won't, or I'll have you back on a boat to Ireland before you know what happened to ya. Go out and get me some coffee, like a good little boy."

Billy scrambled out of the office and John Sanderson walked back to the front door to address the last few people waiting outside.

"Sorry, folks, almost time for the fights. We've got to get ready. I'll be happy to help all of you Monday morning. Yes, you can meet with me personally; I had business at Tammany Hall today. I hope you're all going to the fight. The smart money is on Pretty Paddy—mountain of a man. Can't be beat." With that he closed the front door, and then opened the back entrance to the small office where a different kind of a line had formed. The five sluggers who worked for Sanderson from time to time hadn't yet received their assignments for the weekend. The Boss had a good eye for sluggers and a knack for picking thugs who weren't totally without intelligent thought. He called them all in together.

"Okay guys, we've got one big job this weekend and we're going to need you be available next week when the Draft starts. This weekend, you'll be my security. We heard the Bowery Boys put money down on Johnson and may try to get to Pretty Paddy before the fight. The boy doesn't live in the Five Points. Watch out for him when he arrives. I want one of you to stay with him at all times, and the rest of you will help me keep an eye on things at the event tonight. It starts at 7, so I'll need you in place by 6 pm."

"Sorry boss, too late. The kid got there early and two guys jumped him. No problem though—just a warm-up for him. After we saw what happened, we got rid of them."

"What did you do? We don't need a war. What did you do?"

"Nothing too bad, one was already out cold, so we just touched the other one up so they were a matching pair."

"Promise." The biggest one tried to look honest. "We dropped them right at the border with the Bowery. They learned not to come down to the Five Points and cause trouble." All of them offered their broadest grins. John Sanderson took a minute to consider what they'd done and came to the conclusion they did use their limited smarts to the best of their ability.

Billy Conklin arrived with his drink and wondered why the Boss wanted hot coffee on such a sweltering day. "Here you go Boss. Are we okay about the desk thing? You know I didn't mean anything by it."

"Sit down, and show me what you did while I was gone."

Billy meekly walked toward Sanderson's desk and said, "Again, sorry boss, but all of the stuff is on your desk." Sanderson offered a sarcastic smile as he let his aide gather up his materials from the desktop.

"Okay, we had about forty people come in—nothing out of the ordinary. Ten were looking for jobs and if we add them to the twelve from earlier in the week, we've got the twenty they wanted over at the iron works as laborers. Do you want me to make the arrangements?"

"Yes. Are these first timers or have we helped them before?"

"Mostly first timers—just off the boat."

"Okay, give them the official welcome packet, talk to them about citizenship, and make sure they know we own their votes. Okay?"

"Yes, sir."

"What about the rest of the people?"

"They all asked about the Draft–either wanting to get out of it, or wanting money to get into it."

"Boss Tweed gave me a list of five rich midtown men who are looking for substitutes for less than the $300 it would cost them to get out of the Draft with the government. We'll set the price so that there's a little something for us. How many of those who want to join up are legitimate?"

"I've got four on the list, but one looked so sick I didn't even want him in the office. I'm guessing at least two are for real."

"Okay, let me meet them Monday morning. I have to make sure they aren't scammers and they'll need to actually report for service."

"That's why I said two. One is definitely a scammer—Thomas McPartlin—I think he's done this in another city and run off. He's playing games."

"Send one of the sluggers to visit him this weekend. We can't let out-of-town Mr. McPartlin think he can play games with Tammany Hall. Anything else?"

"Yes, we've got a longer list of men who want to get out of the Draft."

"No shit. Put together a profile of the ones we should help with the money along with your ideas about how they will pay us back. Be creative, but nothing's free. Understand?"

"Yes, sir, Mr. Sanderson. I've learned from the best."

"Finish up here, Billy, and then head over to the fights by 5:30 pm. I'll arrive right before fight time. Looking forward to seeing Pretty Paddy do his thing."

"Will do, Boss. Will do."

CHAPTER 32

Edward and Jason

THIRTY YEARS AT the Tribune—his life's work, and he never wanted to do anything else--until recently. At the age of 60, however, Edward Simmons didn't have many career options. The lifelong newspaperman began his career as a typesetter and worked his way up to senior editor. Those outside the paper considered Edward's position to be prestigious, but those on the inside understood he was nothing more than the hired help. The true power at the paper rested with the publisher, Horace Greely, who was well known and involved in the intimate affairs of the local, state, and national governments. He was the one who mattered.

Greely knew Edward well, but did not consider him an equal either intellectually or socially. People like Edward Simmons could manage the day-to-day affairs of the paper, but the big groundbreaking public activities were better handled by the man himself. The publisher's image often adorned the pages of his paper and many city residents came to recognize his drooping posture, white hair, and spectacles. Not a real looker, but the cameras loved him indeed.

Edward Simmons kept to the Republican party line at work, because to do anything else at the Tribune would be career suicide. This was why he enjoyed expressing other viewpoints at the Friday breakfast club meetings. Edward didn't agree with all of the political opinions of his boss, but did his best to represent them when he was dealing with the public.

Edward had to admit, however, that his Democratic friends in the breakfast club were having an impact on him, and he wondered on more than one occasion if a shift in party affiliation might be in his future. The idea that a man of his age and long held political beliefs could grow to embrace some of the positions he'd opposed for years fascinated Edward. The key was to actually listen to the merits of opposing arguments, which sometimes made a good deal of sense. As with many things in life, the answer never seemed to be at the extremes, and often hovered somewhere near the middle. He was careful, however, to never express any Democratic views at the Tribune in the interest of working a thirty-first year.

"Edward, please join me in my office." Edward Simmons didn't like the tone, but stood to follow his boss.

"Edward, I don't check everything we print in the Tribune. I trust my senior editors to be my eyes and ears so I can focus on other things of great importance outside of the paper. I can't do everything myself and I need to be able to place my trust in individuals like you."

"Why of course, Mr. Greely. You can count on me. I've been at the paper for thirty years and one of your senior editors for the past fifteen."

"Yes, this is true. So do you care to explain the story you wrote about this Irish giant? Is this news?"

"This story may not be news, but it profiles a different kind of young man. Someone who we assume is all about his brawn, when, in fact, he is quite intelligent. In my interviews with him, I gained real insight into the thinking of the Irish immigrant. Stories like this will go a long way in helping the city better understand the tremendous number of Irish immigrants who've arrived after the Great Famine."

"So, you are doing interviews—no longer just an editor? You go out and interview young Irish men so we can all have a better understanding. How nice for you! Perhaps I need someone who has more time to devote to being a senior editor for the New York Tribune. Is this some type of career capping exercise? Did your days as a columnist leave you unfulfilled? What is it Edward? I don't have all day to try and figure you out."

"Mr. Greely, with all due respect. You can still count on me. I write pieces from time to time. This is not so unusual."

"Perhaps not, but I always thought you understood the political position of the paper and for you to attempt to publish something like this over this weekend, it is nothing short of irresponsible."

"Irresponsible, how dare you. I've served this paper for…"

The publisher jumped up from his chair and interrupted his editor, "Yes, yes…over thirty years. Edward, your long tenure might be about to come to an end. How could you write a piece, which describes the Irish fear of freed slaves coming up to the Northern cities to take Irish jobs. I told you to report facts, but this is opinion, and you don't have the right as editor to take this newspaper in this Democratic direction. We must support President Lincoln and stay true to our Republican principles and not rile up the masses the weekend before the Draft."

Horace Greely tried to calm down and returned to his seat. "After all these years, you are forcing me into a position where some might think I'm censuring my own paper. People who work for me at your level must share my views and positions. We must stay together. I'm worried we've drifted apart."

"Mr. Greely. My piece doesn't say whether the Tribune agrees with the viewpoints expressed by those interviewed, it simply presents a contrary point of view, which I think is helpful in a period such as this."

"I have no squabbles with free speech. It would be a terrible thing if I did, but I'll be damned if I am going to carry the flag for views inconsistent with the agenda of this paper and this country. There is a place for your article, Edward, but it is not the Tribune. I think it will be best for you to begin your summer vacation right away. If I see your piece appear in any other local newspaper, I will take that as a symbol of your desire to resign. If on the other hand, your article does not appear, I will welcome you back in two weeks from your holiday. We are done, Mr. Simmons. Enjoy your vacation."

Edward Simmons got up, walked back to his office, and placed the picture of his deceased wife and adult child in his bag. Edward wondered if this would be the last time he would be inside the Tribune office and how the world might accept an old washed-up newspaperman. He walked out of the office—hat in his left hand and bag in the right, much the same way he left every day. It was hard to believe he was carrying the baggage of thirty years. Edward headed home to Brooklyn.

--==◉ ◉==--

Typically, Friday was a quiet day at Columbia College. Classes didn't meet and most of the local students headed home for the weekend. Today, however, the college was teeming with life. The very popular professor, Jason Timbers, was holding a special "current events" symposium and the topic was the Draft. Given the ages of the male student body, a discussion of the Draft was of tremendous interest.

Professor Timbers surveyed the crowd of over 100 college students and realized the rules of wealth and political orientation had already taken hold here. With none of the lower class groups like the Irish, Germans, or Blacks present, the young men congregated in two distinct camps based on their political affiliation. The first group---the offspring of "Old New York Money." The fathers of these young men were staunch Republicans in favor of the Draft, the war, and the President, in particular. They also espoused a strong anti-slavery position.

The other group consisted of the children of the Democrats. Most of these young men were also wealthy, but as recent arrivals in New York, their families were not accepted in the same circles as the Old New Yorkers. They had found their success in business, and despite their short time in the city, the wealth of these families approached or eclipsed that of the more established Republican elite. This wealthy Democratic group held an anti-Draft/anti-Republican position, and were fairly neutral on the matter of slavery.

Professor Timbers called the anxious students to order. "Today we will be less formal and this will be more of an open forum with the next generation of New York leaders and a professor, who I understand you consider to be years past his prime." The students offered a muffled giggle in response to this remark, which did ring true. Jason Timbers' tenure at the college was so long, the joke among the students was that when he spoke of "the war," he likely referred to the Revolutionary War. Professor Timbers had graduated from Columbia College in 1819, and had been associated with the college ever since. He lived downtown, much closer to the old location of the school.

The college had moved to 49th Street and Madison Avenue in 1857, so the well-liked professor had a commute. He enjoyed his trip, however, and never went directly from Point A to Point B. This morning's stop at the Friday Breakfast Club was one of his favorites. On the way home in the early evening, he often found himself getting parched, which required him to stop at any number fine bars and restaurants to quench his thirst. The professor had become a lady's man after the passing of his wife Genevieve in 1845, and normally had at least three women in regular rotation on his social calendar.

"All right, settle down," Professor Timbers called out as he tapped an over-sized book on his desk to gain the group's attention. "We are here today to talk about the Conscription Act. First, who would like to tell us the structure of the Act?"

A tall young man, who was not known to the professor stood up to speak. "Professor Timbers, my name is Timothy Stewart and I am the son of an acquaintance of yours, Johnston Stewart. I am actually a recent graduate of Harvard..." The room was immediately filled with boos and hisses. The professor had to once again tap his book on his desk to regain control. "Mr. Stewart. Yes, I do know your father, and I would venture to guess many of the fathers of the students in this room either know of him or have actually worked with him. He is a master merchant here in the city, and despite your somewhat questionable educational credentials, we welcome you. Please proceed."

The professor's comment about "somewhat questionable educational credentials" sat well with the proud Columbia College student body and settled them down. Young Mr. Stewart continued, "The act requires all able bodied men between the ages of 20 and 45 to register for the Draft. Names will be picked at random from a wheel to identify those who will be drafted. There are some notable exemptions, however."

"Mr. Stewart, thank you. I imagine all of the young men in this room stand a strong chance of being drafted. How likely is it that they will serve? Will these exemptions perhaps apply to this group? Let's have someone else respond."

The group started to smirk, giggle and whisper. No one stood to speak, and the professor actually overheard one of the whispers, which offered a suggestion that the war should be fought by the expendables. The professor knew within a few years, everyone in this room would have positions in industry, which would rank them among the elite in the city. Right now, they were pissy little privileged children, who would take a little shit from their professor and perhaps learn a life lesson. The smile left the professor's face, as he addressed the student who whispered the expendables remark, "Mr. Webber, I just overheard that you have a brilliant plan. It appears that none of you should serve and the war should be fought by the expendables. A curious comment, please explain."

A few of the students laughed as they heard the term, expendables, and the professor took note of their names. The rest of the group anticipated the professor's response.

"Professor, I didn't mean for you to hear that. Many apologies."

"Mr. Webber, never apologize for saying what you think or developing a plan to spare all of your classmates from risking their lives in this terrible war. Please tell us about your expendables. Who are they and why do you refer to them in such a manner?"

Webber stood. "Professor, I meant to say the Irish and maybe the Blacks. The Conscription Act excludes the Blacks because they're not citizens, but I think they should all fight, because, after all, the fight is about their freedom."

"Why are these groups expendable?" The professor changed his tone as he asked this last question in order to imply he was intrigued and anxious to understand. This put the previously nervous student at ease and he returned to his naturally cocky attitude.

"Thousands of Irish arrive in the harbor every day and they do not perform any work of substance. The same will be true of the Blacks except they won't be arriving from overseas, they'll be coming up from the South. We'll probably have too many Irishmen and Blacks fighting for the same low-level jobs. Thinning the herd is probably the right thing to do."

The professor, now enraged, spent the next 20 minutes preaching to the group about how the Irish built the railroads, dug the Erie Canal, and provided service to this country, which was of true substance. He explained, at one point, that he was Irish and that his mother and father would not agree with how expendable he was. The professor also suggested that Mr. Webber might not view him as being so expendable when he failed him in his senior year and found himself returning for another year in this expendable's classroom. Then the professor announced proudly to the class he was also partially black and born into slavery. As a proud black man, he railed against Mr. Webber's suggestion that his "herd needed to be thinned."

The professor knew this rant was one of his better performances–almost at the level of his famous "I am Chinese" performance of a few years prior, which resulted from a similarly elitist remark. He looked at the faces of the future leaders of New York, and thought he might have gotten through to a few of them. Perhaps today's lesson would make them a little more enlightened as they assumed positions of power in the city in the years to come. The professor understood that despite his long tenure and fine academic reputation, it was these rants that prevented him from ever becoming a senior administrator at Columbia, but that never bothered him. If he got through to even a few of his brats with his sensational remarks, that would be a good day's work as far as he was concerned.

CHAPTER 33

The Stewarts

ANXIOUS TO TELL his father about the lively group discussion at his alma mater, Timothy Stewart made the short walk from Columbia College to his posh Fifth Avenue home in record time. The elder Stewart, a graduate of Columbia College, had attended the old downtown location. Timothy remembered how excited his father became when the college moved to 47th Street because it would be so convenient for his son to follow in his footsteps, but every time his father told him how close he would be, the more Timothy wanted to go away. Like many young men on the verge of adulthood, Timothy yearned for some independence. Johnston Stewart was devastated when his son decided to go to Harvard, but didn't protest because, as much as he wanted his son to be a Columbia man, he understood the need for a little distance. He felt much the same way when he disappointed his own father, a Dartmouth graduate, and went to study in New York City.

Timothy rushed into the house to find his father and almost knocked over the butler, who was carrying the afternoon tea into the parlor. Johnston Stewart, seated at his desk, was poring over ledgers and financial statements, wondering how he would get out of this mess.

"Father, Professor Timbers put on quite a show. He is a remarkable man."

"I expected no less."

Timothy spent the next several minutes giving his father a detailed account of the discussion. Johnston listened to his son and smiled as he realized Timothy had become a thoughtful and analytical adult—one who would be able to understand the different sides of an issue and handle whatever advantages he had in life with class and tact. The professor had made an impression on Timothy with regard to the Draft question. It was time for Timothy to understand the challenges of the current business environment. After they both settled into their comfortable chairs for their afternoon tea, Johnston began to speak.

"Timothy, you received a first class education at Harvard and learned much in terms of theory, but you need to appreciate the realities of our business. Take a seat, listen, and learn. I'm not as dynamic as Professor Timbers. I won't claim to be either Irish, Black or Chinese, but I will claim to be concerned about how we will settle back after the war."

"What do you mean, Father—how we will settle back after the war?"

"Our entire business involved cotton before the war. We had a vast network of southern plantation owners who used my services to export their cotton to Europe. I gave them loans for working capital, and their assets secured those loans. Our books include $1 million in receivables from my former business associates and each of them politely wrote to me soon after the start of the war, indicating they had no plans to repay their debt."

Timothy swallowed hard. "I didn't know about this, Father. One million dollars is a fortune! How have we survived?"

Johnston sighed. "I started running up some serious debt of my own in the early days of the war. I wanted to maintain our standard of living and send my talented son," he smiled affectionately, "to Harvard, but the revenue came to a halt."

"No revenue! I didn't know, and you wasted money on me. You should have told me. I would have stayed and helped you."

"Thank you, Timothy, that's very noble, but foolish. An investment in the future is never wasted. You needed to get your education to be truly effective. You're my only heir--I need you to be as prepared as possible when you assume more control of the business. "And," he paused and smiled, "You also needed to grow up. In hindsight, getting away from your somewhat controlling father proved to be a good idea. I am so pleased to see the man you've become."

Timothy barely heard the praise. "Thank you, Father, but what did you do to manage?"

"Well, at first I was tempted to side with our controversial former mayor."

"Fernando Wood?"

"The one and only. He advocated for New York City to secede from the Union and become a free city. I found his argument to be partially logical, but morally indefensible." Johnston paused to take a sip of tea.

"What do you mean?"

"Well, the logical part involved finances. The duties we collect at the ports with all of the goods coming into New York could more than sustain New York as a free city with little additional taxation of any kind. In this scenario, which involved the United States being split into two countries, the finances would work. Unfortunately, there was an equally logical opposing argument—the Union would never allow this to happen. The North would not be willing to forgo the income contributed to government coffers by New York City, and they would never permit us to secede. The movement to break away from the Union was also a minority view, and most people here had a great allegiance to the ideals of freedom and liberty espoused by our founders during the revolution. In my opinion, secession was never going to happen. Even when Fernando's brother, Benjamin, the publisher of the Daily News, threw the support of his paper behind his brother's idea, I realized it wasn't feasible. So as much as seceding appealed to me financially, my practical side told me to let it go."

"I do remember reading about secession, but at the time, I didn't understand the issue so well. Now it makes more sense. What about the immoral part?"

"Our esteemed Mayor publicly stated racist opinions and acted as if he spoke for all of us when he said New York City would never support a war that sought to free an inferior race—the Blacks. Our founders delayed dealing with the slavery issue, but I am absolutely certain they never intended to abandon it. The country simply wasn't ready to deal with slavery at that time, so as much as we spoke of 'Life and liberty,' we should have added the clause, except for the Blacks. The rest of the world has been moving away from slavery for years. The British Empire abolished slavery back in the thirties, and even the French did it over ten years ago. It's true that I became wealthy trading on slavery during the last 20 years, but it never felt right, even though the profits did. We are one of the last major countries to still embrace slavery. How can we justify that if we were founded on a life and liberty platform?"

"So you are in favor of the war and the abolition of slavery."

"Never think I'm in favor of this war! The carnage is beyond anything the world has ever seen. We are killing off an entire generation. I hoped we would abolish slavery, and in some way transition from free slave labor to a system of wages and more equity for Blacks. In my perhaps naive way of thinking, the additional costs of wages would be included in the cost of production and the only down side would be an increase in prices. I believe Europe would be willing to pay a few more pennies for the shirts, pants, and other materials made from our cotton."

"Actually, your naive way of thinking does make sense."

"The problem, however, is that slavery is a way of life--a terrible way of life. It is embedded everywhere. And you cannot underestimate the other financial piece of it."

"What other financial piece is there other than wages?"

"Take a look. Let's see what your Harvard education has taught you." Timothy sat behind the desk. "Take some time to review the books, especially the receivables—the loans outstanding to our former southern business associates. Tell me what you see." Timothy settled in, anxious to prove to his father that he could find the answer. The review didn't take long. Timothy realized he didn't need a Harvard education to understand his father's point. After a few moments he looked up and said with confidence, "It is all about property. In accounting terms, we would say assets. Am I right?"

"Yes. And a plantation's most valuable asset?"

"Slaves."

"Right. Slaves are actually the collateral for all of our loans--and everyone else's loans--to the plantation owners. Without compensation for the loss of their slaves, they would never even consider the end of this horrible practice. Much like a factory owner being asked to give away all of his facilities and equipment—this won't happen without compensation. While the southern plantation owners espouse the same racist views as our former mayor, ultimately it is all about finances, as you will learn, most things are."

CHAPTER 34

God Bless You, Pretty Paddy

THE SLUGGERS SENT by the Ward Office provided Patrick and his mother with some much needed security. Three of them stood guard and joked about how big, strong Pretty Paddy needs his Ma to hold his hand on fight night. After spending some time with Paddy's Ma, however, it started to make sense. She even seemed tough enough to do a little fighting herself. The makeshift dressing room in the back of the warehouse provided mother and son with the privacy they needed to discuss the events of the day. Patrick also tried to explain what he'd been doing for the past year and how he'd made his money. According to Patrick, he didn't have much boxing talent or speed; his only real fighting skill was his ability to absorb punches, and once he connected a couple of times, his smaller opponents went down for the count.

People liked his fights because they enjoyed the early rounds when the opposing fighter ran circles around him while he missed his mark. Patrick always gave the crowd this portion of the fight. Once he fought a skilled fighter who was 100 pounds lighter and much faster. He literally could not catch the man and looked the fool for the first ten rounds. His opponent tired in the eleventh round and the first time Patrick connected with an upper cut to his jaw, the fight ended in a knockout. This fight established Patrick as one of the best because the man he defeated had been the reigning champion in the back alleys of Five Points.

The reality was that Patrick did have excellent boxing skills and above average speed for a man his size. Given all of the time and effort that went into these fights, however, he knew his career would be short-lived if he ever appeared invincible. This is why he let the smaller men dance around for a few rounds before he knocked them out. While the money earned fighting could be substantial, the big money came from gambling.

Grace stopped her son before he finished his explanation, "Patrick, your father viewed this nickname as an insult because he was disfigured by scars. People only saw the scars on his face, neck, and arms, but I can tell you, they were all over his body. He didn't have those scars as a young man— they came from *his* prizefighting--he was also a fighter. He got in with the wrong lot and was supposed to throw a fight, didn't, and they strung him up for hours as they beat him, cut him, and taunted him with that damned nickname, Pretty Paddy. Is that what you want, Patrick? Don't you see that you're at risk here? Earlier today, those men wanted to do you harm. Do you understand what I'm telling you, boy? Do you understand what and who you're getting involved with?"

→═ ◐═←

The professor enjoyed these outings. As he left his apartment in the Fourth Ward, he walked past places he would often frequent when in his proper suit and interacting with the world as the professor. If he planned to continue walking toward the Sixth Ward for a certain kind of an evening, he would change into a more pedestrian outfit and adopt a whole different identity. On these evenings, he would never be honest about his profession. Actually, he never told anyone what he did, but let people assume something questionable in nature–this added to his mystique. On those nights, he was just "Tim." Not the most creative alias…you would think a Columbia College professor might do better, but it was just the first three letters of his last name, and Jason wanted something he would be able to recall even if he was a few cocktails into the evening.

As he walked down Mulberry Street and passed all of the bars and restaurants, he remembered the lovely women whose acquaintances he'd made over the years in each establishment. He liked Mulberry Street for these "Tim" nights, but didn't often wander all of the way to the end, because even Tim had his limits. Tonight, however, was different.

→═ ◐═←

One of the sluggers poked his head into the dressing room. "One hour until fight time. We've got your meal. We figured we'd get something for your Ma as well." Two trays arrived with steak and potatoes. "Better eat fast and start getting ready."

"Thanks, guys. I do get hungry from time to time." Everyone laughed because if you knew Patrick at all, you knew he could eat. Mother and son settled in for their meal. Grace had calmed down, and Patrick thought it was time to fill her in on the rest of his plans.

"City life isn't for me. I need space and don't want to be stuck in a tiny apartment. Out west is my kind of place–I'll be able to stretch out my arms and have the room I need."

"Out west? What will you do out west? We're New York people, Patrick. There's no dock work out west."

"I'm not sure yet, Ma, but I'm studying with a professor from Columbia, and I've got a girlfriend who I want you to meet because she's the one. I'm sorry I didn't tell you before, but I wanted to be sure. Come with us, come out west... I'll take care of you."

Grace was shaking her head. "I don't know as I can leave. And why do you mock your Da with that name? It has nothing but bad memories and bad luck."

"I knew about Pretty Paddy because I remember people calling Da that when we were in the works project back in Galbally breaking stones. While you say the name was given to mock him because of how he was disfigured, I heard the people Da helped say, 'God Bless you, Pretty Paddy!' and I can tell you they uttered his name with the utmost respect. I use it to honor my Da, not mock him."

"You'll not honor him if you're a dead man. Everything bad in the city happens here in the Five Points. This is the most dangerous part of New York and you're in with all kinds of criminals here. Never think they're here to protect you. Everyone is looking out for themselves. Never forget that. You'll need someone to look out for you."

An unexpected voice added, "Exactly my thought."

Patrick was shocked by the presence of the professor. "How did you find me? How did you know I was a fighter?"

"Patrick, I've enjoyed tutoring you—you are one of the most remarkable students I've ever had, and you're not even enrolled at the college. One night I came down here for a fight." He smiled at Patrick's reaction. "Yes, we all have our secrets, don't we?...and you were on the bill, so I started following your fighting exploits. You're close to reaching the big time, and I thought you might need some help. So here I am, but you already have some able assistance. Who might this lovely lady be?"

"Quite the charmer, professor, I am Patrick's mother, Grace."

"Ah, yes. A fine Irish lass from Galbally, I believe!"

"Careful who you call a lass, professor, she's the one who taught me how to fight."

"Point taken, my boy. What's the plan for tonight?"

CHAPTER 35

The FiveP Dance Hall

MOSELEY JOHNSON, THE founder and proud owner of the FiveP Dance Hall, told everyone who would listen, "You got to have a plan." The first part of Moseley's plan, owning his own business, had been achieved, and he focused on the second part, making sure his two sons became more successful than he was. *That's how it should be. A father does a good job for his sons, they grow to be prosperous men with children of their own, and then those children grow to be better off than their parents, and so on. After a few generations,* Moseley thought, *the Black man would take his rightful place in society.*

Moseley, born to a free Black man in upstate New York, relocated to the Five Points in the 1820's to get a taste of city life. He chose New York City and the Five Points section, in particular, because the area had a reputation as being a place where free Blacks coexisted with whites. The explanation seemed odd at first, but after some time began to make sense to Moseley. Just like Black on Black discrimination based on skin tone, the Irish, who lived side by side with Blacks in the Points, didn't appear to be white enough in many circles. Moseley couldn't see it himself, *had to be something about white eyes,* he thought, because in the white world, the Irish were the Blacks.

FiveP and a few other dance halls brought the two cultures together to create a new style of dance. The Irish Jig, when influenced by the Black Shuffle, created tap, and FiveP had some of the best tap competitions in town. Moseley always said, "You got to have a plan," and dancing was the plan for Moseley's oldest son, Jimmy, who was regarded as one of the best tap dancers in the city.

Moseley worried the simple name he gave his first son, Jimmy, might somehow limit his possibilities and potential, so when Moseley's second son came along, he named him Belvedere. *A fancy name for a fancy boy,* he thought, but he got it wrong—Jimmy was the fancy one. He wore his upscale clothes to go uptown for his performances, and spoke better English than any other Black in the Five Points. As a homosexual man, Jimmy's way of life was more readily accepted in the Points than anywhere else in the city. Moseley loved Jimmy, but realized he should have been named Belvedere. The actual Belvedere was anything but fancy and over the years, the nickname of Belvy seemed to fit him just right.

"Belvy, come over here. Tonight the night!"

"I know, Dad. Getting ready long time for this."

"Belvy, you ain't done nothing for long time—you only eighteen boy, everything new to you."

"Yeah, Dad, everything new. Except my plan. Everyone got to have a plan, Dad. Belvy got a plan. Dad. You told me, Belvy got a plan. No worries, Dad. I got a plan."

Belvy Johnson squeezed his enormous frame through the doorway, which had been constructed in the late 1700s. Even Moseley had to duck as he entered the room. Belvy stooped and turned sideways to fit through the opening. At 6'5" and well over 300 pounds, he didn't fit well most places, and certainly not in this odd apartment built on top of the dance hall. A single staircase in the back of the hall led upstairs to a maze of dressing rooms. Moseley and Belvy needed to pass through four of these rooms to get to the small doorway, which led to their living quarters.

Belvy was slow—that's how his father characterized him. He didn't think fast, he didn't move fast, he didn't learn fast—a giant with the mind of a child. Known as a plodder in the ring, smaller men danced around him and hit him at will, but Big Belvy—as he was known—hardly felt a thing. Eventually, Belvy would hit his man, and down he would go. No one had ever beaten Big Belvy, and with one more win, he would earn the payday, which would secure his future.

Jimmy had moved out five years ago and lived in his own apartment a few blocks away. His current and occasional boyfriend, a wealthy, married white man, paid the rent and came to visit from time to time. Moseley didn't understand that aspect of Jimmy's life, but loved him, and hoped he had a plan for that as well.

With one more impressive victory, Big Belvy would be set. There was only one man who might be able to beat him, and that was Pretty Paddy—just as enormous—and some said as mean a son of a bitch they'd ever met. Everyone's got to have a plan, and Belvy had his—the problem, however, was his plan had to go through Pretty Paddy, and not much ever went through that animal.

CHAPTER 36

Molly's Surprise

MOLLY HAD SO much to do. Patrick had promised to take her out for a picnic in the morning, and she wanted to look her best—a bath and a new hairdo were on her agenda. Ten more minutes and her shift would be over. She walked around the Great Hall of the Colored Orphan's Asylum, straightened the chairs, and tidied up as the evening shift settled in and prepared for the long line of children who would soon file in for their supper.

"Molly, I need to meet with you before you go. Please stop by my office on your way out," the day manager, Joshua Redden, called out from the doorway to the large room.

"Yes, Mr. Redden. I'll be there in a few minutes."

Charles, often the first in line for dinner, always had little Carla by his side. When she first arrived, Carla had been bullied by the other children. Under the protection of Charles, no one would dare mess with her. Charles was a big man like Patrick, and big men took care of good people. One day, Charles would leave the orphanage and go live with Patrick. Two big men—they'd straighten things out. They'd take care of good people. For now, Charles had to do his best from inside the orphanage.

The path to entry into the Colored Orphan's Asylum was almost always littered with grief and heartache. Carla's mother died at childbirth and her father was killed on the docks by an Irish mob when he tried to report to work. Carla couldn't understand why these men killed her father—he was going to work, just like them. No one ever explained what happened to her satisfaction and they all wanted her to act like everything was okay. How could she smile or laugh? Daddy was gone. They killed Daddy.

Carla had no one, except for Charles. He understood she didn't want to talk, laugh, or run. She didn't even want to play—she only wanted to be left alone. The taunting from the other children didn't bother her so much, but she had to admit, things were easier because of Charles. Carla mustered the courage to raise her head ever so slightly to glance at Charles, who offered her the warmest smile in exchange. Carla wanted to sneak her first look, but Charles noticed her glance and offered a wide return smile—she was almost ready to smile back.

Charles stepped aside, and Carla filled her tray with food. They both sat together and started to eat—no talking—just chewing—all business. Carla decided to look up again, and Charles, who had just put a big spoon of oatmeal in his mouth, quickly offered his big return smile, which caused some of the oatmeal to slip out the side of his mouth. For some reason, Carla found this to be hysterically funny and worthy of both her first smile and laugh. Charles took a chance.

"Hi. I'm Charles."

"I'm Carla."

It was the most interaction she'd had in a long time. Charles appreciated the moment and didn't try to push it. Molly took note of the exchange, offered Charles a smile of approval, and placed an apple on his tray as she walked by on her way out of the Hall. One more stop—she needed to meet with her boss, Mr. Redden.

"Molly, please have a seat. This is Mrs. Camille Vanderway, she is a patron of the orphanage."

"Pleased to meet you Mrs. Vanderway. " Molly turned to her boss and asked, "Am I in some kind of trouble?"

"We're not sure. Let's give Mrs. Vanderway a chance to explain."

"We are doing our best at the Colored Orphan's Asylum to provide a wholesome environment for these unfortunate children who have nowhere else to turn. Do you understand how important this is, my dear?"

"Yes, of course, Mrs. Vanderway, and I think that I am a good person. Quite wholesome."

"That may or may not be the case. Tell me about your boyfriend."

"My boyfriend? I don't understand. Why are you asking about my boyfriend?"

"Molly, please answer Mrs. Vanderway's question. I've already explained he has become a volunteer at the orphanage and the children love playing with him."

"Well, Patrick Allen is not just my boyfriend, he is my fiancé."

Shocked at what she just heard from this Irish peasant, Camille Vanderway interrupted, "Please do not use words you do not understand. What do you think fiancé means?"

"Mrs. Vanderway, I may not be school smart, but I know what the word means. We plan to marry in the near future. He works on the docks and lives with his mother over on Tenth Avenue."

"Mr. Redden. Please show her."

Joshua Redden, reached down to the floor behind his desk and picked up the poster which advertised the double bill of prizefights for that night, which read:

BIG BELVY VS. HELMUT BEHRMAN &
PRETTY PADDY VS. TIMOTHY JOHNSON
FIVE POINTS – JULY 10TH @ 7 PM
WINNERS MEET JULY 17TH @ 7 PM!

"Why are you showing me this? I don't read. What does it say?"

Mrs. Vanderway responded, "Of course, dear. I should have understood someone like you couldn't read. It is an advertisement for a barbaric fight this evening in that horrible part of the city called the Five Points. Your fiancé, as you refer to him, is fighting tonight at 7 PM. Are you telling me you didn't know about this?"

"What do you mean, he is fighting? What are you talking about? He works on the docks. My Patrick works on the docks. Where does it say his name?"

Joshua Redden jumped in, "The poster doesn't list his actual name, only the name he fights under, Pretty Paddy."

Molly knew it could be true. Patrick told her stories of his beloved father and how his nickname was Pretty Paddy. *How could he lie to me? What does all of this mean?*

"I see from your expression you understand. We cannot let this type of person have anything to do with the orphanage. Your boyfriend is an animal. He will never be permitted to step foot in this building again, and word to the wise, animals like that don't marry gullible Irish girls like you. He is talking marriage to get into your knickers, my dear. I suggest you leave him, but no matter what you do, he can never come around here again. And if you stay with him we cannot guarantee your position here. Do you understand?"

Molly didn't know what to make of all of this, and felt like slapping this anti-Irish, rich bitch squarely in the face, but when she glanced at Joshua Redden, his demeanor and body language were clear—this woman had the power to make the rules, and her boyfriend was no longer welcome at the orphanage. She said her goodbyes to the bitch and her boss, who seemed to forget much too quickly all of the good work Patrick had done around the orphanage.

She had so many questions in her mind as she left the office. Some were things she should have asked long ago. *Why didn't I ever meet Patrick's mother? Why didn't he ever talk about his job? Why was he free so much during the day?* Others were new questions. *Does Patrick actually fight under his father's old nickname? Why did he lie about what he did? Why would anyone think he was an animal?* It had become clear that it was time for answers. Molly's plans for the evening had changed. The bath and the hair would have to wait. She had a fight to go to.

CHAPTER 37

Fight Night

"Is THIS IS a Tammany event? What makes you think you're in charge?"

Billy Conklin noted the pattern, back in the office with his boss and out in the warehouse with gang leader John O'Seary. People thought he was angling to take over, and they were right. Billy had no doubt he would do a better job than any of his "bosses." Time to smooth things over—lots of ways to do that, but often kissing ass and a little laughter did the trick.

"John, my friend, I would never overstep. This is a Dead Rabbit production, through and through. I'm here to make sure things go well with the police and I brought a few of my men—added security for Paddy. I'm sure you heard the Bowery Boys sent some guys over earlier today to soften him up for the fight."

"Ah, yes. Those fucking Bowery Boys. I piss on them. The nerve of them, coming into the Points. Too bad your boys found them. They would have never gotten back to the Bowery if we did."

"I'm sure you're right, but then we wouldn't be here tonight, making lots of money with these fights. We'd be dealing with all of the Bowery Boys/Dead Rabbits bullshit. Chances are we'd be in the middle of a riot. Am I right?"

"Ah, the wisdom of Tammany Hall! There is a place for it, but you're not running my event. Take your men and go and protect Paddy, but stay out of my way. The Dead Rabbits are in charge. Don't forget, the Dead Rabbits rule the Five Points."

Billy Conklin walked toward Pretty Paddy's dressing room with his sluggers and thought about O'Seary's claim of ruling the Points. To a great extent, he was right. About ten years before, many groups vied for power in the Points.

The Dead Rabbits, who could be identified by the blue stripes running down the side of their pants, were powerful, but often fought with the Roach Guards, who wore pants with red stripes, for supremacy within the Points. In the last few years, the Roach Guards became absorbed by other Irish gangs. The Shirt Tails, another Irish gang who wore their shirt tails out in the back, joined the Dead Rabbits a few years ago, and the Daybreak Boys, violent young teenagers known for raiding ships in the harbor before daybreak, also became extinct. The Dead Rabbits had assumed total control of the Points.

Even in the old days when the different Irish gangs vied for power, they all became allies bound together by pure hatred when they squared off against the Bowery Boys, who controlled the area just to the north. The Bowery Boys considered the Irish and the Blacks to be the lowest forms of life. This made their picks on fight night simple—they bet against Irish Pretty Paddy and Black Big Belvy. A lot of money rode on the outcome of these fights. In the eyes of the leaders of the Bowery Boys, invading Dead Rabbit territory for the purpose of roughing up Pretty Paddy was well worth the risk.

Despite the early hour, the warehouse buzzed with activity. Many people arrived before 6 pm to find a good spot to watch the fight and place their bets. They also hoped to assess the condition of each of the fighters as they entered the warehouse. Given the likelihood of foul play at any Five Points fight, knowing if a fighter arrived beaten up, drunk, or sick before you placed your bet was inside information of the most valuable kind.

Big Belvy arrived with an entourage of about twenty Blacks—mostly relatives, employees of FiveP, or hired sluggers much like those working for Tammany Hall—just Black. When Belvy first started fighting, he didn't travel with such a large contingent. Since the Emancipation Proclamation, however, the peaceful coexistence of the Black and Irish in the Points had changed for the worse. Now, there was only safety with numbers. Every fight Belvy had against a white opponent was symbolic, and any Belvy win could turn into a riot. Moseley and Belvy had to be prepared.

"Daddy, did you see the bunnies?"

Moseley stared at his huge son, who often reverted to childish behavior and speech. No matter how many times they came upon the same scene,

Belvy couldn't remember the fate of the cute bunnies on fight night, and his reaction was bad for his image as a fighter. Moseley ushered his son into the dressing room seconds before the inevitable transpired—one of the Dead Rabbits gathered up the three rabbits, snapped each of their necks, and impaled them on a pole. The Dead Rabbits entered all of their brawls carrying spears similar to this, and John O'Seary thought having the spear with the affixed dead rabbits in place for the opening announcements of each fight made for good theatre.

⤙⬤ ⬤⤚

A thousand miles west on the prairie, the sun was about to rise and Patrick welcomed it. Another bright day, a good day, a day to remember—he glanced to his side, and admired Molly, who sat sidesaddle on her horse, smiling, enjoying the space and the fresh air. Molly and Patrick rode toward the rising sun. A good day, indeed. The scene was interrupted by Grace, "Patrick, are you ready, boy? You've got to be strong like your father. Today, you're not my son—you're the man people fear when you walk the streets of the Five Points. Today, you're Pretty Paddy, understand, boy?"

Patrick growled and began his transformation. The loveable smiles and the good natured, dumb looks were gone. The mother studied her son and realized the other Patrick, an intimidating and ferocious version of his typically amiable self, was emerging. *Why had it taken it this long to resurface,* Grace thought as she remembered the first time she witnessed the other Patrick at the age of fifteen. A drunken man on Tenth Avenue offered to give her a "roll in the hay" as long as she put a bag over her head. Her teenage son, already well in excess of 200 pounds, beat him to a pulp. Several men in the vicinity tried to stop him, but he tossed them to the side like they were little children. Punches and kicks seemed to be natural movements to her son—just like his father. He needed to learn to control his temper, but Grace hadn't told him to stop at first because she was so shocked. Then she didn't tell him to stop because—it was hard to admit—she approved of his behavior. Finally, she did stop him, because if she didn't, he would have killed the man.

After they returned home, Grace had taught Patrick how to calm down by transporting himself to another place and time in his mind. She didn't realize that when she suggested he let his mind travel out to the wide-open spaces of the West it would never return. Grace wasn't surprised to hear his future plans involved moving out west, but she did worry that his dreams were nothing more than the fantasies of a young man. Life was tough for the Irish wherever they went, but the vision of the West served him when he needed to relax. At this moment, however, relaxation was not the objective; Patrick needed to channel that ferocious 15-year-old boy.

→⟫ ⟪←

"Mr. Conklin, I believe?" asked the uniformed police officer.

"Yes, Billy Conklin at your service. How are you today, officer?"

"I'm quite all right. Do you understand prizefights are illegal, Mr. Conklin?"

"Well, I understood with a donation, they might be legal for the next few hours."

"Why, yes. Still wrong, but as long as you assure me it is all good clean fun, we will look the other way."

"Here you go, officer." Billy handed the officer an envelope. After inspecting the contents, the policeman pulled out two bills, and gave them to Billy Conklin. "Put one of these on Big Belvy and one on Pretty Paddy. Who do you think will win when they go head to head next week?"

"I would never get ahead of myself, but I hope for your sake they win tonight. Have a good night, officer."

→⟫ ⟪←

Molly knew better than to come to the Five Points alone and arrived with all three of her brothers.

"Sis, I can't believe you're dating Pretty Paddy. He's a fucking animal who'll kill you. We can take care of you tonight, but if you marry Pretty Paddy...nothing we can do for you. He's a natural killer."

"Careful what you say, he's a good man, but he's been lying to me. Time for the truth." Molly didn't know what to expect and wondered whether this could all be some kind of terrible mistake. Maybe Pretty Paddy was not her Patrick. It was all confusing, but thankfully, one way or the other, the confusion would soon end.

The announcer walked to the middle of the makeshift ring—four poles connected by rope, strung together in a square shape with one side of the ring flush with the wall. This was a special feature in this particular fighting venue; some fighters learned how to build the wall into their strategy and knocked the backs of their opponents into it, while they pummeled their fronts, thereby causing pain on both sides of their body. Oddly, a wide open door, which opened to a ramp leading to the street, created a substantial gap in this special wall.

The timekeeper sat outside the ring with a bell, and a Dead Rabbits gang member, who stood inside the ring, had the job of making sure the fight didn't get boring. If the men got locked in a wrestling match, he had orders to break it up. Other than that, the crowd would be treated to simple bare knuckles fighting with very few rules. The announcer held the long spear upon which the three dead rabbits were impaled, and introduced Helmut Behrman, an overweight 35 year-old German, with a barrel chest and a pot belly. Moseley told Belvy not to look at the announcer because he would see the dead bunnies—Belvy lowered his head when introduced. The crowd roared for Big Belvy, which surprised Billy Conklin who mistakenly assumed the mostly white crowd would cheer the German boxer. The consensus of the crowd, however, was that they wanted a match-up of Big Belvy vs. Pretty Paddy the next weekend, and for that to happen, the German had to lose.

Belvy had both his father and his brother in his corner and Moseley tried to get him to focus.

"Belvy, looks like he's real slow, so you should be okay, and he's big, but not as big as you. Just protect yourself and look for your punch. Do you understand?"

"Belvy got a plan, Daddy. Everybody need a plan."

Moseley hated moments like these, which forced him to question whether he did the right thing with his youngest son. They knew Belvy wasn't normal and Jimmy had tried to convince his dad Belvy was not cut out for boxing. Moseley agreed but wanted Belvedere to get one big payday before he stopped, and that payday might be just a week away if he beat this German. The timekeeper hit the bell, and Belvy sprung off his stool. Moseley had conditioned his son to under-stand when the bell rang, he needed to fight, and when it rang again, he should rest. Things had to go right one last time between the ringing of those bells.

Grace left Patrick with the professor in the dressing room because she want-ed to get acquainted with the format of the fights as well as Patrick's next op-ponent. She couldn't believe the speed at which these two men were moving... slow and slower. The German was well past his prime, overweight, and almost out of breath after throwing his first punch. The black man was a physical speci-men—as big as Patrick, but not as quick by any stretch of the imagination. Patrick may have presented a lack of speed as his weakness as a fighter, but she had witnessed him in action against the two thugs a few hours earlier, and thought Patrick might have been a little too self-critical.

The German charged back in the ring and threw another wild punch, which connected and hit Big Belvy on the shoulder. Belvy barely flinched—his strength and ability to absorb a punch was impressive. Three more missed attempts by the German and then, right before the bell rang signaling the end of the first round, Belvy threw one upper cut which connected with the underside of the German's jaw and literally lifted him off of his feet and knocked him backward. Helmut Behrman was knocked unconscious by this one well-placed punch. The fight was over and the crowd roared again for Big Belvy. Both Moseley and Jimmy ran into the ring to stop Belvy from going to help the German fighter or do anything else that might not seem warrior-like, because his one punch knock-out cemented his reputation as a ferocious fighter. *Pretty Paddy here we come,* Moseley thought to himself.

Grace went back into the dressing room with great respect for Big Belvy, who seemed just as strong as her son. She hoped, however, Patrick had the ad-vantage of speed.

The unlikely trio walked out of the dressing room, surrounded by the Tammany Hall sluggers; Pretty Paddy in the middle, his mother to his left, and the professor to his right. The plan—Grace would keep an eye on Patrick while the professor paid more attention to the crowd. Jason Timbers' familiarity with the Five Points would enable him to pick up on all of the groups and any more troublemakers immediately. He noticed the large number of men with red striped pants—all Dead Rabbits gang members who ran the event. He even noticed one with blue stripes, an older fellow who the professor assumed refused to let go of his Roach Guard roots. Similarly, he noted a group of three men with their shirttails out—again a little older—most likely former members of the defunct Shirttails. The professor scanned the room for any sign of the Bowery Boys, but didn't expect any would be present, given the strong presence of the Dead Rabbits and Tammany Hall sluggers.

One man caught the professor's eye—someone he recognized as a resident of the Bowery. Jason Timbers always made a point of understanding who he should stay away from, and this man was definitely one of those people. He wasn't wearing the signature silk stovepipe hat, red shirt, or brocaded vest for which the Bowery Boys were known, but the professor did take note of the oiled back hair, which was peeking out from under his cap and the calfskin boots which were also part of the standard uniform of the gang. The professor tried to whisper the location of this intruder to Billy Conklin in such a way he would not be obvious, and within a few minutes, two of the sluggers left Paddy's security detail and walked toward the man, who quickly made his exit. Had the Dead Rabbits been aware of his presence, all hell would have broken loose.

Grace, no stranger to prizefights, squatted in front of her son and took note of the fire in his eyes. Her fifteen-year-old boy who defended her honor returned just in time and needed to put on a better show than Big Belvy. Grace grabbed her son's hands, stared at him straight in the eyes, and offered her only pre-fight instruction. "None of this wait a few rounds and let the fight drag on shit. That big black fella did it with one punch at the end of the first round—you need to beat that. Understand?"

Patrick nodded just as the bell rang. The mostly Irish crowd started chanting, "Pretty Paddy! Pretty Paddy!" Thomas Johnson, a 25 year-old, well-toned man started circling Paddy and showing off his speed. At only 170 pounds, he had no business being in the ring with Paddy, who started stalking his prey and slowly forcing him into the corner. Thirty seconds into the fight, Paddy threw his first punch, which turned out to be the only one he would need, and knocked his opponent through the ropes on the side of the ring with the wall. Johnson was propelled through the opening, rolled down the ramp, and eventually landed head first on the sidewalk outside the warehouse. Grace picked up his stool and threw it down the ramp after him screaming, "You forgot your stool, sweetheart!" Paddy had literally knocked him out of the building. The crowd had never seen such a display of pure power and chanted, "Pretty Paddy! Pretty Paddy!" in an endless loop.

Paddy stood in the center of the ring and trained his fiery eyes on Big Belvy, who returned an empty blank stare. Moseley caught the exchange as did Belvy's brother Jimmy. The crowd assumed Paddy inherited his killer instinct from his beast of a mother. While Grace was a formidable force, Patrick was really his father's son.

Billy Conklin and John O'Seary knew they needed to have the mother back next week. Pretty Paddy may have been the fighter, but his mother was the show. O'Seary turned to Conklin and whispered, "I'd be willing to bet $50 the mother would have kicked Johnson's ass too. Probably would have taken two rounds." The men laughed, and started counting dollar signs in their heads—Pretty Paddy vs. Big Belvy would be the biggest prizefight ever in the Five Points.

Moseley's smile after his son's fight turned to a look of concern as he wondered if Belvy would survive his ordeal with this animal of a man with the devil as a mother. Moseley assumed Patrick came from a line of killers. Still in the moment, Grace and Patrick couldn't deny the vicious display felt good; they both had a violent streak which they learned to manage as best they could, but when an Allen had the chance to legitimately kick some ass without any concern for consequences, it was a party, and what a party they had that night. Mother and son left arm in arm. The professor also left, pleased to have been of service, but concerned about the severity of his student's alternate personality.

The only person in the Pretty Paddy camp who left devastated was Molly. This wasn't the man she loved. The rich bitch at the orphanage was right. Molly turned to her brothers as they left and said in a muffled voice, "You're right. He is an animal and so is his Ma. I'm done with him." They all responded together, "Thank God for that."

Chapter 38

Edward's Friends

EDWARD SIMMONS REFLECTED on his day, one of the busiest Fridays ever at the Tribune. Most of the increased activity involved speculation about what would happen with the Draft, which was scheduled to begin Saturday morning. The office consensus: the first day might be uneventful, but Monday would go down as a day to remember.

The local importance of the Draft made it hard for the Tribune to devote more lines of the paper to the big victory in Gettysburg, which had taken place a few days earlier. The Tribune hoped it would make the Draft more palatable. Perhaps people would view the Draft as the last step in the victorious war effort-- nothing more than the final manpower needed to guarantee a Union victory. Until Gettysburg, many logical and informed men had predicted a Southern victory. The official spin at The Tribune was that Gettysburg would be the turning point.

The Draft coverage at the Tribune and all of the other major papers focused on Manhattan, the nation's largest city, and Edward couldn't understand how the third largest city, Brooklyn, simply got lost in the shadow of Manhattan. Perhaps the proximity was to blame—the daily ferry ride from Brooklyn to Manhattan took all of twelve minutes from start to finish. Edward often made the case that Brooklyn had its own story to tell, but the Tribune didn't seem interested. He laughed at himself during the ferry trip home. *Even though I may have worked my last day at the Tribune, I can't stop looking for the angle.*

The short walk from the ferry station to Edward's apartment took another six minutes, and then hanging up his suit, a final four minutes. He glanced at the clock mounted on his wall–he'd done it again! Exactly twenty two minutes from his departure on the ferry and *voila*...he was officially bored to tears.

He walked toward the back of his large four-bedroom apartment, with a lovely balcony facing Manhattan–exactly the specification he provided to agents and landlords during his apartment search. One landlord asked him about his family, and Edward thought to himself, w*hy would this man ask such a personal question?* It took a few moments for Edward to realize the apparent absurdity of his apartment search—a widower with one grown son, no siblings, not even a cousin he was aware of–looking for a four-bedroom apartment. He responded by telling his potential landlord he had no family, but did have many special friends who liked to stay with him.

Edward got up from his chair by kitchen table and thought he would take a moment to visit with his friends. The first bedroom by the front door contained friends he met in college, and the second bedroom contained friends whose acquaintance he made through work. The living room had friends perched all over with whom he simply liked to relax. The third bedroom was where he slept and sadly, never entertained any friends. The fourth bedroom was totally empty and reserved for friends yet to be met. Edward reflected on his five years in this apartment and realized it had served him and his friends well.

Time to dine—who would be his companion? Ah, yes, after a day like today, some poetry to free the soul. Edward went into the first bedroom and started to scan the stacks of books from his college years–books lined up on shelves occupying every inch of the wall and floor space. Poetry dominated his collection from that period. He found it–a book of poetry by one of his favorites, William Blake. Edward Simmons and his date headed downstairs to dine.

"Mr. Simmons, right on time. Good evening." Edward smiled at Wanda, the friendly proprietor of the small café where he dined almost every evening. After all of these years and countless meals, Edward didn't even know her last name. He settled into his special reserved table beneath a small lantern, which provided enough light for reading. The water arrived first, whiskey second, and his food third. The fourth, fifth, and sixth rounds were more whiskey.

Wanda found Edward, who was much older than her 40 years, to be impressive, well-read, and disciplined–he arrived at the same time every day, always with a different book. After four glasses of whiskey and dinner, he got up, no worse for the wear, said good night and walked back up the stairs to his apartment. Edward Simmons was a mystery, and a dapper mystery at that. Wanda tried yet again to connect.

"What are you reading, Mr. Simmons? Looks like poetry."

He smiled at her. "One of my favorites, William Blake—an English chap. He died while I was finishing college, which is often a great career move for a poet. Not so famous during his life, he…"

Wanda interrupted. She didn't want the William Blake life story, just the Edward Simmons story. "Can you read some for us?"

The other waitress chimed in, "Yes. Please Mr. Simmons, read some for us. Please."

The four other customers nodded —they were all curious to meet this mysterious man who sat under the lantern night after night with his whiskey, food, and books. Some people thought he was a writer; others thought he was a professor; only a few knew of his job at The Tribune. Regardless of what he actually did, the group at the café considered him to be highly intelligent and well spoken. Edward flipped through the book and found the page, which he had marked forty years ago with a small piece of paper. He stood and walked to the center of the small dining room to recite his favorite William Blake poem from college. Wanda called into the kitchen and asked the staff to come out, and the sixty year-old, possibly retired newspaperman, felt twenty again as he cleared his throat.

"A Little Boy Lost, by William Blake…

Nought loves another as itself,
Nor venerates another so,
Nor is it possible to thought
A greater than itself to know

'And, father, how can I love you
Or any of my brothers more?
I love you like the little bird
That picks up crumbs around the door.'

The Priest sat by and heard the child;
In trembling zeal he seized his hair,
He led him by his little coat,
And all admired the priestly care.

And standing on the altar high,
'Lo, what a fiend is here! Said he:
'One who sets reason up for judge
Of our most holy mystery.'

The weeping child could not be heard,
The weeping parents wept in vain:
They stripped him to his little shirt,
And bound him in an iron chain,

And burned him in a holy place
Where many had been burned before;
The weeping parents wept in vain.
Are such things done on Albion's shore?"

The small audience applauded Edward for his superb delivery. He thanked everyone for their kindness, placed a bill on the table, and tucked his friend under his arm as he left the café. Wanda looked at him as he exited and wished with all of her heart she could walk up those stairs with him. Edward loved the poem from start to finish, but connected most with the title, "A Little Boy Lost." Despite all of his career success, Edward Simmons realized he had continued to be that little boy, and he was determined to make a change. No more going through the paces, no more business as usual. Edward Simmons had plans to make.

CHAPTER 39

Friday Night in the Points

MANY PEOPLE THOUGHT that well-heeled Republicans, whose idea of a night out on the town was good food, wine, and sophisticated company, did not socialize in the Points. While this may have been generally true, those with more peculiar tastes could be found just beyond the public eye. They did not seek sophistication, however, they sought release. Married men who didn't get what they needed at home frequented the brothels. Sexual preferences and practices weren't judged in the Points—they were celebrated and serviced. Booze, opium, poker and other games of chance were available to all interested parties. A plan for a night in the Points might start with drinks in a dancehall, a minstrel show, some poker, and then a brothel. Opium tended to be left for an all-nighter, which kept the opium dens busy until daybreak.

The challenge of the Points did not lie in finding a particular vice, but rather in being able to enjoy the vice without getting robbed or conned, and leaving at the end of the night with health intact. Veterans of the Points understood how to meet this challenge, but those new to the scene became targets for all kinds of unfortunate acts, which would, at best, relieve them of their money and, at worst, their life.

The FiveP Dancehall provided a variety of entertainment depending on the evening, but live music and dancing took place every night. This is where Moseley's son, Jimmy, developed his chops as a tap dancer, and it is also where he realized, at the end of a particularly action filled night in his sixteenth year, that he was more attracted to men than women.

Jimmy was the kind of homosexual man who appealed to the wealthy New Yorker with similar inclinations–presentable and not overtly feminine. He cleaned up well and moved around the city as easily as any Black man could. Jimmy had plans to buy out his father and turn the FiveP Dancehall into the premier spot for the best entertainers in downtown New York. Moseley often complimented Jimmy on how well his "plan" seemed to be coming together.

Jimmy managed and promoted Friday nights at the dance hall, which meant Moseley had the night off. Sitting in a little apartment directly above loud music and next to active dressing rooms was not exactly restful. Still, Moseley appreciated the break and had to admit Jimmy's "He She Be Me--Friday Nights" were a hit–the most profitable night of the week.

The live music had started over an hour ago and the crowd downstairs danced at a frenzied pace despite the extreme heat. Jimmy had already performed two solos and had had a dance-off of sorts with another established tap dancer from the Points. Most people agreed Jimmy got the better of him, as he typically did. Moseley walked out of his little apartment to stretch his legs and needed to pass through several dressing rooms to do so. The five men in the furthest room, who should have been making their final preparations with make-up and clothes for their performance as a female singing/dancing troupe, were all gathered together, laughing, and having the time of their lives.

"Here you go, baby, a little more blush and a touch more lipstick. Your face is simply beautiful!"

"Excellent work! Let's put on the wig...yes, what a pretty girl!...put these socks in the top for the boobs. Oh, God, he doesn't need them. Look at the size of that chest. Make it bounce for us honey. You know how to do it. Make it bounce, baby."

Moseley stormed in, which put an end to the fun. The five performers scampered out of the little dressing room and Moseley came face to face with the source of their laughter–Belvedere, seated on a flimsy wooden chair, flexing his pectoral muscles up and down with an empty smile on his face. He was never sure when people were making fun of him and he only wanted to be liked. With his father standing before him with the "bad look," Belvy understood he'd been embarrassed, yet again.

"Daddy, they said they needed one more girl because someone got sick and you asked me to fill in–I'm just trying to help you, like you help Belvy. Did I do something wrong, Daddy? Why you stare at me like that? Belvy got a plan, Daddy. You know I do. Why you stare at me? Belvy got a plan!"

Moseley tossed a towel to his son and started removing all of the female make-up and clothing from his massive boy as he consoled him, "Yes, Belvy has a plan, but this isn't it, Belvy. Be careful who you trust, boy. Trust your Daddy, trust Jimmy, but be careful with everyone else–careful with everyone else. You got that, Belvy? Tell me you understand."

Tears streamed down Belvy's face as he came to grips with being fooled again. "Why they do this to me, Daddy? Belvy never hurt them. Belvy never hurt them. Never, Daddy. Just like you told me. Only hurt when I hear bell. Only bell, Daddy! No bell rang–never hurt anyone, why they do this, Daddy? Why, Daddy?"

Moseley walked Belvy back to their apartment and planned to stay there for the rest of the night to consider all the events of this particularly momentous Friday evening. He needed to get Belvy out of the dancehall--that much was clear--and set up in a more wholesome environment. The first step was to get the funds to do it. In one more week the money would be there as long as Belvy survived his fight with Pretty Paddy. Moseley knew he didn't have much time left. As a matter of fact, his doctor told him he was already living on borrowed time. Children should do better than their parents–that's what Moseley always said, and that's what he wanted for his boys. Jimmy would be fine as the owner/ manager of FiveP, but Belvy had to get out of the Points, and this last episode was a good example why.

Belvedere started to calm down as Moseley sat next to him. Despite the music, the laughing, and all of the other background noise, he fell asleep with a smile on his face--Belvy was in his bed and with his Daddy, and that was all he needed. A tear fell from Moseley's eye as he leaned over to kiss Belvy goodnight, just as he'd done every night for the last eighteen years. "I understand, Belvy. I do understand. Belvy got a plan. Sleep well, son."

CHAPTER 40

The Unlucky Few

THE FIRST AND third largest cities in the United States, New York and Brooklyn—well over one million residents—were essentially unguarded. The substantial New York-based militia had been called to Gettysburg and played a major role in the Union victory. The administrators of the morning's Draft at the Provost Marshal's office on 49th Street & Third Avenue were understandably concerned with the prospects for violence because their security detail consisted of only twelve officers.

"Keep looking out the window. Tell me if there are any mobs of people. We're unprotected. How the hell could they leave us with only 12 policemen? They must be crazy." The junior member of the Provost Marshal's staff fretted, but no crowd gathered, and the initial day of lottery picks went on without any problems or interruptions. The process was simple and began with a spin of the large lottery wheel, during which a card containing the name of the draftee was extracted. Fifty names selected and recorded–all fifty men would be quickly notified of their selection through ads taken out in local papers. Most of the fifty would hear the bad news in this manner the next day, but one of the unlucky men, who had a recognizable name, knew almost immediately. Within a matter of an hour, this one gentleman decided how he would let his displeasure at being selected be known.

Patrick and Molly never introduced each other to their families. As a result, they always met at their destination. Today, they planned to meet at their favorite spot in Central Park and Patrick, who brought the blanket and a jug of iced tea, enjoyed the cool morning air as he patiently waited for his date to arrive. After an hour passed, and still no Molly, Patrick decided to head toward her apartment on the East Side.

Patrick wasn't sure what to do. Should he knock on the door or should he just wait outside and try to catch a glimpse of Molly in the window and perhaps motion for her to come outside? Patrick opted for the latter approach and had his eyes trained on each of her windows, which faced the avenue. After a short period of time, Molly's silhouette quickly crossed the window as she walked by. Patrick couldn't understand. *Could she have forgotten about their picnic? That would be out of character for her. No, it had to be something else,* Patrick thought, and decided it was time to meet her family.

"Hello sir, my name is Patrick Allen. I am here to see Molly."

The older man who opened the door offered no response and had a look of fear in his eyes. A male voice called out from the back of the apartment, "She doesn't want anything to do with the likes of you!"

Patrick quickly responded, "What do you mean by that?"

The source of the voice, a man in his twenties, appeared from behind the shadows and stood next to the father and explained that Molly found out he was Pretty Paddy, not some run of the mill dock worker, and didn't want anything to do with him. Patrick understood the message, but did not accept being dismissed by anyone other than Molly.

"I would like to speak to Molly, please. I can explain everything."

The father finally spoke up, "No, I think she's had enough contact with you. Go on. Off with ya."

Patrick didn't know what to do—he always feared things would end badly with Molly because of the secrets he kept from her. *Maybe I'm not good enough for Molly.* His version of Pretty Paddy was not like that of his father—he couldn't imagine anyone saying, "God Bless you, Pretty Paddy," unless they were under threat of physical harm. *Molly is right…I'm not good enough for her…I'm not good enough for anyone.* Patrick realized he'd been dumped, and while his inner voice agreed with Molly's decision, he didn't want to let go because Molly was both his present and his future. Even his dreams, which took him a thousand miles away out West, would be nothing more than fantasy without her.

Patrick thought back to his courtship of Molly--the thrill of his proposal, the delight in her acceptance, and then the celebration. *Ah, the celebration*, Patrick thought to himself as a smile spread across his face. Patrick loved to celebrate.

Molly's father sensed he was not dealing with a ferocious man, but a confused boy, and took a step toward Patrick, who instinctively stepped back into the hallway. Molly called out to him, "You big animal, you lied to me—you're nothing more than a dirty street person. Stay away from me and take your shitty little ring." The ring came flying out from behind her father and hit Patrick in the back of the head. Patrick walked down the stairs clutching the ring, which he never thought would leave Molly's finger, as he continued his internal dialogue. *I'm no good. She's right, I'm nothing but a dirty street fighter. I don't deserve someone like Molly. I'll let her down. She's better off without me.*

⇢▸⊙ ⊙◂⇠

More than just a place for a haircut, Washington's Barber Shop served as the primary meeting point for the leadership of the Black community in the Five Points. Moseley and Belvy came in for haircuts along with other assorted Five Points residents and businessmen. The conversation turned to the fight as Moseley and Belvedere got situated in their chairs.

"Man, you knocked the shit out of that German last night. How do you think you'll do against Pretty Paddy?"

"Pretty Paddy good boxer, Big Belvy good boxer."

The barber turned to Moseley and raised his eyes in such a way as to ask if that was the best answer he would receive. Moseley nodded in the affirmative, so the barber didn't press for further clarifications from Belvy. Moseley tried to change the subject back to the Conscription Act, a very unpopular topic. One man said Blacks should be allowed to serve, another predicted the Irish would become violent with Blacks over the act. Everyone agreed the Irish had a real reason to be upset, but not with them.

⇢▸⊙ ⊙◂⇠

Saturday night was not a happy one for the fifty men selected earlier that day for the Draft. There was one well-known draftee who was particularly furious at being selected and had been in meetings all day planning his response. The Black Joke Volunteer Engine Company--named after a ship--was powerful in the city, and he was its chief. He'd assumed firemen would enjoy the basic exemption they'd always had over the years. No exemption was being offered, however, and the captain's last meeting of the night with the men in his company was productive. They had their plan and were confident their voices would be heard loud and clear Monday morning.

CHAPTER 41

Mommy's Rule

TENTH AVENUE AWOKE more slowly on a Sunday morning, but the familiar sounds of horses, foot traffic, and horns from steamers on the Hudson reminded Grace she, too, needed to begin her day. She sensed that her health had taken a turn for the worse the night before. This morning she felt such a weight on her chest, and she couldn't even sit up in bed. Grace's doctor had told her extreme exhaustion would be the sign the end was near. As long as she didn't exert herself and got lots of rest, the doctor estimated she might be able to live another several weeks. Unfortunately, her seven hour walking tour of Manhattan on Friday, which culminated in working the corner in her son's boxing match, triggered a bout of exhaustion she was unable to overcome. Unsure that she could get out of bed, Grace struggled once more to at least sit up. She needed to speak with Patrick, who didn't have any idea how bad her health was – he wasn't the only one in the family who liked to keep secrets.

"Patrick, my dear. Pull your chair closer to my bed. I want to talk to you and I don't have so much strength today."

Patrick always did as his mother said, but sometimes, he took his good, sweet time. He didn't like his Ma's shaky voice and pale color, however, and in an uncharacteristic move, left some of his eggs uneaten in his plate as he went to his mother's side.

"I'm really not well. The last 15 years of hard labor on the docks have taken a toll and I think I need a much deserved rest."

"Oh, Ma." He smoothed a hair back from her face, "Of course you do. You can lie in bed as long as you like. No need to get up at all today. I'll take care of you, Ma. No worries."

"I know, *a ghrá*, I can count on you for sure, but I need you to listen to me." She stopped to breathe, then continued. "You learned Daddy's Rules and they served you as a young boy. It was good to see them grow you into a man. But those rules were basic things. The way things are going in the city and with my...weakness," she paused again and breathed slowly. "I don't think I can take any longer to offer your final lesson, which we'll call Mommy's Rule and should serve you well as a man."

"Ma, you're not weak. You just need some rest. I can get the doctor..."

"Patrick." She laid a hand on his arm. "This is serious. I'm worried about you, and I want you to make good choices. Do you understand me?"

"Of course, Ma. But I'm not so sure what else you can teach me."

"Ah, so when did you come into all of this wisdom? When you became a teenager, or when you left your teenage years and became twenty a few weeks ago? Don't be cocky, boy, you've got a whole lot to learn. You may be able to handle yourself in the boxing ring, but the world outside the ring is where I have greater concerns." She closed her eyes for a moment, breathing hard.

"Okay. Teach me Mommy's Rule."

"First, pour a little water for your Ma."

Patrick walked away to get the water and Grace organized her thoughts. She had learned what she was about to explain to her son back in Ireland, but it seemed as valid today in New York as it ever was in the old country. She had a sense that Patrick might soon be tested and she might not be by his side to offer the benefit of her experience.

"Here you go, Ma, a tall mug of water." Grace took a few sips and rested the mug on the small end table next to the bed. "Back in Ireland, we never got along with the Protestants. Physically, we were no different, but we quickly learned who was who because we hated them and they hated us. Then, after genera-tions of Protestants mistreating the Catholics in terrible ways, a funny thing hap-pened. For the first time, an actual visual difference distinguished the Catholics and Protestants. After 150 or so years of them preventing us from owning land, serving in the government, and fully participating in society—we looked differ-ent. By the early 1840s when I met your father, the Irish Catholics had no shoes, no coats in the winter, and starved to a much greater extent than the Protestants.

The Catholic children, however, displayed the biggest difference of all; extreme starvation caused a black fuzz to spread over their faces. We called them the bearded children and wondered what this terrible start to their lives would mean down the road if they survived. Generations of mistreatment finally showed on our bodies. I always wonder if the Protestants who put us in that state realized beating down a group so severely was not in the interest of either side."

"But then we came here to the United States and left those problems behind us."

"Really, Patrick? Is that what you actually think? With all of the books you read, and all of your high level conversations with your intelligent friends like the professor, do you truly think we left all of that behind us in Ireland?" Grace paused to take another sip of her water as she realized this was going to be harder than she imagined.

"The Irish who came to New York were again at the bottom of the social ladder. We were offered the lowest jobs and treated like dirt most places we went. It's better than Ireland, but in comparison to the rest of the city, we're shit, and we're Catholic shit, to boot. The only thing that makes us think we're better off is the fact that another group here is below us. They are just like we were in Ireland–no legal rights, can't own property, and can't vote. And they have always looked different. At first, I think we did relate somewhat to the free Blacks. We lived side by side with them in the Five Points for years, but we eventually started to believe that they were different and we were better."

She shook her head and took another sip of water. "Now the politicians are pitting us against each other for their own gain. The Irish hate the Blacks in much the same way the Protestants hated the Catholics. It is happening all over again. The Draft, I fear, will push this tension to the boiling point. Our men will not accept being forced to fight in a war to free the people who the politicians say will steal their jobs. People will take sides. People will fight. I want you to be on the right side and do the right thing."

"Ma, I don't think I'm going to be on any side. I'll be like New York City a few years back during the talk of secession. I'll be neutral. Not my fight, Ma. Not my fight."

"Not your fight, Patrick? Look at the size of ya, people know you–you are the feared Pretty Paddy. When you can make a difference, it is your fight. You can't stay out of this because if you do, you're no better than the Protestants who looked the other way. I don't hate all of the Protestants: you can't help what you're born into or change what happened before you, and some of them helped us. I've no use for the people who made the laws that kept us down or the ones who stole our land. But more than anything I hate the ones who could have helped us, but looked the other way. Pretty Paddy can't do that because it *is* your fight. You can't change the world by yourself, but when you can make a difference, you have to—that's Mommy's Rule. I need to know that my mountain of a big-hearted son, with all of his intelligence and physical gifts, will use what God gave him to make a difference. Your father set the example —he made a difference with everything he did. We wouldn't be here today if not for his sacrifice. Don't let him down, Patrick and don't you let your Ma down either. It is your fight, Patrick. It is."

Grace finished and was out of breath. Patrick sat, thinking. After a few moments, he got up, ate the last bit of eggs, and then returned to his mother's side. He reached out and held her hand as he said, "You're right, Ma. I won't stand by, and I'll make you proud, which is all I ever wanted to do. It's my fight too, and one day you'll talk about me like you do about Da. Not to worry, Ma. This is my fight too."

Patrick occasionally "yes'd" his mother along as many children do, but this was different. Grace acknowledged her son's response with a smile, closed her eyes, and got her much needed rest. Patrick sat quietly with her as her hand grew cold to the touch. It wasn't until her jaw began to stiffen that panic started to set in and he felt his heartbeat picking up in speed. Then he remembered the mind game his mother taught him and took his mind out West to the prairie, another sunset and so much wide-open space. His heartbeat slowed as he realized that his mother would always be with him. *I won't forget, Ma. I promise.*

CHAPTER 42

An Unusual Meeting

SUNDAY NIGHT. A highly unusual time for a meeting of the Friday Breakfast Club, Margaret Kilpatrick thought. She noticed the professor first, as he wandered the streets of midtown after stopping by his office at the college. After just a few short blocks, he confirmed what he always suspected– wandering was so much more fun downtown. Next, Johnston Stewart came strolling by with his son Jonathan and took note of the activity inside the store. The next surprise was Edward Simmons, who decided to start his vacation with a night in Manhattan. He knew the morning would bring the demonstration against the Draft and worried about being unable to get into the city. Even though he considered himself to be a man of leisure–at least for the next two weeks–he would always be a newspaperman, and had to be close to the action.

Margaret Kilpatrick and the four men settled in for a chat, but needed refreshments, and dispatched Jonathan Stewart to buy some iced tea and cookies. *What an impressive young man,* Margaret thought as she made a mental note to consider him as a possible permanent addition to the club. The shopkeeper had an eye for influencers and enjoyed this group she so carefully assembled. Despite the fact she had plenty of opinions of her own, Margaret never contributed much to the political discourse–she kept her remarks on a personal level and only got involved as a peacemaker when needed. She considered herself to be more the social scientist, and thought it possible for reasonable men with radically different points of view to find common ground if the dialogue remained ongoing and cordial. Margaret knew she did well with this group; they had all moved from the political extremes toward the center and had become like-minded old friends. The opportunity to spend time together on the eve of a highly explosive day comforted them all.

New York had a long history of riots and talk of another one in the morning, permeated the city. It seemed like just the other day the *Dead Rabbits Riot* pitted the city-run police against the state-run police, with each force supplemented by either Five Points or Bowery gangs. The underbelly of New York enjoyed a good riot, and it appeared they might have their fun in the morning.

At different points in the conversation, each of the men came to the realization they were sitting with their very best friends in the world, and what had begun as a social experiment had truly brought them together. Each of them started out with such extreme views tied to their affiliations, but found themselves on either side of the center. Margaret Kilpatrick called it the sweet spot—a place of agreement in which problems can be solved. Jonathan Stewart heard the tapping on the glass, and was a bit concerned to see the giant Irishman standing outside. The older men saw Jonathan's fear, started to laugh, and assured him everything was okay because it was only Patrick.

The group realized something bad had happened to Patrick and the conversation quickly turned from political events to his life. He couldn't bring himself to say the words, but Margaret Kilpatrick understood and kissed Patrick on the forehead while offering her condolences, "She's at peace, Patrick. No one could have been a better son." Patrick had held back his tears until that moment, but once they began to flow, the group appreciated that everything about this young man was big, even his tears.

Margaret sat next to Patrick and held his hand. Her touch reminded him of his mother, and all of the advice offered by the Breakfast Club members sounded like genuine counsel from the uncles he never had. He wasn't sure how much he retained, but he sat in their circle, munched on their cookies, and smiled for the first time that difficult day. The advice came from the heart and felt like a loving arm draped around his broad shoulders. He was with family and wasn't alone after all.

CHAPTER 43

The Irish Ready For Their Fight

PERHAPS BECAUSE IT was so long in the making, the morning of Monday, July 13th, 1863 had an extraordinarily early start. Everything moved fast, even the weather; the heat and humidity, which had recently been more forgiving in the early morning hours, was already unbearable by 8 AM. The air was so thick, people had the sensation of wading through it as they congregated. Shirts became soaked with sweat even before they'd begun their work for the day, which would not involve loading/unloading, hammering, or any of the other tasks expected of Irish laborers. Today's work would be different and to many, much more meaningful.

The gangs from the Five Points knew the feeling as did battle-tested ex-soldiers. Some experienced it for the first time, but everyone handled the preparation for battle with expressions of either intoxication or fear; no one was indifferent. The Irish were rising up and they might not win the war, but they would have their fight. Nerves and fear simmered under empowered outrage–the Irish were ready. The more extreme factions intended to inflict bodily harm, and no one anticipated offering any respect for property or discourse. No more talking–those responsible would pay.

The culprits were numerous, so targets would be easy to find; Federal officials who made the Civil War the South vs The Irish; the rich who turned their noses up to the Irish for years and who would buy their way out of the Draft; Blacks who would have them fight just to steal their jobs; even their supposed Democratic leaders in Tammany Hall, would answer for their inability to stop this day from coming. The level of frenzy was exactly what you would expect from a mob on the verge of violence. Some were so confused they planned their revenge against the Protestants and the British in the old country. For this one day, the Irish would be invincible.

The Confederate President, Jefferson Davis, would have been cheered by the crowd while Abraham Lincoln, ripped to shreds. Lincoln had engineered this death sentence called the Conscription Act. He would pay. They would all pay.

A somewhat organized uptown group, which assembled in Central Park approached on Third Avenue and proceeded south in two columns. Everyone had a job. Signs which read "No Draft" had to be carried, telegraph lines needed to be cut, stores had to be looted for axes and crowbars, the tracks of the Third Avenue trains needed to be uprooted, and any Irishmen who had the nerve not to be part of the battle, had to be recruited. Irish productivity would be up to the task.

The downtown masses originated from various points and lacked the same level of organization, but included many from the Irish gangs in the Five Points who would add much needed combat experience to the mix. The two groups arrived from either direction on Third Avenue to where they would make their stand at the symbolic location of their enemy, the Provost Marshal's Office. They were all present and accounted for at 49th Street and Third Avenue by 10:00 AM, just as the Draft was scheduled to begin.

CHAPTER 44

254 Children

OUTSIDE THE PROVOST Marshall's Office, the scene was set. Inside, however, was anything but–the major problem being a lack of security. The soldiers assigned to guard New York had been redeployed to Pennsylvania in late June for The Battle of Gettysburg, and had not yet returned. As a result, security in the city depended on a small force of 550 Metropolitan Police. The twelve officers assigned to the Provost Marshal's Office that Monday morning would need to control a mob of over 1000 Irishmen.

At 10:30 AM, the Draft began with the selection of the first fifty names of the day. The level of agitation had grown on the outside, but the mob did not have the leadership to move beyond yelling, screaming and generally being a nuisance, until the Black Joke Engine Company appeared on the scene. Their captain had been drafted on Saturday. After their arrival, a pistol shot rang out, which prompted the mob, led by the firemen, to break through the windows and the doors of the office. First, the mob destroyed the Draft Wheel and then vandalized the office. In an ironic twist, the firemen set the building ablaze.

A Confederate sympathizer addressed the Irish with an anti-Draft, pro-Confederate speech and the crowd cheered his message. As the blaze started to spread to the tenements next door, another fire company arrived on the scene, but the mob prevented them from doing their job.

Someone in the crowd pointed out the Superintendent of the Metropolitan Police, John A. Kennedy, in plain clothes outside the office. He was beaten, dragged through the mud, and eventually saved by a Tammany Hall politician.

By 11:30 AM, the Draft officially ended for the day and the Irish finally had a win.

With their objectives met at the Provost Marshal's Office, the large crowd broke into several smaller groups and began roving the city looking to attack the wealthy and the Blacks. The rich, sarcastically referred to as *$300 Men*, because of the price they paid to be exempted, were targeted because of the way that they treated the Irish and rigged the Draft so they would not serve. Their punishment: beatings and stolen or destroyed property.

Blacks, the second group to be targeted, had to pay for the sin of threatening Irish jobs. The mobs beat both young and old alike and lynched a number of adult Black men. One of these poor souls was even set on fire after being hung and then dragged through the streets by his genitals after his execution.

The Irish didn't carefully weigh the magnitude of the sins of each group in determining the punishment. More pain could be directed toward Blacks because they didn't matter. Killing a Black in New York was like killing a Catholic in Ireland—who would really care?

One mob attacked The Bull's Head Hotel—they had the nerve to withhold free liquor. The mayor's residence and many other Republican Fifth Avenue homes were attacked as well. Johnston Stewart's house had the unfortunate luck of being next to the residence of the most well known New York Republican and publisher of the Tribune, Horace Greely. After the mob left the publisher's house, they broke down Johnston's front door. Johnston, his son, and three servants barricaded themselves into one of the upstairs bedrooms. All of the men had rifles with plenty of ammunition, and their most prized possessions had been quickly moved into the room. Everything else could be replaced. They heard the intruders enter, ransack for a few minutes, and leave. The Stewarts were safe. Other Fifth Avenue families were not as lucky, but as out of control the Irish were that day, they knew their limits—they only beat the $300 Men. Order would eventually return and the rich still had power.

As each hour passed, the composition of the roving bands of rioters changed. Some came to their senses and returned home; others who thought they had missed out took their place. By the late afternoon, there were fewer people in the streets but the groups became more violent. By the late afternoon, the Irish had already been at it for well over eight hours—time for one last attack, and this one needed to be special. The mob arrived at 4:00 PM exactly. The choice, perfect— 44th Street and Fifth Avenue—The Colored Orphan's Asylum.

Joshua Redden, Molly Morrison, and the rest of the staff had been on guard all day. The children stood in line for so long that many of them, including ten-year-old Charles, fell asleep and curled into a ball on the floor. He remembered putting his head down on little Carla's shoulder and closing his eyes after seeing another of her hidden smiles.

"Charles, wake up. We have to leave. Everyone has to leave though the back door."

"Wait. Ms. Molly, where's Carla? She was right next to me when I fell asleep. Where is Carla?"

"Don't worry Charles, she must be further back in the line. I'm sure she's okay."

"You don't understand. I'm a big man. Big men take care of good people. I take care of Carla. Where's Carla?"

"Charles, we have no time for this—move. Carla is fine."

The evacuation was a logistical miracle. The mob entered the lobby of the orphanage just as the last of the children exited through the back to safety. Twenty minutes later, when the entire entourage from the orphanage found safety in a nearby church, they did the official count. Only 254 children. One was missing.

CHAPTER 45

Further Out West

PATRICK BARELY SLEPT for most of the night, but couldn't bring himself to get out of bed. Eventually, hunger provided enough of an incentive and he folded his outshot back into the wall, and ate his first meal of the day. The clock mounted above his mother's bed confirmed his late start. 11:00 AM.

He couldn't remember much about Sunday. After having his Ma's body removed, Patrick walked the streets, wound up at the bookstore, and remembered the warmth and compassion of his friends. He needed to regain his focus and decided to start with an accounting of his finances. The can wedged under the kitchen cabinet contained the $500 in cash he managed to save. Patrick counted the bills and coins as he thought, *more than enough to pay for my exemption if I get drafted with plenty left over to finally move out of the city. Maybe I don't even need my final payday from the Big Belvy fight.*

Patrick left the apartment and started walking south on Tenth Avenue. As he went, he decided to change his daily routine by turning west and heading toward the river. By the time he arrived at the docks, however, he realized he wanted to change more than his routine, and for that to happen, he needed to get out of New York.

Where is everybody? Patrick thought, as he found the docks to be as deserted as Tenth Avenue. He overheard a conversation on the street about the riots and this confirmed Patrick's decision to leave the city. He didn't need riots—he needed peace and quiet in wide-open spaces.

"Hey buddy, I'm heading up to Canada and then further out west. Everything's already loaded, but one section of the cargo area has to be repacked before we head out. Most of my crew left –someone your size might be able to do it alone. You can have passage in trade. May take a while, though. What do you say?"

Patrick didn't even ask about the pay. Once he heard "further out west" he went on board, and spent the next four hours lifting, moving, and rearranging large, heavy crates. The captain of the ship marveled at how one man accomplished all of this work in such a short period of time. He told Patrick he had enough time to go home and pack a bag. It was 4:30 PM–they'd be pushing off in about an hour.

Billy Conklin headed back to his old Tenth Avenue address because he wanted to be as far away from the Sixth Ward as possible and passed his old friend in the street.

"Paddy, thank God you're all right. Riots in midtown. The rich and the Blacks are being attacked. A mob stormed The Colored Orphan's Asylum!"

Patrick thought about the ship in the harbor. Then he thought of Molly, Charles, Carla, and all of the innocent children at the orphanage. Finally, he thought about his mother. It was his fight. Sometimes you had to get involved. With that, and despite the heat, the humidity, and the fact he'd performed hard labor for the past several hours, he began an all out sprint to the orphanage. The streets cleared as he ran. No one, not even one of the small roving mobs, wanted to get in his way. He needed to run five avenues east, and as he got close he noticed some familiar faces outside the church on Sixth Avenue. He stopped to investigate.

Patrick was relieved when he walked into the church and saw Molly, who ran into his arms and started crying as she asked for Patrick's help. "Carla is missing, you have to find her."

"I'm sure she's with Charles." Molly motioned to the first pew where Charles sat with his head down, hysterically crying. Patrick started his sprint again, one more block. He was in the orphanage within minutes.

The strong smell of smoke gave Patrick a sense of the fire's intensity. He knew exactly where to look and worked his way past the debris toward the small prep table covered with the long tablecloth in the back of the lobby. The cloth, now more gray than white, looked as if it hadn't been disturbed. Perhaps there was hope. He uncovered the table and found her—she wasn't burned. As a matter of fact, she appeared almost untouched. But she didn't move.

Carla must have fallen asleep in her favorite hiding place, and died of smoke inhalation. Patrick wrapped her in the tablecloth, cradled her in his arms, and began his slow walk back to the church. He cried and whispered his apologies as he walked, but did not direct them to Carla—he asked his mother for forgiveness. "I've already let you down, Ma. I'm sorry. I almost left. This is my fight. I'll make you proud, Ma. Take care of Carla, she's a good girl, but don't worry, Ma, I understand. It is my fight, and I'm ready for it."

CHAPTER 46

Making the Rounds

AFTER FINDING CARLA, Patrick decided to check on the short list of people who mattered to him. Molly was upset, but safe, and Patrick had hope he could win back his girl in time. He just had to make sure his Breakfast Club friends had survived. The swagger of Pretty Paddy returned as he began the brief walk to the bookstore where he found Mrs. Kilpatrick barricaded inside her front door. Patrick tapped on the window to get her attention.

Mrs. Kilpatrick. It's me, Patrick. Are you okay?"

Margaret Kilpatrick smiled and called out through the glass, "I'm okay. So far they left me alone. Go check on the Stewarts on Fifth Avenue. They're going after the rich. Edward Simmons is also in town. I hope they're all unharmed."

"Don't worry, Mrs. Kilpatrick. I'll check on them. Keep yourself safe."

The next stop–the Stewarts, a short walk from the bookstore. Patrick found the family and servants in fine condition, busy boarding up broken windows. Johnston gave Patrick the professor's address in the Bowery, and told him he'd find Edward Simmons there as well. Patrick headed out. One last stop.

⸱⟶▣ ▣◀⸱

"Edward, it is such a shame the streets are so dangerous tonight. I know all of the spots for two good looking older gentlemen like you and I."

Edward laughed, as he had no desire to go carousing with the thrill-seeking professor. The lovely owner of the café on the first floor of his apartment building was the only woman in which Edward had an interest. He would love to spend the night out on the town with the charming Wanda, but never had the nerve to ask her out on a date. Often a pessimist, Edward focused on what could go wrong and never considered the benefits if things went right. *What an idiot I am*, he thought to himself. *I won't ask her out because if it doesn't work out, I'll have to find another place to have my dinner. That's pathetic.*

The professor and the editor returned to their projects at the large kitchen table. Jason put the finishing touches on a lecture about the social significance of the riot, while Edward worked on the second article in his series about the thoughts and feelings of a "young Irish man." With every word he wrote, his decision became clear—he would not return to the Tribune, and planned to follow his own political philosophies from this point forward.

→▶◉ ◉◀←

Initially, Moseley thought it was a good idea. If the Five Points erupted in racial violence, the bloodshed would be extreme. The plan—stay in a rented room for the night in the neighboring area to the North, The Bowery. Moseley didn't expect to be refused a room because he'd seen Black folks staying at the boarding houses in the Bowery from time to time. Tonight, however, the rules had changed because businesses that permitted Blacks to be patrons were being targeted for violence by the Irish mobs. Father and son had been turned away from two different houses and had no choice but to head back to the Points. Moseley stood behind Big Belvy as they maneuvered the dangerous streets trying to steer clear of the Irish mobs, who were everywhere.

→▶◉ ◉◀←

"Come in my boy! Not the best night for a boxer in training to be out and about, but you're right on time for a beverage!" It had been a while since the professor entertained at home. Given the general Irish themes of the day, Irish whiskey was the obvious choice. The group settled in for their drink.

Edward used the unexpected visit to continue his ongoing interview with Patrick. The professor listened in between sips of whiskey and realized Patrick and Edward were two of the most intelligent people he had the pleasure of knowing. Edward's series of articles describing the plight of the Irish as seen through Patrick's eyes, was truly groundbreaking material. If he only reached a small percentage of his readership, he would still make a difference and change minds.

His young friend showed a different kind of courage with his gesture in checking on his breakfast club members despite the danger. Of course, both his size and ethnicity were of some protection, but still, it was impressive that young Patrick was so concerned about his friends. Things always seemed impressive to Jason Timbers when he drank, but given he was still sipping his first tumbler of whiskey, he was confident in his assessment of his companions.

After they spoke for about an hour, Patrick announced he was leaving. The professor, now on tumbler number 3, joked, "What kind of Irishman are you? You're going to leave without even finishing your drink?"

"I guess I'm an Irishman who knows I may have some trouble tonight, so I've got to think clearly. Mr. Simmons, keep an eye on the professor. I'd cut him off after one more."

The three friends chuckled; the light moment was a welcome relief from the night's violence. Patrick headed out and started to make his way up Mulberry to head back home to the West Side.

⇥◉ ◎⇤

"Daddy, almost home. A few more blocks and we back in the Points. Stay behind Belvy. Belvy keep you safe. "

"I don't feel good about this Belvedere, we never should have left. My mistake, boy. If we get stopped, just protect us, but don't kill anyone. I think we can get a pass on throwing some punches, but a Black man can never get a pass on killing a white man, even if they're Irish. Be careful, boy."

"Belvy careful, Dad. Belvy got a plan."

⇥◉ ◎⇤

Ten Bowery Boys stood in an alley about eight blocks outside the Points on Mulberry. They looked like they were dressed for an unusual wedding party—red shirts, brocaded vests, and calfskin boots. When they each removed their silk stovepipe hats, they revealed identical oily, slicked back hair. The leader of the group practiced kicking back so the blades he'd installed in the soles of his shoes would extend. He'd been waiting for an opportunity to use his new toy and knew he'd get his chance in the next few minutes. Two Black men were approaching.

CHAPTER 47

Here's the Bell

THE TEN MEN paused momentarily to decide how to best have their fun. The biggest of the bunch charged in and Belvy lifted him up over his head and tossed him back into the wall. Another man, much smaller, darted in, punched Belvy in the stomach, and quickly ran away. The men enjoyed the spectacle of seeing the massive Black man miss his mark. Belvy's lack of speed prevented him from retaliating with any real effect. After some time, the game lost its charm, so it changed.

Moseley became the target and Belvy started to cry as he did his best, but failed, to defend him against the Bowery Boys, who dashed in from all directions. When Belvedere wrapped his arms around his father and turned his back to his attackers, all ten men pummeled him and the father and son fell to their knees. The gang leader kicked back, the blade extended from his shoe, and sunk deeply into Belvy's calf as he kicked forward. The abuse stopped as the gang stepped back to take a moment to enjoy Belvy's pain.

Enough with the games, the gang leader thought, as he backed away and looked around the immediate area. The old man wouldn't be a problem; any pole would do, but the large man would be a challenge. The rope arrived with a noose fashioned wide enough for Belvy's neck. One of the Bowery Boys stated the obvious, "This is Big Belvy. He made us lose a whole lot of money last Friday night." Another of the attackers yelled back, "Of course it's Belvy, you idiot, who the fuck else is this big?"

The answer came from behind, "I am."

Patrick witnessed the assault made with the bladed shoe and remembered Daddy's Rule about weapons—you've got to take care of them first. He had surprise on his side and brutally stomped on the calf of the leader. The entire gang winced as sound of shattering bones filled the air. Patrick followed the kick with a punch to the leader's head and he was out cold.

Patrick realized the irony of coming to the aid of the man he was scheduled to box in a few days, but the fight that mattered was happening right now. Belvy stood up, smiled at Paddy, and the two men stood side to side in front of Moseley. Their combined six hundred pounds of muscle and thirteen feet of height gave pause to the leaderless Bowery Boys. Pretty Paddy and Big Belvy stood their ground.

The Bowery was no place for an Irishman and a Black man to pick a fight. The Bowery Boys considered both groups the lowest form of human existence. Dozens more gang members appeared from various locations on Mulberry Street and things started to look bleak. Moseley, still incapacitated, grabbed the metal pipe by his side and screamed, "Belvy, here's the bell" as he struck the pipe against a broken cast iron kettle, which also lay on the ground. The resonant bell-like sound prompted Belvy and he swung into action. Paddy followed suit and the two Five Points boxers more than held their own. The gang backed away and realized the price to pay for fighting hand to hand was too high. The next wave of reinforcements had weapons—a variety of chains and knives.

Belvy smiled at Paddy and said. "Belvy good boxer. Pretty Paddy good boxer. We have good fight, right?"

"Best fight ever, Belvy."

As they braced for what might be their final round, a voice in the distance called out, "The Bowery Boys are going after Pretty Paddy." Five members of the Black Joke Engine Company, the same group that started the whole mess at the Provost Marshal's Office, broke through the crowd brandishing axes and crowbars.

The firemen were surprised when they realized Paddy sided with black men, but the presence of Belvy and Moseley provided an even greater inspiration. The Black Joke men knew what they triggered that morning had become a race riot, and while they started the day as bigots who had been sold the party line that Blacks were going to steal their jobs, there was nothing about the lynchings and the violence of that day that felt right. Helping Moseley and Belvy went toward balancing the scales.

The firemen stood in front of Belvy and Paddy with their axes and crowbars and the Bowery Boys backed down. The standoff over, the firemen walked the last few blocks down Mulberry Street into the Points as a security detail for Belvy, Paddy and Moseley. They said their goodbyes in the Plaza.

As they entered the FiveP Dancehall, Belvy's smile turned into a frown as he started to feel the pain in his calf. Patrick scooped him up and carried him up the back staircase and into his bedroom. Within the hour, Belvy was patched up, in his bed with his Daddy sitting by his side and his new friend, Pretty Paddy, in the next room. Moseley kissed his son good night, but knew this was not just any day. What Pretty Paddy and the Black Joke Firemen did for them was nothing short of heroic. Moseley went to sleep with a greater sense of hope than he'd had in a long time. He couldn't claim the events of the day were part of his plan, but something like this didn't happen by accident. For the first time in his adult life, Moseley Johnson knelt by his bed and gave thanks.

CHAPTER 48

Life After the Riots

THE VIOLENCE IN New York came to an end as Federal troops returned from Gettysburg and restored order, but the relationship between the Irish and the Blacks would never be the same. Thousands of Blacks fled the city, and the Irish still viewed them as threats to their livelihoods. Nonetheless, Patrick and Belvy remained notable exceptions. The events of July 13th made them brothers for life with a bond that could not be broken.

Patrick moved in with the professor and eventually received a full scholarship to Columbia College. After he graduated, Patrick and Molly married, and began a family of their own. The second Pretty Paddy realized the first's dream of a political career, and became an elected official at both the city and state levels. He never had an interest in seeking a Federal post in Washington, however, because he believed the things that mattered most were in New York. It might be a little cramped for a big man, but there was simply no reason to go anywhere else.

His theatrics in the boxing ring along with his Monday evening exploits during the riots made Pretty Paddy a legend in certain circles, and Patrick never shook the nickname. Wherever he went and whatever he did, he was Pretty Paddy, which kept him grounded as his father's son.

Soon after the riots, Patrick introduced Belvy and Moseley to Margaret Kilpatrick and sparks began to fly. Quiet and reserved Margaret became a new person when in the company of Moseley. Within ten minutes of meeting, they politely disagreed. Within thirty minutes, their conversation became animated, and within 45 minutes of their very first meeting, heads bobbed, and fingers pointed–they had each met their match. Patrick reminded Margaret about her rules regarding cordial discourse, but then saw the smile form out of the side of her mouth, and noticed a return smirk from Moseley. They enjoyed each other's company immensely and became the best of friends.

Johnston Stewart lived into his eighties and came to the club every Friday morning with his son, Jonathan, who took their post-war business to new heights. In his final years, Johnston didn't say much, but just enjoyed the company. The professor continued to be a member of the Breakfast Club for years until his unfortunate passing in the bed of one of his female friends. Edward Simmons combined all of his articles about the young Irish man into a book, which became a best seller. This book, however, would be the last publication of a political nature for the former editor of the Tribune. While he never got the nerve to ask the lovely Wanda out for an evening on the town, one night she simply did not accept his "goodnight" and followed him upstairs after he finished his fourth whiskey. All of his writing pursuits from that point forward involved poetry. He was a changed man.

Moseley lived much longer than the doctors predicted, but turned over the day-to-day management of the FiveP Dancehall to his eldest son, Jimmy, soon after the riots. He proudly told anyone who asked that he was a retired man of leisure. This gave him more time to spend at the bookstore with Belvy and Margaret Kilpatrick. Moseley died about three years after the riots, and Margaret three days later. Patrick joked at her funeral that she still had a bone to pick with Moseley and wasn't going to let a little thing like his death get in the way of having the last word.

Margaret, Moseley, and Patrick had it all worked out, although Moseley claimed it was his "plan." Patrick became the owner of the bookstore along with the associated building from Margaret. Jimmy inherited the dancehall and made small monthly payments to Patrick, which purchased a fifty percent stake in the bookstore for Belvy. The two men, who had already become brothers, would be business partners. Moseley, pleased with his plan, expected both of his boys would do better than he did.

When Belvedere moved into one of the apartments above the bookstore, he only took a small bag of clothing and one piece of furniture–his bed. At the end of most days, Patrick walked Belvy upstairs to say goodnight. Belvedere would quickly climb under the covers and fall asleep with a smile on his face. Moseley came to him in his dreams with a good night kiss and the same comforting words he'd heard his entire life, "I know, Belvy. I know. Belvy got a plan. Sleep well, son. Sleep well." He did.

Patrick and Molly took the upper level of their inherited building as their home and converted the roof into a fabulous outdoor space. His favorite spot, though, was the northwest corner of the rooftop, where he'd built what he jokingly called his rampart, by extending a retaining wall in order to form an enclosed area. The openings in the wall were similar to windows he'd seen in drawings of medieval castles. The view of the city was excellent from the vantage point of his chair in the rampart, which he always faced to the west, but not because he still needed to transport his mind to the wide-open spaces to relax. Patrick was just a Wet Side boy and wanted to remember that simple, but important fact.

PART V

Patrick

.

CHAPTER 49

The Trio

ONCE AGAIN, PATRICK had no idea how he arrived in the lobby of the elegant Boigen Hotel. The buses pulled up to the Tenth Avenue entrance and the large, happy group began their ritual as each peeled off a single white tulip petal before exiting. Patrick silently wished them well and hoped they would all be up to the challenges of their next lives.

The elegant chandelier lit the multi-layered table below, which held a decimated bouquet of tulips. What seemed like borderline vandalism to Patrick before, now appeared celebratory--the tulips off on another adventure of learning and achievement. He appreciated the symbolism as the young hotel employee replaced the bouquet.

Aunt Grace sat with a gentleman in the Reflektions Café and seemed to be flirting. From behind, the man looked to be in his seventies, quite age appropriate. *Could there be dating at The Boigen?* Patrick laughed as he thought of the odd concept of souls in transition going out and "shooting the shit." *Maybe the hotel disco is on the second floor, and the piano bar on the roof!* The possibilities were endless, but all equally absurd. *Probably not a date, but she's certainly enjoying herself.* Patrick came around to the other side of the table and realized she was in the company of the same front desk agent with the monogrammed P.S. on his sleeve.

"Mr. Walsh, Bravo!" the agent said as he straightened his already perfect tie.

"Yes, my dear. Excellent effort," Aunt Grace added.

Patrick took a moment to absorb the compliments and realized what he'd called flirting was nothing more than the joy which follows success. After all, Aunt Grace was being tested as well. In both of Patrick's do-overs, the information or encouragement from her soul had pushed him in the proper direction. He still had free will, but her guidance played an important part in his success.

"Thank you. And I must also thank you, Aunt Grace. You always gave me the advice I needed."

"You're welcome, my dear. We're not quite done yet, though. It's time to go backward in order to move forward. Are you ready to see what happened the first time around?"

"Yes, let's go."

Patrick, Aunt Grace, and P.S. took each other's hands, concentrated, and within a few moments, they were flying–this time so much faster and at a higher elevation. The experience was exhilarating and Patrick didn't want the ride to end, but the trio landed on the windowsill of Pretty Paddy's Tenth Avenue apartment. He recognized his Aunt's beautiful red feathers and slumped posture–her tail, as always, pointed downward. The front desk agent was a head taller than Aunt Grace, and in addition to the black coloring around his eyes, he sported streaks of white feathers in his wings, which gave him a more majestic appearance. Patrick landed next to the agent, and the three spectators peered through the window at Grace and Paddy. It was Sunday morning.

Grace couldn't get out of bed, and failed in each of her attempts to do so. Extreme exhaustion was the sign that the end was imminent, and Grace hoped to muster the strength for one last conversation with Patrick. The unmistakable sounds of her son, a knife and fork clicking on a plate, emanated from the far side of the small apartment–he was up. Grace tried again to rise, and barely budged from her resting position. *What am I to do, I have to tell him that some things are worth fighting for. I know he'll be tested.* Grace tried one final time and had the same disappointing result. *Let me just rest for a bit and gather some strength.*

As time started to pass, Patrick realized his Ma would never wake from her nap. The trio turned to fly away as the son sat by his mother's bedside, clutching her lifeless hand.

Airborne again. The sky went from light to dark, and back to light again; it was Monday afternoon as they landed on a railing on the West Side docks.

Patrick disembarked the cargo ship drenched with sweat. Billy Conklin ran up to him and said, "Paddy, thank God you're okay. Riots in midtown. The rich and the Blacks are being attacked. A mob stormed The Colored Orphan's Asylum!"

Another short trip—the trio trailed Patrick as he ran down 44th Street toward The Colored Orphan's Asylum. He slowed down when he approached a church on 44th & Sixth Avenue. No reason to land…they just continued to circle. Patrick, on the move again, entered what remained of The Colored Orphan's Asylum and Aunt Grace wanted to rest, but P.S. insisted they continue to circle. Patrick exited the orphanage cradling little Carla in his arms and headed back toward the church. The trio followed every step of the way. The awning next to the church provided the observers with a perfect vantage point to hear Patrick's thoughts:

If only I'd gotten up sooner and followed my normal routine. I knew something like this might happen. What's wrong with me? How didn't I know about Ma's illness? I could have made her follow her doctor's advice. Instead, I made her worry and the day she spent following me around town must have been too much for her. I'm no good. No one should count on this big man. I've got to get out of here.

Pretty Paddy was running again—this time straight to the docks to board the cargo ship headed for Canada. The birds ascended to the point that nothing could be distinguished below. Finally, they leveled off, and the changes from light to dark came so quickly, the horizon blurred into a constant gray. The trip was so much longer this time, but Patrick's realization of what he'd done wrong dampened the thrill of flight—he just wanted to get back to The Boigen, but P.S. insisted on one more stop. Finally, they descended yet again, and the gray lifted as the alternating light and dark returned. The trio arrived at a warehouse in Toronto, Canada in 1878 and took positions on the rafters.

The years had not been kind to Paddy—he was only 35-years-old, but his grizzled and scarred face gave him the appearance of being 50. At a weight of almost 400 pounds, his fighting no longer inspired the roar of the crowd. He would battle another young man today and likely lose. He just hoped he wouldn't be embarrassed. Paddy paced in the ring and the crowd mocked him as he readied for his fight.

"Hey old man. Time for a new nickname. How about Punching Bag Paddy, you old piece of shit."

"Hey Paddy, ready for another ass-kicking?"

"Damn, who hit you in the face with a hammer?"

"You're nothing but a big, fat, Irish drunk."

The younger fighter came into the ring and the crowd cheered. P.S. took pity on Patrick and fast-forwarded the action to the end of the first round. Paddy lay unconscious in the center of the ring. The promoter of the fight walked over and stuffed a bill in his belt and dropped a bottle of Irish whiskey by his side. Paddy eventually sat up and clutched the bottle. He looked around the abandoned warehouse, took a long swig of whiskey, and felt comfortable for the first time that night. He was alone.

The trio returned to their seats in the Reflektions Café, and considered what they'd witnessed–Patrick understood. The first time around, he didn't have Mommy's Rule to help harden his resolve after Carla's death, and he just listened to his negative thoughts, turned away from the conflict, and ran away to Canada. The life he lived from that point forward was all he deserved. No Molly, no Belvy, no career as a politician. He ran away like a coward and paid the appropriate price. The second time, he had his mother's words to guide him, and he stood his ground, fought, and made all the difference. Patrick looked at Aunt Grace and thanked her–she answered with a hug.

The front desk agent spoke first, "You should both know that Patrick has never been an independent soul. The two of you were always connected as a team, but were also part of a larger group. Patrick, you made grave errors in your last two lives because of your own bad choices, but we never intended for you to make those decisions independently. You always needed an advisor, and your Aunt Grace was supposed to be that for you. In your most recent life, however, your Aunt's decision to move to California effectively ended her role as your advisor and pushed you over the edge. Grace, we gave you a few good years in California, hoping you would come back on your own, and when you didn't, we made things uncomfortable. While you stayed in California, Patrick fell apart here in New York. It wasn't that some of his choices were bad–they were all bad."

"Do you actually think I don't understand? Why are we dwelling on this?"

Patrick laughed to himself. If this was a first date, the dapper gentleman just blew any chance of a second. He decided to remain silent and let the grown-ups work out their issues.

"My dear Grace, don't be upset. We aren't dwelling, we are reflecting. This is what we're supposed to do in the Reflektions Café. Take no offense. You are right, it is in the past. A past you've corrected."

Quick recovery, Patrick thought—*very smooth.*

"I simply wanted to make the point that you required some encouragement to correct your mistake. We needed to get you back to Patrick, in New York."

Patrick and Grace nodded and Grace took a sip of her tea, while Patrick ordered another coffee. Both wondered why they needed to rehash all of this. Mr. "P.S." continued, "We were all afraid something had gone wrong with your chemistry. You lived good lives, but when it came to moments of truth, Patrice Beaumont and Patrick Allen did the wrong thing, and his coach was ineffective in preventing it. Sometimes the matter at hand is of such a magnitude it is worth risking everything. But enough of that, both of you did do well. Let's toast the two of you!"

The mysterious P.S., Aunt Grace, and Patrick each raised their respective coffee and teacups, clicked them, and took a hearty sip. The smiles returned.

"But it wasn't just the two of us. Shouldn't we have toasted the group?" Patrick asked.

"Well, yes, the group was important to both of you. It is common for us to travel in small groups from lifetime to lifetime—always together, but in different relationships and roles. There are also other souls, with whom we individually connect, and this is where you found your romantic love. This type of love does not come automatically and must be earned. Do you understand?"

"Yes, I believe I do."

"Fine, let's take a look at the 20th Street exit and see who is about to go to their final reward."

Patrick turned his head in the direction of the group seated by the side exit—the souls who really had reason to celebrate. Three former members of the Breakfast Club, Edward Simmons, Professor Jason Timbers, and Johnston

Stewart had learned their final lessons, achieved a high enough level of purity, and were moving on. He might have guessed the three of them were a team. He nodded to his old friends, and received a smile from each in return.

The front desk agent paused for a moment and extended his hand to Patrick. *What is his name?* Somehow Patrick didn't think it appropriate to ask, but didn't leave his new friend hanging. As their hands connected in a firm shake, P.S. offered, "You've succeeded in your moments of truth, my boy, which means you'll resume your old life and emerge from your coma in much better shape than when you entered it."

P.S. paused and took another sip of his coffee before he continued, "When you return, you'll be less explosive. Perhaps those heart palpitations of yours won't be so troublesome. Enjoy it, Patrick. You've earned it. I'll be happy to keep your Aunt Grace company here at The Boigen. Maybe we'll go to the Piano bar on the roof!" He laughed at Patrick's expression. "Don't be so surprised, Patrick. I know what you think and feel–I always have and I always will. Don't rush back. Time passes quickly here and by the time we finish this cup of tea, you'll be standing once again in the lobby. So go up to your room and take a well-deserved nap. When you wake up, you'll return to your life as Patrick Walsh."

PART VI

Going Home

CHAPTER 50

Welcome Back

FIRST, HE COULD hear.

"Mother, if you just wrote things in the calendar I gave you, you wouldn't be so late all of the time. Keeping a calendar gives you a plan for the day. I've always told you, everyone has got to have a plan. Everyone, even you mother. I can't wait for you to show up whenever you want."

"Listen, my dear, I waited nine months for you to show up, so I think you can wait ten minutes for me. How's that for a plan?"

Gloria and Diane were at it again—Patrick had missed their lively back and forth banter, which was quickly drowned out by uproarious laughter coming from a slightly further distance away. Patrick picked up another familiar voice, "...so that's why you never eat an ice cream cone while driving!" Clearly, Patrick's brother, Frank had just delivered one of his famous punch lines. The timing and delivery was so familiar—Patrick had the urge to laugh even though he missed the front end of the joke.

Patrick's lack of vision changed in an instant as his dark movie theatre became flooded by lights so bright, they blinded him in a different way. After a few moments, he regained focus and scanned the room. Gloria and Diane, Patrick's mother and sister, were already onto another topic of disagreement, and his brother continued to hold court in the doorway with three nurses. Diane offered two words, "Welcome back!"

→══● ●══←

The doctors were surprised when Patrick woke up from his bullet-induced coma so soon after surgery. Patrick's mother made the decision. The odds of him surviving the procedure were slim, but if they did not remove the bullet, Patrick would live out his remaining days on life support. Gloria wanted her son to have a chance to live a normal life. Frank and Diane had suggested they wait a little longer before making a decision, but Gloria had pulled rank.

Patrick's family took note of his changed disposition—not as nervous, although quite emotional at times. In addition, he seemed more connected as he suggested where they would all go, and what they would all do once he was back at home. While his family enjoyed the talk, they wondered what would happen once he was on his own, fully functional, and back to his old ways. Patrick sensed their skepticism as his discharge date approached.

"I'm leaving the hospital tomorrow and not going back to the East Side. I'm a West Side boy. That's where I belong."

Frank raised his eyebrows. "You're a West Side boy? You could also be a downtown boy, or a Harlem boy. You've lived in almost every neighborhood in the city! Where did this West Side thing come from?"

Patrick had no logic other than it seemed right when he thought of it, and even better when the words came out of his mouth. He decided to tell the truth, "I don't know."

Diane whispered to Frank and her mother, "Let's humor him." She then walked over to Patrick, gave him a kiss on the top of his shaved head and said, "Ok, my little West Side brother, whatever you say." Patrick's mother and brother nodded in agreement.

Frank handled the discharge from the hospital and things became strange as soon as the brothers entered Patrick's old apartment.

"Patrick, what are you doing? Why are you packing?"

"I told you. I'm going back to the West Side. I'll be staying at the Yotel Hotel on Tenth Avenue."

Patrick's plan made absolutely no sense to Frank, but he remembered Diane's advice to play along. Frank assumed he would likely be picking Patrick up to bring him back to his East Side apartment after he got this West Side thing out of his system.

Frank began to make his way to the elevator with the three packed bags, when Patrick told him he needed a minute and walked onto his favorite terrace, which he sarcastically called The Castle. He admired the walls, and his cut out medieval era windows. The westward facing chair appeared so inviting, but Patrick resisted the temptation to sit. Today was a day for action, not reflection, and he called out to the city, "This is not the best terrace I ever had." *Yeah, that sounds right*, Patrick thought as he smiled and headed to the elevator to meet Frank.

Frank helped his younger brother settle into his tiny room at the Yotel Hotel in the Times Square area, and Patrick became excited as he admired the view from the window, "Frank, look at this."

"Boy, what a beautiful old church. Classic."

"No, not the church…that corner apartment with the wraparound terrace, don't you remember? That used to be mine."

Frank paused for a moment and took a breath. "Patrick, I wouldn't know. You never invited me over, but it does seem special."

In the past, Patrick would have offered creative explanations as to why he never extended invitations, but the new Patrick refused to repeat his old mistakes. He turned, faced his brother, and apologized, "I'm sorry, Frank. I haven't been the best brother." Frank smiled and broke the tension with one of his jokes, "Patrick. It's all good, buddy. Did I ever tell you the one about the traffic cop who pulled over the Pope for speeding outside the Vatican?"

Patrick perked up. "No, you didn't!"

Not Frank's best joke, but good enough, and the two brothers shared a laugh before they headed out for their next errand.

"Where are we off to, Patrick? The doctor told you not to overdo it at first."

"We're only walking across the street to my old building, and then a quick taxi ride down to 18th street."

"Okay. Then right back here. Agreed?"

"Agreed."

--•=◎ ◎=•--

"Is that you, Mr. Walsh?"

Patrick paused as if he planned to answer the doorman, and surveyed the lobby, which featured a wonderful multi-level glass chandelier. He sighed and opened his arms while he took a deep breath. He'd sensed it the moment he stepped through the door, and now he was steeped in the feeling. There was no doubt. *I'm home.*

"Mr. Walsh? Are you okay?"

Frank jumped in, "Patrick, the doorman said hello. Do you remember him?"

"Yes, Frank. I do. How have you been, Henry? Your friendly hello was one of the nicest things about my time at The Victory."

Henry noticed the delay and sensed something was wrong. *He's a percentage of his old self. Must have lost 40 pounds, and all his hair. I hope he's okay.* "So nice of you to say, Mr. Walsh. What can we do for you today?"

"Well, I'd like to go to the leasing office."

"Sure thing. Do you remember where it is?"

"Twenty first floor. Am I right?"

"Absolutely, Mr. Walsh. I hope you're coming back."

Patrick winked at the doorman and proceeded to the elevators—a bank of only three cars, which serviced The Victory's fifty floors. Often residents waited a minute or two for a car and today was no different. Patrick didn't mind.

The leasing agent informed Patrick that his old unit, Apartment 1010, would be available within two months. *That won't do*, Patrick thought, as he asked to speak with the current occupant. The agent made a call, and after a short discussion, the deal was made. The tenant agreed to move out early in exchange for a substantial payment from Patrick. Everything was set. The timing would be perfect. Patrick would move back into his old apartment in two weeks.

CHAPTER 51

Dance New York

"PATRICK, WHAT'S SO special about this diner? You've got a perfectly good one right next to your building. I don't know why we had to come down to 18th Street for a cheeseburger."

"Sorry, Frank. This is part of getting re-acclimated to my surroundings. I spent some time at the dance studio across the street."

"So that's why you're staring at the entrance?"

"Yeah, I'm hoping to catch someone who works there."

"Patrick, we can't stay here forever, but we've got a few minutes. I'm going next door to the market to pick up some things. I'll be back."

"Ok, Frankie."

Patrick remembered his first time visiting Dance New York. Kasandra worked as a teacher in the studio and made arrangements for a surprise Tango lesson with her colleague, Elizabeth.

"Mr. Walsh?" Patrick turned in the direction of the voice and discovered a petite woman, who was all belly—she had to be close to her due date.

"Yes, please call me Patrick."

"Hi, my name is Elizabeth. Ms. Kasandra asked me to escort you to the *practica*. She told me you might fight the idea of taking a Tango lesson, but I assured her a real gentleman would never fight with a pregnant lady. Was I right?"

"A Tango lesson?"

"Yes, this is her little surprise and present for you. Please follow me."

Patrick entered the large room where 15 to 20 people clustered against the far wall. Two instructors, a man and a woman, were addressing the group. The male, a tall, pompous looking man with long black hair, blocked Patrick's view of the female instructor. As he stepped to the side, Patrick realized Kasandra was his partner. She wore a gold top and black pants with her hair pulled back. Patrick caught her eye for a moment and she offered her cute, innocent smile, which Patrick considered to be her signature look. *God, she's beautiful.*

The music began and Kasandra stepped backward as her partner moved forward. The man stopped, extended his left foot to the side, and snuck his right foot between her legs, which caused Kasandra to stop, step backwards, and then transfer her weight forward, while kicking between the man's legs with a flourish. The male instructor announced, "This sequence, which we call a Parada leading to a Gancho, will be the focus of the advanced class tonight."

When Kasandra kicked, Patrick noticed the long slit up the side of her pants, which showcased her long, lean legs in the best possible way. The students applauded, and Kasandra took a laughing bow before she addressed the group, "Okay class. All the advanced students, come with me, and the beginners, stay with your own instructors. Work alone with them for a while. In 30 minutes, we start the *practica*."

Patrick didn't have a chance to approach Kasandra, who was immediately surrounded by the advanced dancers. Elizabeth came to Patrick's side and said, "That's our cue. Follow me please."

Patrick spent the next half an hour learning how to walk as if he were holding a dollar bill between his legs. He also learned how to stand erect while leading with his chest, and how to offer an embrace that would support, but not bully, his partner. At times, he seemed to get it, but often felt awkward and out of step. Patrick didn't think he had any talent, but Elizabeth told him he was excellent for a beginner.

The thirty minutes came to a close, and Elizabeth bid her farewell. Patrick offered to pay for the lesson, but everything had been taken care of by Ms. Kasandra, who appeared by his side with one of her signature smiles. Before he could say a word, the music began and he started dancing with his girl. Patrick moved as if he did, in fact, have potential and Kasandra smiled again. Just as the *practica* was about to end, Patrick stepped to the left, and snuck his right foot between Kasandra's legs. She then went into a Parada, and with one fancy kick with the flashing legs, the *practica* concluded with a Gancho. Patrick always preferred to end things on a high note, and pulling off his first Gancho with his beautiful Kasandra by his side, made the memory of his tango lesson something he would always cherish.

Patrick's smile turned to tears as he remembered his visit to Dance New York. He didn't have the courage to charge into the studio and ask for a second chance—he'd blown it with Kasandra. There was no going back, and there would be no new memories to cherish.

Frank saw the tears on his little brother's face when he came back into the diner and handed Patrick a napkin. "Here Patrick, you got some ketchup on your cheek. Did I ever tell you the one about the penguin who wanted to go sky diving?"

"No, I don't believe you have, Frankie." Patrick laughed all the way back to the taxi.

CHAPTER 52

The Barbecue

THE WEATHER COOPERATED–79 degrees and sunny–*one less thing to worry about,* Patrick thought as he scanned the terrace as a final check for the big event—everything was set. His eyes started to roam. The view to the east, outstanding, and the view of the Hudson River to the west, the best he'd ever seen. *Yes, this is the finest terrace I've ever had. This is the one.*

"Nice haircut."

Patrick quickly turned away from the railing. *My God, she came.* He rubbed his bald head as he responded, "Thanks, I hoped you would like it."

"So sorry to hear about your troubles, Patrick, but I do have one question."

"You can ask as many questions as you like."

Kasandra walked toward Patrick, tilted her head downward, and offered her fabulous smile. He opened his arms, and she rushed in. The embrace suggested what the kiss confirmed–she was back. Finally, Kasandra asked her question, "Why does it take a bullet in the head for you to contact me?"

Patrick didn't want the embrace to end and offered no answer. A single tear streamed down the right side of his face and Kasandra wiped it away with her finger. "I got your letter and I understand, but I'm not going to stay. Our first date should be just you and I. So here's my famous cheesecake for you and your family. Have fun today, Patrick." Her final kiss–still more hello than goodbye. Patrick smiled. *I've got another chance.* This time, however, the third date would not be the highlight because, as the comedian suggested to him so long ago, he planned to "close the deal."

Almost time for the festivities. Patrick had invited a few people from the building to fill out the space, but this barbecue was for his mother, brother and sister who he always planned to host on his fabulous terrace overlooking the Hudson. The first round of burgers sizzled while Patrick sprinkled Adobo, his secret ingredient, on top. Perspiration spilled down the sides of the coolers. The beverages begged to be consumed, and Patrick's partiers seemed up to the task.

Gloria and Diane arrived together, as they always did, and were off in the corner enjoying their first argument of the day. Patrick noted the discrete side smiles–they were having a ball.

Frank entered the terrace escorted by his highly trained dog, Cheyenne, who walked on his hind legs. Three young children ran over to meet Cheyenne and Frank asked if they knew how to whistle. They did, and every whistle was a signal to Cheyenne to make a face. The children erupted with laughter.

Cheyenne took a break–time for the master to perform. Frank joined a group of four people and introduced himself. Within minutes, they hung on his every word and erupted in laughter with each soundbite. Approachable and lovable, Frank was in his element, and as always–the life of the party. The old Greek Orthodox Church across the street rang its bell signaling high noon, and Frank jumped out of his seat and almost spilled his beer over his audience as he assumed a fighting stance. Cheyenne barked and the group laughed. Ringing bells always caused this reaction in Frank. No one ever understood it. Frank turned his quirky reaction to the bell into a joke, and the partiers exploded in laughter, yet again.

The westward facing chair called out to Patrick and he took a break from his duties at the grill. Instinctively, his family joined him and soon stood by his side. Diane draped her arm around her mother, and Frank put his hand on Patrick's shoulder. A beautiful red bird with black feathers around its eyes circled the group a few times before landing on the railing directly in front of Patrick. No words were spoken because nothing needed to be said. Patrick wished he could hold onto that moment forever.

CHAPTER 53

The 20th Street Exit

PATRICK HEADED FOR the Reflektions Café as soon as he arrived. Aunt Grace pointed to his coffee and joked that since he'd become a calmer version of his old self, it wasn't decaf. They had a good laugh. Within a few moments, they walked over to the side entrance by 20th Street and settled into two empty chairs across from Gloria and Diane. Oddly, the two ladies were not arguing—they were holding hands. Diane noticed Patrick's surprise and whispered, "We were always holding hands." Laughter filled the lobby and Patrick spotted Frank chatting up the confused souls on the registration line—he must have just delivered his punch line.

The well-groomed front desk clerk with the monogrammed shirtsleeves walked over to Frank.

"How've you been, Frank?"

"Very well, Peter, and how about yourself?"

My God, Frank knows everyone. So his name is Peter—the name suits him, Patrick thought. Peter chatted with Frank as he escorted him to the empty seat next to Diane.

"Frank, we do appreciate your patience and the fact you've been ready for a long time. Here they are."

Peter's face lit up as he turned to Patrick and winked. The wink meant, good job and congratulations. It also asked, have you figured things out yet? Frank settled into his seat.

The nonverbal communication began, and Frank took the lead by directing his gaze at Patrick, who studied his brother and realized it all made a good deal of sense. Frank's form slowly morphed from Frank Walsh to Big Belvy and Abraham Julian. Patrick smiled as he relived his lives with each of them. He understood—it was nothing more than different packaging for the same soul.

Grace offered no surprises as she toggled back and forth between Camille and Grace Allen. Gloria was both Giselle Archambeau and Margaret Kilpatrick. The most extreme transformation, however, involved Diane, who went from her current form to Chantal Archambeau, and Moseley Johnson. The group sat, smiled and enjoyed themselves as they relived their adventures. Patrick understood why the souls seated by this exit always seemed so content, but subdued in their expressions—they had reason to be happy, but not to celebrate, because what awaited them as they exited The Boigen, would be the true cause for celebration.

Diane hugged Gloria as she recalled the day she flew onto the branch of a tree outside her mother's bedroom and witnessed her being beaten and raped at the hands of Philippe Archambeau. Patrick then thought of his great love, who he'd known as Marie, Molly, and Kasandra. Images of dancing and smiling filled his heart. Frank understood his question and told him not to worry—she would be passing through the 20th Street exit soon enough with her own group, and the next time he met her would be forever.

The group continued to reflect, no longer about mistakes to be corrected the next time, but about how the packaging of their souls created such unique challenges in each of their lives. Their White, Black, Jewish, Irish, and Catholic labels meant nothing in the end. They were always the same good souls trying to find their way. Ultimately, the group met these challenges. Patrick and Grace simply needed a second chance.

The charter bus pulled up on Tenth Avenue and the excited group under the chandelier peeled their tulip petals, and headed out for their next adventure of learning and growth. It was time. Patrick and his family prepared to leave the hotel. Peter said goodbye as they departed through the 20th Street exit, and then hello on the other side. He welcomed them home.

Author Bio

 A. Robert Allen is a longtime New York City college administrator with a lifelong passion for writing. When he traced his family tree back hundreds of years and uncovered roots that were white, black, Catholic, Protestant, and Jewish, the seed of a story began to grow. *Failed Moments* is a fictional account of the exploits of his ancestors during racially charged periods in the past.

Find out more about the author and his works at his website: http://arobertallen.com/.

Made in the USA
Lexington, KY
14 June 2015